MW01134927

Dawson Howard

1: Australian Desert

The sun was intense on the baking red bull dust of the desert as the temperature climbed into the high forties. He had been walking since early that morning and was concentrating on thoughts of The Dreaming. Not being aware of anybody in the nearby vicinity, the sudden pain in his left calf that swung him around and threw him to the ground was completely unexpected. The familiar sound of a 7.62mm SLR round cracked, like a stockman's whip, and he realised he'd been shot.

On the ground he rolled across to the cover of the Porcupine Grass. It was a clean, straight-through shot. The burning sensation crept up his leg and he started the mental process of finding something to stem the blood flow. Lying on his back he used his trusty double-bladed hunting knife to cut strips off the Paperbark Tree. The first as a tourniquet and the wider second strip was wrapped to secure the muscle. He found a stick to tighten the tourniquet. Then, to stop infection, crushed Billygoat Weed and spread it over the entry and exit holes along with a further wider strip of Paperbark as a bandage.

The whole time he remained astutely alert to further shots or movement. He had calculated that the shooter was to the southwest and was most likely scanning his vision from west to east. Trusting his hunting skills and having not picked up a scent he knew if there was more than one shooter they were not to the north.

Eight minutes had elapsed, since the shot. Watching through the Porcupine Grass a rifle barrel reflected off to the southeast. Being unarmed he needed to level the playing field. He found a long stem Black Boy plant that would act as a decoy. Lifting the plant up and down gave the appearance of somebody moving. As the rounds were slashing and penetrating the Porcupine Grass he deduced where the two shooters were located. He doubled back and crawled along a dried up waterway that meandered behind them.

With the sun directly overhead and the ground like a furnace the shooters would not have much patience and would need to find shade. Using this to his advantage, lying four metres behind the first shooter he waited. It had been fifteen minutes since they had fired their volley of shots. The shooter became frustrated and stood. Wiping the sand and sweat from his eyes he grabbed his two-way and instructed his mate to follow suit.

The shooter had raised his water bottle to his mouth as the knife lodged directly into the side of his neck, killing him silently and instantly. Rushing across to the fallen shooter he reached down grabbed the rifle; checked a round was chambered and spun around to sight the second.

The second shooter had left his hiding position and was scampering across the sparsely vegetated, iron ore encrusted landscape. Without missing a beat he aimed the long range scope and fired a direct headshot.

Twenty minutes later he had found weapons, ammunition, GPS scanner and water on both men and a photo of him taken at the Darwin Marina, nine weeks earlier.

Wade Ross is a trained Special Forces soldier who had just spent the last nine weeks wandering through the desert of Central Australia on a journey of Aboriginal spiritual enlightenment. He knew these two shooters had been sent as his assassins.

It was time to return to civilisation and first point of duty was to find out who these hitmen were working for and why he was targeted.

Using the vehicle of his would-be assassins, he headed back to Darwin.

2: Darwin

Darwin, the northern most city of Australia, considered the gateway to the Australian outback and therefore a prominent area to find aboriginals. Wade Ross the half-caste aboriginal, adopted and raised by a full blooded aboriginal mother had always called Darwin home. He had spent a youth enjoying the fruits of learning the aboriginal beliefs and ways, whilst having the opportunity to be educated in the white man system.

Wade, his mother Martha and adopted sister Camira had not been afforded the creature comforts of wealth but they had experienced the happiness and joy, as a family, that money could not buy.

Since the murder of his family Wade had decided he would never return to the family home so he made his way to the harbour to meet up with his old friend Stefan. The French Foreign Legionnaire, who lived on a disguised fishing boat and operated his undercover missions out of the Darwin harbour, throughout the Timor Sea and into Indonesia. Wade and Stefan had worked together on numerous occasions whilst Wade was on temporary attachment from the SAS.

At six foot eight and two hundred and sixty pounds Stefan is an extremely large and muscular man. This works to his advantage in most situations but not on the one particular night when they had been instructed to eliminate two Egyptian males, who had been suspected of leaking classified French documents. The five man assassination squad had come ashore at a marina, sixty kilometres south west of Alexandria, Egypt. Part of the mission required them to crawl through a boat repair area. The area was extremely tight. Stefan became trapped and in turn alerted the guards. Whilst trying to escape he was shot in the hip and only through Wade's skill and strength were they able to rescue him. A strong bond had developed and Stefan felt he owed Wade his life.

Halting the car on the concrete hardstand of the derelict area within the harbour, Wade watched as the last rays of sunlight disappeared over the distant horizon. Darkness in the Topend comes over like a blanket shrouding every ounce of available light and within minutes it had gone from a sunset to complete darkness. Wade waited until his night vision had focused and then started the onerous task of searching for Stefan's early warning detection devices.

Disabling a tripwire activated flare, an electric current to the wharf access ladder and a movement sensor; he stepped up to the side of the boat.

"Hello you big ugly critter," said Wade as a surprised Stefan swung around. At the same time pulling a Heckler & Koch 9mm pistol from his waistband.

With the gun aimed straight at Wade's head he cried out, "Oh *mon Dieu* … Wade you could have got yourself killed sneaking up like that."

"I think I was fairly safe," he replied stepping on to the boat.

The mention of Wade's name caused an almighty scream, and the dropping of plates, as a gorgeous brunette scampered up the galley ladder.

"Hello Crystal," said Wade as she wrapped her arms around his neck like a spider that had caught its prey.

"I'm so glad you're back. I missed you so much," she said in her Mid Atlantic Virginian accent while not letting go with her head buried in his chest.

"Well it's good you two are excited to see me and it's nice you waited around," he said easing Crystal from her grasp.

Kissing her gently on the lips and shaking hands with Stefan all three sat down.

"I'm surprised you're still here. I would've thought you would have returned to the states by now?" asked Wade looking at Crystal.

After nine weeks living in the tropics, on a boat, with limited showering, spending most of the day swimming, eating, reading and dressed only in a sarong and bikini top; Crystal had become very tanned and Bohemian looking. Wade had missed her gorgeous emerald eyes and continually smiling face.

Stefan answered first, "Buddy, let me tell you that was never going to happen. In the time you've been gone I've had HQ contact me with three missions that I'm supposed to be on and each time, this young lady has told me I'm going nowhere. So here we have waited," replied Stefan, with an exasperated look but smiling all the same.

With his arm around Crystal, Wade said, "Well even so, I'm glad you're both here."

Crystal, the US Navy helicopter pilot had been assigned to deliver Wade into Sierra Leone whilst serving aboard the USS George H W Bush, stationed off the west coast of Africa. Approaching the drop off zone they were attacked and shot down by a SAM (Surface to Air Missile). Wade utilized his remarkable hunting, jungle and survival skills to rescue her from the burning and sinking Viper. After saving her life a further two times as they forged their way back to the Mediterranean, an attraction had developed. The nature and secrecy of Wade's work caused Crystal to become embroiled in his latest mission.

Now madly in love with this handsome Australian she was happy to be held in his strong arms and she hoped that the moment would never end. Sitting with her eyes closed, she remembered all the adventures and scary, nerve-racking times they had spent together over the last five months.

"So ... how was Walkabout?" asked Stefan.

Unsure how a question like this was answered Wade replied, "I'm glad I went and I'm now ready to move on."

"I know it's something you don't talk about much but what do you do on Walkabout?" asked the big affable Frenchman.

Thinking for a moment Wade looked at them both. "As the name implies it's walking about. We do it in the middle of the outback," as he pointed south to the vast Australian desert, "with no one else. Therefore it gives us a chance to reconnect with our spirit world." He stated as he lowered his head. "We go to areas of tribal significance. We study the cave paintings. It helps us remember the Great Ancestors of the Dreamtime. To us all life is interrelated; everything exists for a reason. There is no distinction between man and nature, life and death, past, present and future. By doing this we can remain focused and at one with ourselves ... It gives us peace."

Crystal and Stefan sat there quietly until Wade raised his head and asked, "What's happened while I've been gone?"

Stefan, switched to military mode and explained how they had a visit early one morning, four nights prior, from two divers who were intent on planting explosives under his boat. His early warning devices enabled him to pick them off and they were left to the salt water crocodiles.

After Stefan was finished explaining the details Wade told them of what happened that day in the desert. Crystal sat in awe as Wade removed the makeshift bandages and Stefan applied a compound field dressing.

"Is that going to be alright?" asked a concerned Crystal.

"Guaranteed. You won't believe what concoctions he can come up with. This will heal in no time," replied the smiling Stefan in his broken English.

Wade showed them the photos he had taken from the shooters and decided it was time to give General Forest a call.

3: Washington

General Forest, head of the CIA, and second only to the President of the United States within the US intelligence sector, had been summoned to a meeting with the three most powerful people in Washington.

Forest prided himself on his punctuality and all of his staff were aware of this. So when a call came from the National Security Council (NSC) that U.S. President Markham (POTUS), Secretary of State, Charlotte Bysmith and Chairman of the Joint Chief of Staff (CJCS), General Burt Razen were expecting him at an oval office meeting, pronto, everybody kicked into gear to make it happen.

The General was leaving his office when an aide approached, "Sir, I have a Mister Wade Ross who wishes to talk with you."

Forest immediately stopped in his tracks and turned back; to the complete surprise of the six man security detail and the three aides who were accompanying him to the White House.

General Forest and his secret CIA team, who operated out of The Warehouse in a derelict area of West Washington, had been entrusted by the NSC, with the task of locating and destroying the Grey

Wolves offshoot group. Initially cautious of the General's intentions Wade had slowly come round.

"Wade … General Forest. Good to hear from you again."

"Hello General … I need some help from you and your resources to track some would be assailants."

"Okay. Where are you and how do I get some Intel on these assailants?"

Wade explained the details upon which the General responded, "I would assume both of these attacks are directed at you and Crystal. Therefore I would strongly recommend you both make your way back here. I'll send some people to the site in the desert and we'll check the bodies for any identification. I also have some good news. The President wishes to thank you personally for your last mission, so when you arrive I'll have it organised."

Waiting for him to respond the General finally asked, "Wade did you hear what I said?"

"Yes General. I heard what you said. Let's not rush to organise too much … okay?"

"Wade I understand but this is a great honour and you deserve it, so please consider carefully before rejecting it?"

"I will. Thanks General." As the line went dead.

4: Pacific Ocean

The luxury Gulfstream G650, state of the art, long range jet made the trip to Washington extremely comfortable. The General had made sure that Wade and Crystal were receiving the best.

Wade was sitting opposite her, in the luxurious club lounge, as she read a magazine. He could not believe how much he had fallen for this beautiful brunette with the rich green eyes and the silky olive skin. He had finally got up the courage to tell her how he felt and was just about to speak, when she raised her head and asked, "Would you come with me to meet my Dad?"

"Of course … why would you think I wouldn't?"

Lowering her head again she replied, "I wasn't sure how you would feel and I thought you might think it too soon."

Wade suddenly realised this was the moment he had been waiting for. He stood up, walked over, bent down, kissed her on the lips and said, "Crystal Carters … I love you." To which he kissed her again.

Standing back up he noticed she hadn't responded. She sat there looking straight ahead and the tears slowly started to swell in her eyes.

Wade watched as she still hadn't responded when he finally said, in a stammering and nervous voice, "I'm sorry ... I didn't mean to upset you."

Crystal leapt to her feet, threw her arms around his neck, and pressed her face against his as she said, "No, don't apologise. It's the most beautiful thing I could ever have wanted to hear ... I love you too."

They kissed and hugged for what seemed hours until the hostess asked them to take their seats for landing.

Crystal held his hand and looked into his eyes as if she was never going to let go. She was smiling so much she felt her jaw ache, but right then, she didn't care.

5: Virginia

It was early afternoon when the jet arrived at Andrews Air Force Base. The two CIA Agents had been instructed to take them wherever they wished.

Crystal gave her father's address and the agents explained it would be a two hour trip.

During the drive over Wade asked Crystal about her dad.

Trent Carters had been drafted into the US Navy in 1970. After obtaining his officer commission and completing his flight training he joined the USS Constellation as an attack pilot, flying F4 Phantoms, during the Vietnam War. In 1974, after three tours and multiple commendations for bravery, he returned home a hero. He met Susanne, the most beautiful woman he had ever seen, at an airport opening function, of which he was the guest speaker. They fell in love and two years later they were married. They were the perfect couple with a wonderful life and were both so happy with the approaching birth of their child. Tragically during the birth Susanne had complications and died. Trent, with the help of his mother, raised his daughter whilst also establishing a very successful career in military weapons technology. He never remarried and currently lived with his dog, Frugal, the shorthaired pointer.

Wade sat and listened as Crystal detailed her father's life story. He noticed how she spoke about him with such respect and love. He watched her expressions go from extreme happiness to great loss and sadness and then back to cheerfulness.

They arrived at the typical American Neo Classical style house in the upper middle class neighbourhood of Clarksville, Maryland. The house was two storey with a portico to the front and a large veranda on the first floor. There was an enormous set of steps leading up to the front patio. The external façade was predominately painted white with the stars and stripes flying in the front yard. The gardens and lawns were well manicured and the elms were losing the last of their leaves as the winter approached. Wade noticed the beat up Ford F250 pickup in the driveway and the shotgun across its back window.

Leaving the car Crystal lead the way and had just crested the top step when the door flew open and a man wearing a baseball cap, burst out, closely followed by an extremely excited brown and white pointer.

Wade was surprised how fit and healthy this middle aged man appeared but he was more delighted to have finally returned Crystal to her Dad.

After much hugging and kissing Crystal looked from her Dad to Wade as she said, "Dad, I want you to meet Wade. The man I've been telling you so much about."

"Hello Wade, it's wonderful to finally meet you. Thank you for looking after her and bringing my little princess home in one piece," Trent responded, as they shook hands.

After a lifetime of either being in the military or associated with military personnel, Trent Carters considered he had a fairly good understanding of the many different types he would expect to meet. He knew the guy standing in front of him, who shook hands not gripping tightly or loosely, who stood with the poise and stance of a jungle cat; he was definitely a soldier to be taken seriously.

"Pleased to meet you too, Mister Carters."

"Please, Trent … come in," he said as he looked toward their car, "What about your friends?"

"CIA. They will want to stay in the car," replied Crystal as she hooked her arms through the arms of her two favourite men and led them inside.

The afternoon and evening flowed on with a beautiful meal and the three talked until midnight. During the evening Trent had organised food for the drivers as they took turns at guard duty on his patio.

The next morning they organised to visit Crystal's mothers' grave. As they approached the gravestone Wade noticed how Crystal had grabbed her father's arm and seemed transfixed on the headstone. Stepping back and allowing the Carter's their due respect he watched as she placed flowers and silently mouthed words to her mother.

Wade, the eternal soldier, was watching with his peripheral vision and constantly scanning the cemetery. Not really expecting any problems, he thought he caught a glimpse of a man carrying an Uzi submachine gun, duck behind a large marble plaque.

Slowly dropping further back with his head directed toward the Carters; he kept scanning when he picked up another barrel protruding from a headstone fifteen metres from the first.

Shouting to Trent and Crystal to get down, as the first silenced shot whistled above their heads, Wade had already started a flanking movement on the two shooters. Moving on all fours and using the marble tombstones as cover he skirted the area to the high side of the shooters. Affording himself a glimpse of what Trent and Crystal were up to, he noticed they had found cover behind Susanne Carters gravestone. The single fired shots were coming in rapid succession as the shooters took turns emptying their magazines.

Wade had spent many years learning the art of rapid, silent, undetected movement and as he came up behind the first shooter he hoped that Crystal and Trent would stay protected enabling him to finish this quickly and efficiently. The first shooter was now only five metres to his front. He had swapped the Uzi for a scoped M15 semi-automatic rifle and was about to attempt to take out his targets in sniper profile.

Waiting until the shooter was transfixed on his target; Wade leapt forward. He covered the distance in two steps and at the same time pulled the wire garrotte from his side pocket. The wire was around the shooters neck and his throat sliced open before he had a chance to turn his head.

Dropping the now limp body to the ground Wade scooped up the M15 and took aim at the second shooter. Firing off a standard Special Forces double tap technique of a shot to the body and one to the head, he started searching for others.

Once certain there were only two and having searched their bodies he made his way back to Trent and Crystal.

Giving a quick summation of events to the startled agents, who had raced from their car once the shooting had stopped, he stepped around the headstone and noticed how scared Crystal was, with her head buried in her father's chest.

"It's okay. You can get up now," said Wade.

"Who were they?" asked a frightened Crystal as she stood and put her arms around Wade's neck.

Wade explained that they were most likely affiliated with the same group that had tried to take him out back in the desert. He showed how each shooter had a photo of Crystal, and it had been taken at the Darwin Marina at the same time as the previous shooters' photos of him.

Having exhausted their desire to stay at the cemetery they headed back to Trent's house. The agents had already sent a report to Langley. They had been in the car ten minutes when Forest called on the in-car secure phone.

"Wade, I've just heard what happened. I think it would be a good idea for you and Crystal to get back here," he said with an unusual level of concern in his voice.

The phone was on speaker and all in the vehicle had heard what the chief of the CIA had just said but they had also heard that it was a request, not an order. With all eyes locked on Wade, he calmly replied, "Why do you think that, General?"

After a slight pause the General said, "I realise that you, more than anyone else, could probably find who these shooters are and what they're up to, but I feel we need a collaborative approach. Also I have some information you might find interesting."

"Okay, we'll drop Crystal's father off at his home. We should be there in about two and a half hours," replied Wade.

"No need. I have a chopper on route. It'll pick you up on the outskirts. I'll organise a detail for round the clock coverage of Crystal's father's house and

I'll meet you at the Warehouse," exclaimed the General as the line went dead.

6: Washington DC

The Lakota helicopter landed on the deserted cargo hardstand in the derelict industrial area of West Washington. The blades had only just started to slow their revolutions as the four occupants leapt from the rear cabin area. With their heads bowed all four raced across to the waiting CIA issue black Suburban.

Wade, Crystal and the two agents had not said a word since they had climbed aboard the helicopter. The Suburban skirted the first two sheds and then accelerated toward the rusty corrugated wall of the third, larger shed. Twenty metres from the wall and appearing not to slow, Crystal grabbed Wade's arm and screamed.

The driver, Wade and the two agents never batted an eyelid as the wall dropped into the ground and the Suburban raced inside. The vehicles came to a stop Wade looked across to Crystal, put his hand on her leg and asked, "You okay?"

"My God, what next!" she nervously replied trying to calm herself whilst also being aware she had never felt safer than when she was with this man.

The Warehouse was a large, rusty, corrugated shed covering nearly twenty thousand square metres. All the windows and doors had been enclosed and welded shut. No natural light was able to enter the facility. Inside the building a bomb proof and radiation resistant structure had been built. The internal walls and roof had been covered with a lead lined and soundproofed material. All communication was through specially designed fibre technology that had been built into the corrugated sheets. Completely self sufficient with its own water, electricity, food and recycling air; occupants could comfortably live for ten weeks. The five metre by five metre door that dropped into the ground was the only means of access. The building was constantly under satellite and drone surveillance. Guarded by highly trained field operatives posing as homeless drunks.

Inside resembled the futuristic flight deck of a Star Trek spaceship. Two hundred people sat facing computer screens, analysing data or communicating with various parties throughout the world. 3D screens hovered above desks covered in maps and large plasma screens showed live images from the world's hotspots. Men and women were in discussion whilst cutting, pasting and dragging information and photos. Forest had organised unidentifiable satellites to be available at all times.

Helping Crystal from the vehicle, Wade made his way toward Forest and Kaitlyn, the Israeli Mossad agent whom he had developed a close working relationship with over the years. He noticed Joe Plant, the CIA Station chief of the Turkish office, standing off to the left. Stopping in front of the General he put out his hand as he said, "Thanks for all your help."

Turning to Kaitlyn he put his arm around her shoulders and said, "Thank you. We'll always be able to work together. Don't forget that."

As Wade headed toward Joe, Crystal noticed Kaitlyn trying to hide the tears that were forming. "Wade told me what happened and what you said. I don't want you to worry or apologise as I believe I am learning to understand how this world you all live in, operates," said Crystal.

With her head bowed Kaitlyn responded, "Thank you Crystal. I'm sorry for the way I treated you. Hopefully I can make it up."

Kaitlyn thought of how she had brutalised Crystal in Darwin, months earlier. How she had stepped outside the boundaries. She also knew that her work, as a Mossad agent, meant she was expected to perform tasks that others would not. But her biggest regret was losing respect from Wade. He was the closest she had to family and it ate at her to think she had jeopardised a relationship that had taken years to develop, all over a jealousy toward Crystal's affections to Wade.

Forest called Wade, Joe, Kaitlyn, Crystal and three aides into the secure meeting room. Looking at the group the General spoke first, "We don't appear to have a lot to go on regarding these shootings but Jade has found something of interest."

A tall, extremely thin, pale skinned young woman who seemed very nervous at addressing the group stood and looking down at her notes, slowly and softly started to speak. With her long, snow white hair hanging in front of her face she tried to relay the information but nobody in the room could understand or hear her. Wade realising her predicament rose, walked around the table and stood next to her as he said, "I understand how hard this might be for you, so sit down and take a deep breath. I'll sit with you. You talk to me as if there's no one else in the room … okay?"

Looking straight into Wade's eyes she saw genuine caring and quietly said, "Thank you."

Commencing again, looking at Wade, "We've examined the bullet casings found at both the shooting sites. They're consistent with casings we found twelve months ago when two of our agents were shot, outside a Berlin diamond cutting house. When we finally gained access to the building it had been wiped clean. The only item worth noting was an indentation in a desk that showed an inverted *Opus Dei* symbol. We've been unable to follow this path any further until now. We don't understand what the symbol implies but we do know somebody outside of the normal production factories has

26

produced these bullets and therefore we feel the casings will be the link we're looking for. We also believe the style of production would more likely indicate Italian manufacturing but we cannot confirm this."

"Why a link between the symbol and the casings?" asked Wade.

"We were able to get some microscopic metal fragmentations from the desk which we know came from the symbol and these fragments match the metals used in the bullets. We know the symbol would not be made from this metal as it would be too soft but there is a possibility they came in contact, i.e. maybe were being carried together. We feel it is too coincidental to ignore."

"Thank you Jade. You did very well. We appreciate all your help," Wade replied as he helped her stand and escorted her, and her fellow workers, to the door.

Crystal watched, as he closed the door and returned to his seat. All the time thinking, 'He never ceases to amaze me'.

"I don't feel we're any closer to who they are and what they want but I think it's time I paid Ryan Cotterill a visit," said Wade.

Ryan Cotterill, the son in law of President Markham, who had received a ninety five million dollar deposit into an unknown Swiss bank account and whose second uncle is Professor Borgias Bart.

Professor Bart, a lead scientist at the LHC (Large Hadron Collider) facility in Meyrin, west of Geneva, Switzerland whose information was instrumental in the group destroying the Grey Wolves production facility.

The Grey Wolves, a Turkish style mafia, that a splinter group was formed from by the ex director of MIT (Turkish National Intelligence Organisation). The group was predominately operating as a mercenary group. They had developed a lucrative illegal arms and diamond business and were also intent on producing nuclear Armalites. The destruction of this group, its leader and two associates had been Wade's latest mission. The two high profile associates, US Vice President Daniel Cooper and Chief of CIA International Affairs Marcus Smithwright.

"Before you leave I need to organise a meeting with you and the President. When are you available?" asked Forest looking directly at Wade.

"General, I do appreciate what the President and you are asking but not right now," replied Wade as he grabbed a 9mm Heckler & Koch from the side table, checked the magazine was full and headed for the door. With Crystal following he turned to Joe, "You coming?"

7: Baltimore

The drive to Ryan Cotterill's apartment, downtown Baltimore, had been uneventful with the discussion focused on bullet casings and the possible location of production facilities.

Joe used his CIA badge to gain access past the security guard and into the luxury facility. Taking the elevator to the twelfth floor they approached the apartment door and Wade immediately noticed the fine scratching's beside the handle. Checking for surveillance cameras he motioned to Joe to move to the side of the door whilst he pushed Crystal back against the wall. Bringing his index finger to his mouth, indicating no noise, he ensured a round was chambered in his pistol and reached for the door handle.

The door was unlocked. Wade pushed it fully open and leading with his pistol, entered the apartment. Ensuring his eyes and the pistol were always as one he scanned arcs of fire and crept forward keeping hard against the wall. The lights were on with the television playing an evening soap. Halfway down the corridor he saw the walls splattered from floor to ceiling in blood and the two bodies. A young girl was lying face down atop a young man and both had been shot at point blank range. The carpet around the bodies was saturated with dried blood. Touching the bloodied carpet and studying the bullet wounds Wade deducted they had been shot twelve to twenty four hours earlier.

Joe and Wade checked the remainder of the apartment and returned to the bodies.

"Any thoughts?" asked Joe.

"Well … they've been shot with a hollow point from about two metres and there doesn't appear to be anything else touched," replied Wade still searching for any further evidence. "Did you notice that something was used to open the door lock?" he asked without looking up.

"I did but that's not going to help us much."

"Look at this," remarked Crystal as she walked from the bedroom unfolding a scrunched card.

The card was the inverted *Opus Dei* symbol with the name IED SUPO and the words underneath Punishment to all for Eternity. SC

Looking at the card Joe was the first to speak. "What the hell does all that mean?"

Still studying the card Crystal replied, "The picture is the *Opus Dei* symbol as viewed inverted or looking from a mirror and IED SUPO is the name *Opus Dei* viewed the same way. I don't know what the words underneath mean because they don't really go with the *Opus Dei* philosophy but I do feel I have seen it somewhere before."

"*Opus Dei*! Second time today we've heard this. What is it?" asked Joe.

"*Opus Dei* is an organisation within the Catholic Church. It teaches that everyone should aspire to be a saint. It is mainly directed to the common people and their ordinary lives. It is predominately a teaching facility but there are many who believe its secrecy hides a cult of deception and cruelty," replied Crystal still not looking up from the card.

"So there is a possibility this is associated with some religious cult?" asked Joe again.

"I don't think so," said Wade as he walked behind Crystal and put his hand over hers and covered the card. "Let's call the General and he can get a team in here while we pay whoever is watching the CCTV a visit."

After discussing with the General they left the apartment and proceeded downstairs to the security comms room. Spending the next hour going over security tapes they deducted that the assassin had come into the building, waited many hours and then dressed in black, and a baseball cap, had gone about the execution. Again waiting many hours he then left the building. The number of people entering and leaving made the deduction process impossible. They noticed no distinguishing features and knew it was a dead end.

8: Warehouse

After sending the information, of their discovery through, Kaitlyn had been using her contacts in Mossad to help with the deciphering. Joe and an aide were perusing forensic reports and discussing possibilities. Wade and Crystal were at the far end of the large meeting room talking about *Opus Dei*.

"I became very interested in the Catholic religion when I was old enough for my father to tell me about my mother's beliefs. My mother was of Columbian decent and her family had strong ties to the Catholic missionaries, who worked in Columbia, and especially those associated with the orphanages. As a young girl, growing up, she saw the missionaries helping the elderly; the sick, the children and she believed they had been sent by god to help her and her people. I wanted to understand what my mother had felt. It was through this studying that I learnt about groups, like the *Opus Dei*. I believe that those associated with it are mostly trying to do good but there are definitely others who feel it is an organisation hiding something and therefore is evil," remarked Crystal.

"What are your thoughts on the symbols being reversed?"

"I'm not sure but the words below remind me of a pagan event, I read about, where the leader was enticing his followers to their death as a means of immortality … or something like that."

"Well that is cheerful news," replied Wade looking up as Forest and a small, balding, stooped, pale man with bulging eyes entered the room.

"Can I have your attention? This is Professor Faux End and he is from the Academy of the Study of Religious Developments at The George Washington University. He specialises in the study of cults. He has agreed to help us try and understand what we are dealing with here."

"Thank you General. Firstly I don't believe this has anything to do with the *Opus Dei* but merely somebody or some organisation using the symbols and the name to throw you off track. What I can help with is the words. Approximately five hundred years ago a Bulgarian monk used them. He had been excommunicated from a religious order and vowed revenge. He set about evoking fear into the local farmers and serfs by hunting them and their families at night; destroying their homes and farms and all the time giving the impression he was the devil reincarnated. He used the words to force them to join him or they would perish into purgatory forever. He was eventually killed but it is believed the cult lived on and still exists today. I also believe the SAC are initials and would most likely be one of their leaders."

"If that's the case, how would you recommend we find this person or cult?" asked Kaitlyn.

"*Opus Dei* is an extremely large worldwide organisation and has a very good reference library within the Vatican. I would imagine if the CIA were to approach them requesting information on anybody who was searching their database for these particular words, I'm sure you would get results. We also believe the words, on the card, are only used and available to senior members of this cult," replied the professor.

Pausing for any response he then went on, "As a word of caution. We believe that when the leader utters these words, the disciples must kill all non-believers that are present."

"Thank you Professor," said Forest as he escorted him to the door.

By the time the General had returned, Kaitlyn had already contacted her Mossad counterparts and had gained access to the Vatican database. It had returned two results.

"It seems we have an interesting response from the Vatican. Their database returned two names; one is a Mexican drug lord who uses the words as a fear tactic against his growers and I would say definitely not our man. The other is a Samantha Cooper who is the older sister of ex-Vice President

Daniel Cooper. We searched deeper and found she is a recluse who lives on Mount Walker, Puget Sound, Seattle. Similar to her brother she is exceptionally wealthy and has built herself a fortress on the side of a mountain," said Kaitlyn as she continued to scour her laptop.

"Is there anything else we can find on this Samantha Cooper?" asked the General.

"There is one small thing but I am not sure it will be relevant. Apparently Cooper had treatment, as a child, for possible schizophrenia but nothing further reported."

9: Seattle

"Hi Colonel," said Wade into the secure line of the Sat phone.

"Hello Wade. I hear you're in Washington DC," came the distinctive British accent of Colonel Jacob Wine.

Colonel Wine the ex-SAS commanding officer who was on mission with Wade, during the Kosovo war, when Wade saved his life. A person who Wade considered a very good friend, mentor and somebody he would trust his life with.

"Actually I'm just about to touch down Puget Sound, Seattle," replied Wade who went on to explain the sequence of events, thus far.

"Kiwi and Jacko are on a mountain skills exercise in Banff. Want me to send them across? They could be there in three hours," asked the Colonel.

"No … I'm not sure what to expect. I'll complete a recce first and get back to you," replied Wade as he cut the line.

The CIA jet touched down Seattle-Tacoma International Airport twenty minutes later. Wade found the CIA car in the staff carpark that Forest had organised, and left heading west.

After three hours of many incorrect GPS calculations and misguided directions, from the locals, he arrived at Mount Walker, Puget Sound. A beautiful area of northwest America. Extremely rugged with steep mountains, large Douglas-fir forests and immense waterways.

Wade noticed there was only one road, on the southern side, leading up Mount Walker. He knew that a wealthy person selecting such a remote and well-protected area would have only one access road and it would be well guarded.

Hiding the car, he made his way around to the lake side of the mountain. As the most rugged and difficult terrain it would also be the least protected. He spent the next two hours searching and disabling early warning detection devices.

During the remaining daylight hours he observed the fortress-like facility suspended on the eastern side of the mountain overlooking Puget Sound, two thousand feet below. Under the cover of darkness he climbed the mountain rock face and reached the monolithic overhanging concrete slab that formed the floor of the building. Using his night vision goggles (NVG) he made his way through the sub floor area. It was utilised as the service area for the air conditioning units, standby generator, lift motor control room, cold storage and wine cellar. At the furthest end he found the stairs and was about to take his first step when he noticed, through the NVG, that the steps had been rigged with pressure pads. Disabling the pads he was then confronted with the handrail wired to heat sensor detectors.

Wade thought the owner of the building was using every means possible to stop intruders. Swinging his grappling hook over the highest point of the handrail he pulled himself up the inside of the stairwell. Ensuring not to touch the handrail, he flipped himself over and stood beside the door. Deactivating the switch sensor, disabling the CCTV activation contact; he slowly opened the door.

The door was into a thirty car garage. Walking between luxury Mercedes, Ferraris and Bentleys he also found an armour plated Hummer and two fully armed Chenowth Scorpion Desert Patrol Vehicles (DPV), normally associated with the US Navy SEALS. Quickly skirting the remaining vehicles he stepped into a hallway that acted as a service port from the main building.

Destroying the lights he made his way deeper into the building where he found storage rooms, workers sleeping quarters and armouries. Hand on the door handle he heard voices inside: three males. Softly knocking and standing to the left, an Asian male, dressed in military clothing, stepped into the corridor. Wade easily slipped the garrotte around his neck and pulled him away from the door. Slowly lowering the body and removing his NVG, he lay on the floor, leant into the doorway and with two silenced .45 rounds from his H&K SOCOM pistol shot out the lights. Within seconds the remaining two occupants burst through the door. Wade grabbed the second fleeing occupant from behind. His left hand around his neck and under his chin, Wade pulled back and up. The man's forward projection and Wade's strength and whiplash motion snapped his neck. As he dropped him he fired a single pinpoint accurate head shot at the first.

Dragging all three bodies into the room he became aware that it was a communications and control centre. There was a table with three chairs and three screens per chair. Above the table were a further eight wall mounted screens. Wade noticed most were fixed cameras except for two on the wall. One was external and appeared to be moving above the buildings on wire support lines but the other was dedicated to following a person. He saw it didn't show the persons face but did show where the person was located, at any time, within the building. It also showed the path this person had taken.

Studying the screens and the maps laid out on the table, he set about determining his location and trying to find Samantha Cooper. Whilst fiddling with the control knob he suddenly heard a male voice and appearing on a screen was a man and woman, seated, facing each other.

The man was of European appearance, short greying hair, a round face covered in frown lines, and dark brown recessed eyes. He wore a pastel cream Mao collar shirt and small gold cross on a thin wild gold chain around his neck. He was holding a pair of reading glasses in his left hand and had a notepad and pen in his right. He was intently watching the woman as he spoke.

"Now Roxy, tell me what happened last night?" asked the man.

"Barney was rude to Cindy," replied the middle-aged woman in a slow, nearly childlike manner.

"And where was Barney when he said this?" asked the man again, in his strong northern European accent.

"He was on the box, being rude. Where do you think he was!" she exclaimed looking down between her legs.

Wade saw she had a small doll and was nervously fidgeting with it as she spoke. He also noticed she talked to the doll not looking up and talking to the man. He realised the man was a doctor, most likely a psychiatrist, and the woman was his patient.

"Has Barney said sorry to Cindy yet?" asked the doctor.

"No," came the barely audible reply.

"Sorry Roxy. I couldn't hear you," asked the doctor again.

Without warning the woman sprung out of the chair and threw the doll across the room into the burning fireplace. Yelling as she stood, "What the hell are we doing here? We have work to do," she said as she started pacing around the room.

Wade heard the voice had become clear, concise, authoritarian and very manly.

"Please Troy, sit down and let's discuss this?" asked the doctor, appearing nervous.

Walking back to her chair the woman sat down but this time with much more control and confidence.

"Doc, I respect you trying to help but I need to get control of things. I can't have any more mistakes. Losing the plant in Djibouti was bad enough but then also Doksal and Daniel. I need to get rid of this blasted soldier and his girlfriend and focus on Bart," replied the woman.

"Troy, I know you are struggling with Roxy and Samantha getting in the way of your plans but you need to settle down. We can work our way through this," stated the doctor.

"I pay you a lot of money so why can't you get rid of these two?" responded the woman once again becoming agitated and annoyed.

Pausing and staring at the doctor with incredible intensity she continued, "It took me a long time, and plenty of hard work, to get the family fortune and then get rid of my father. So you start delivering some of those psychiatry skills or your little family secret will be made public."

Wade's study of psychology helped him realise what was going on. Samantha Cooper had multiple personalities. The two women, Roxy a child state and Samantha a middle aged recluse, were being dominated by Troy, the strong-minded, intelligent, business-oriented and power-hungry male.

After determining their location, he destroyed all the CCTV system and any associated security alarms.

10: Mount Walker

Wade moved through the building, avoiding two staff members, until he came upon a door with the nametag 'Roxy'.

About to open the door, he noticed the handle appeared to have never been touched. There was a small alarm activation contact at the base of the door. Removing a matchbox size piece of foil from his carry pack he slid it across the alarm; thus ensuring the circuit was not broken when he opened the door.

The buildings security and surveillance system was state of the art. Wade knew there would be a backup or failsafe option protecting the room. Searching the hallway he found the six inch by two foot sheet of material that was blended to match the floor covering. Picking up the sheet the reverse was lined with a reflective foil. Sliding it half under the door he heard the deactivation and the magnetic catch release.

Slowly pushing it open, he was confronted with an enormous room lined from floor to ceiling in dolls. It was laid out as a shrine. Walking through the room he realised that the dolls had been placed in specific locations and were obviously Roxy's pride and joy. All indications of somebody suffering

OCD. Removing blocks of C4 he rigged the explosives to detonate in thirty minutes. Leaving the room he ensured that the alarms were reactivated.

He had progressed a further twenty metres down the hallway when the building was suddenly filled with the screaming sound of what seemed a fire alarm and was thrust into darkness. He heard voices and shouts. Boots scuffing and scraping on the linoleum floor as people scurried for the exits. Following the sounds Wade emerged at a rear entrance and saw the staff running toward a dimly lit car-park.

Checking his location he saw a larger building, further up the mountain, off to the north. Avoiding the crowd of people pouring out the opposite entrance he ran across the manicured lawns.

The building was a hangar and a plane was being readied for take-off. The first of the two propellers had started its spinning motion. Wade saw a group of four men and a young girl standing at the entrance watching the pilot and waiting for the plane to leave the enclosure. Using the cover of darkness he quickly climbed the planes rear stairs and hid behind a tarped box that had been secured to the rails.

As the plane left the hangar he heard the guards, three large bulky Russians and a smaller, wiry Asian climb the steps and help the young Eastern

European girl aboard. The girl's eyes were glazed over and she had all the attributes of being drugged.

They took their seats as the plane taxied down the short runway. The flight lasted forty five minutes. Wade's GPS showed that they had headed in a north westerly direction and landed near Ucluelet, Barkley Sound, British Columbia.

The group, including the pilot, exited the plane and made the short walk to a bunker like facility, three hundred metres east of the runway and on the shores of a lake. Waiting until the bunker door had closed and the area was plunged back into darkness, Wade crept out of the plane and circled the building. His NVG showed no sign of guards or early warning detection devices. When convinced the surrounds were secure he climbed on the roof of the bunker. Using the exhaust duct he climbed down inside the bunker to be confronted with what appeared to be some form of sacrificial ceremony.

The cavernous arena was lit with thousands of candles and wall fires. The air was thick with overpowering, hallucinogenic incense. There were seventy males and females who were all dressed in white flowing robes. The heat and their sweat had the thin material clinging and clearly showing off their naked bodies. On the front of each robe was a blood-formed image of the inverted *Opus Dei* symbol. All members of the group had their hair pulled back tightly which was dyed black and glossy. The heat was intense and the group was chanting, sweating, and thrusting their hands in the air as they built to a crescendo.

He saw the three bulky Russians remove the clothes of the girl as the Asian delicately cut the inverted symbol onto her chest. They lay her, supine, on an altar and stepped away as the leader approached with a red hot glowing branding iron. Wade noticed how all the attendees continued to look between the altar and a large screen. The hundred square foot screen displayed Samantha Cooper smiling as she watched proceedings.

"The time has come for us to enjoy the fruits of our labour," came the distorted voice, of Cooper, from speakers strategically spread throughout the cave.

With that the leader dropped his robe and standing naked in front of the girl, raised the branding iron above his head and was ready to plunge.

From fifteen feet above Wade aimed his silenced H&K pistol and with one clean shot, hit the leader between the eyes. He instinctively swung to his left and a further two shots took out two of the bulky Russian guards. Leaping from his higher vantage point he landed directly in front of the third Russian. The Russian swung his arm in an attempted Haymaker. Wade ducked under the blow and as the huge fist passed he struck from underneath with a reverse Tiger Claw that shattered the Russian's throat killing him instantly.

Bringing his vision back to the group and expecting an onslaught of attackers he was surprised that nobody had moved. With their fists held in the air and the sweat cascading down their face and bodies they all remained rock solid.

The girl was stationary on the altar with the naked leader lying across her legs and the blood from his head shot spread over her chest and face. The entire group was transfixed on the scene at the altar. Samantha Cooper's voice screamed, "Get him. Get him. I want him dead. Punishment to all for eternity."

Still nobody moved, until the wiry Asian appeared and adopted the pose of a very experienced martial artist.

Wade and the Asian traded blows with both delivering decisive contacts throughout the fight, until a movement in Wade's peripheral vision momentarily distracted him. As he returned his focus the Asian struck out with a very controlled Tornado Kick that connected to the side of his head, knocking him unconscious.

11: Barkley Sound

His head hurt, his back and chest was stinging and he could feel his arms pulled above his head. Slowly opening his eyes he noticed he was still in the bunker and was suspended over a pit, hanging by his arms.

He was naked and the stinging sensation across his back was from a whipping he'd received. His blood was dripping into the pit and the crowd seemed fascinated by this.

"Well, well mister soldier or whoever you are. I finally get the chance to get rid of you and your tampering in my affairs," said Cooper watching from the screen.

Wade deducted by the tone of voice that she was speaking as the personality Troy and he knew from his studies that triggering the onset of one of the other personalities when the patient least expected it could sometimes cause the patient to enter a state of confusion.

"Hope your dolls didn't suffer too much," said Wade.

"It was you … you will pay … I hate you … I want you dead," she screamed in her childlike state.

Still screaming and yelling, 'Kill him … kill him.' Wade felt the support rope cut as he plunged into the pit.

Falling twenty metres into a pitch black hole and not knowing what to expect; he suddenly smashed into the freezing water. The force of the impact caused temporary concussion.

Coming to his senses, as he reached the deepest part of his fall, he knew that going directly back to the surface, from where he came, would be suicide. He started breaststroke kicking and five metres later crashed into a wall. Changing direction he kicked ten kicks knowing he would have covered ten metres and then started for the surface.

He could feel the pain in his head and he knew he was in the early stages of oxygen depletion and hypothermia. The lactic acid had built in his legs as he struggled to keep moving and he started to lose focus. Concentrating on his US Navy SEAL underwater training, slowly releasing air and relaxing he pushed further toward the surface. With everything around him still completely black and without warning his head smashed into a concrete base.

Concentrating on holding his bound hands against his stomach and using his back as a guide against the concrete, he tried desperately to kick. He knew his kicks were losing their strength and he was drifting in and out of consciousness.

Wade had shown he was one of the most gifted Special Forces soldiers throughout his various training regimes. He had proven to be the strongest swimmer, had the greatest endurance, the highest pain threshold and could sustain concentration well after others had succumbed.

With his head about to explode and the screaming desire for oxygen about to send him into a subconscious and consequently deadly state; he heard the spirits talk to him. They told him you don't give up; you will only die when you have served your time and now was not that time.

His belief and faith in the spirits was so strong he gave it one last effort and with that the concrete stopped and he burst through the surface. Gasping for air and struggling to stay afloat his first priority was to get out of the water.

He saw the shore thirty metres to his front as he kicked and lunged himself through the water. Eventually reaching the rocky edge of the lake he pulled himself out of the water. Exhausted, involuntarily shaking and trying desperately to stay coherent.

Wobbling to his feet, he used a rock to cut the rope binding his hands and headed for the hangar.

Entering he saw the plane had gone. With the air temperature approaching freezing point, he was naked, wet, beaten and had suffered doses of concussion. He knew he needed to get his core temperature up. Staggering to a change room he found soiled overalls, boots and an emergency Space Blanket. Donning two pair of the overalls and wrapping himself in the blanket, he used a towel and hot water to warm his head. The steam billowed from the shower as he drank copious amounts of the warm water.

Thirty minutes later he started to feel his energy levels rise, the warmth had returned and the shaking had stopped. A further thirty minutes passed and after more searching he discovered a tattered flight jacket and beanie.

Returning to the now deserted bunker with the last of the fires at the flickering stage, he located his pack, weapons, GPS and NVG.

It was midnight when he arrived at the Ucluelet harbour, after a steady paced twelve kilometre run from the bunker. The harbour was deserted. He found a forty foot, twin engine Scarab. Ensuring it was fully fuelled he released it from its moorings and let the outward flowing current drag the boat down to the open sea. Once passed the harbour master tower he engaged the engines and commenced the five hour trip.

12: Seattle

"Excuse me, sir. You cannot tie up here, this is US Naval property," stated the guard standing on the wharf.

"I need to talk to your Commanding Officer," replied Wade as he tried to keep the boat from contacting with the two IRB's that were tied further along the wharf with men scampering from.

"I'm sorry, sir but you'll need to go to a public wharf and then arrange to speak with the CO from the main gate."

"I understand the SOP (Standard Operating Procedure) Seamen but it's very important I get information to the NSC ASAP," yelled Wade once again trying desperately not to hit the IRB's.

With that Wade heard a voice from ten metres along the wharf, "You two, grab those mooring ropes," as he turned to see a fully kitted and camouflaged man pointing at his boat.

As the boat was secured, the person in charge stepped up to his boat. "Wade Ross ... what a surprise to see you here!"

"Hi Joe," replied Wade as he stepped from the boat and they shook hands.

Joe Carr, SEAL Team 6 Commanding Officer and a very good friend of Wade's. Joe was ten years senior to Wade and renowned as a tough taskmaster. He expected only the maximum from his men and would push everybody beyond their limits. Wade was one of the few people who Joe genuinely admired.

"I'm guessing you're not here for a visit and what the hell has happened to you?" Joe asked looking at the state of Wade's clothes, face and hands.

"I had some bad luck with a sacrificial ceremony and had to swim to get out," replied Wade smiling.

"Well … is there anything we can do to help?"

Wade explained the chain of events but left out the reason why. After some discussion Joe agreed to help Wade get back into the compound on Mount Walker.

Wade, Joe and the four SEALs got some breakfast, checked their weapons, prepared their gear and left Bangor Naval Base, Hood Canal.

Wade contacted General Forest and after a thorough detailed account, explained what he and the SEAL team intended to do.

13: Mount Walker

"What can I do now … they're all gone … my babies are all gone?" sobbed Roxy with her head in her hands.

"I understand but we need to put that behind us and look toward the future," responded the doctor calmly.

"You don't understand," she screamed.

Suddenly Samantha Cooper stood and the personality Troy took over.

"Okay, Doc, we're out of here. Grab whatever you can and be at the chopper in ten minutes. We won't be coming back … ever," he ordered.

Leaving the room Troy spoke into his mobile phone. Ordering his staff that a Code One was now operational.

Immediately the staff started loading documents, money, jewellery into carry bags, computers were erased and anything of importance that was not going on the flight was destroyed.

Exactly ten minutes later, two heavy haulage helicopters and a state of the art Bell 525 Relentless, carrying Samantha Cooper, the doctor and the Asian guard lifted off.

Not aware of his plans, Troy had instructed his staff to prepare for their return in ten days. They were to increase security details and surveillance.

14: Mount Walker

Wade and the SEAL team reached the cliff face, on the eastern side of Mount Walker, early afternoon. Wade had already explained the climb, the below level services area of the building and the early warning devices.

Having bought the proper climbing gear they went higher than the services area and entered from the perimeter fence.

The six men split into two three-man groups. Wade and the two SEALs coming in from north of the house using the water tanks as cover. Joe and the remaining two SEALs would enter from behind the hangar. They would have more protection both visually and from enemy fire but they also had a one hundred metre open lawn area they needed to cross.

Two metres from the fence. The team connected by throat mics and earpieces, Wade called a halt.

"What's up?" asked Joe through the mike.

"Something has changed … I'm not sure what but I have a feeling we might be walking into a trap," replied Wade with his head spinning from side to side.

"What do you want to do?" asked Joe again.

"I'm calling in a drone gas drop."

All six men backed away from the fence as they grabbed for their gas masks. Wade called through to General Forest the coordinates.

Six minutes later the single, grey, radar reflecting, unmanned drone took off from Fairchild US Air Force base carrying three gas canisters and two infrared disabling devices.

Using his portable GPS and radar tracking signal from Washington DC, Wade was able to watch as the drone approached. At 50,000 feet and directly above its target, the drone shot its package towards earth. Travelling at the speed of sound, the missile encased package got to 300 feet, exploded and the three canisters and two devices slowly floated into the compound.

With the knockout gas spewing from the canisters and all the infrared inactive, Wade and the team waited until the occupants rushed from the buildings.

Picking them off and when convinced there were no more; they proceeded to cut an opening through the fence and into the compound.

Entering Wade noticed the cameras were still operational and realised they were being watched. Ordering the team to hide from the cameras and put on a dead guards clothes, he explained they were to act as normal as possible and keep away from the buildings.

One of the SEAL members, found the power supply and set a C4 block. As the small explosion eliminated all power, Wade watched, as the cameras remained operational. Aware the whole facility was being controlled remotely and probably wired to explode.

"We need to get out of here … now," ordered Wade.

Special Forces operatives worldwide know that if somebody orders a withdrawal you react instantly.

With the two group's running back to their respective entry points, Wade suddenly heard the distinctive sound of a landmine exploding. Turning he looked across the lawn to see what remained of the two men who had been following Joe.

Without warning, the buildings and various parts of the perimeter erupted. Troy had pre-empted a possible attack could occur and had prewired explosives to be remotely detonated.

Wade, Joe and the two SEALs had survived the explosions but were suffering the consequences of blast concussion. No matter how hard they tried they could not get to their feet or keep their balance. The ringing in their ears was excruciating as their noses bled.

With the haze from the gas and the explosions starting to clear, Wade saw the fence and the welcome sight of the remaining SEAL Team 6 coming to their aid.

Joe had become concerned when Wade had called in the drone strike and thought it relevant to advise SEAL command, who then deployed the balance of the team.

The new arrivals cleared and checked for further activity, gathered the remains of their fallen comrades and called in a helicopter evacuation.

15: Washington DC

"Hey mate ... you been having fun without inviting us?" came the bellowing New Zealand voice from behind him, as Wade turned to see his buddies Kiwi and Jacko walking out of the airport terminal.

"What the hell, Wade ... what happened?" asked Jacko the ex-US Delta Force soldier who was looking at the cuts and bruises on Wade's face and hands.

"Nothing much, just ran into a door."

"Must have been a door packed with C4 and wielding an axe by the look of you," said Kiwi, the ex-Australian SAS soldier, as they all shook hands and slapped backs.

"The Colonel told us you'd be here and we've come to help," stated Jacko expecting a non-acceptance from Wade, who was renowned for getting results by working alone.

"Thanks guys, I appreciate that," he replied. "Come on ... time to pay Crystal and her dad a visit."

The three men climbed into the CIA Suburban as Wade called Crystal and learnt she was at the hospital. Her father had been attacked, beaten and left for dead with the CIA guards shot and killed when unknown assailants had broken into his home early the previous morning.

With her father on life support and knowledge that the family dog had been shot; Wade knew Crystal would be emotionally fragile and he would need to keep her as distanced as possible from the Samantha Cooper affair.

"My god Wade … what happened?" asked a concerned Crystal as he walked into the intensive care room.

"I'm okay … how's your dad?" As the three men stood back and looked at the pulverised body lying on the bed.

Trent was nearly unrecognizable with his head bandaged from a blunt instrument strike, his nose, cheek and jawbones shattered. Both eyes were blackened, bruised and swollen closed. Both arms and legs had been broken and his lungs were punctured from multiple broken ribs. The machines that were keeping him alive whirred and ticked as the intensive care nurse continually monitored his progress.

"They are not even sure he'll live," replied a scared Crystal as the tears flowed and she buried her head in Wade's chest.

They spent the next two hours at Trent's bedside until Wade said, "Crystal we need to do something about this. These people are not going to stop until either we're all dead or they're dead … I'm sorry

I've involved you and your dad but we must go," he said pointing at Kiwi and Jacko.

With her eyes red and puffed from all the crying she replied, "I'm coming to. There is nothing I can do here and I know it's what dad would want me to do."

Looking across at Kiwi and Jacko he noticed how they both nodded in agreeance.

"Okay let's go," he apprehensively replied.

The drive to the Warehouse gave Wade the opportunity to explain events. On arrival they noticed the massive increase in security details. Wade recognized the distinctive presence of the President's Secret Service as an aide ushered them into the secure conference room.

Entering Wade saw seated at the head of the table U.S President Markham, to his left General Razen and Charlotte Bysmith. To the Presidents right was General Forest, Kaitlyn, and Joe. Standing behind the President, against the wall, were two Secret Service agents and on the opposite wall two ceremonial dressed, rifle held, military MPs. At the far end of the table sat a well-dressed middle aged male Wade didn't recognise.

Upon seeing Wade President Markham stood and walked toward him. "Hello Wade," he said holding out his hand.

"Mister President," replied Wade shaking hands.

"I know you were trying to avoid catching up with us so we decided to find you instead," remarked Markham smiling and looking across at Bysmith and Razen. "And I assume this lovely lady is Crystal."

"Yes Mister President, lovely to meet you. Sorry about how I look," replied Crystal bowing her head as she shook hands.

"Please don't apologise. You look very beautiful."

"Mister President. I would like you to meet Kiwi and Jacko. Unfortunately due to operational reasons I cannot divulge their real names."

"That's okay Wade, I understand. Pleased to meet you gentlemen."

"Alright if everybody could take a seat we can get this briefing started," said Forest.

"I realise there are a few here who do not know others in the room and I will not delay proceedings by individually introducing but there is one person I do need to introduce." Looking across at the unknown male Forest said, "I would like you to meet Barry Olsen. Barry is from the Department of Homeland Security and has specialised in the study of the Cooper family and all its associated interests."

"Thanks General. The Cooper family is a self-made multi-billion dollar enterprise. The late grandfather who died of suspicious circumstances about thirty years ago started it. His son, the current benefactors father, who also died along with his wife suspiciously six years ago, succeeded him. They had three children, two sons and a daughter. One of those sons was Vice President Daniel Cooper who lost his life in an explosion in Darwin, Australia three months ago. His brother Thomas has not been seen or heard of for nearly twenty five years and his sister Samantha is a recluse in Seattle. Samantha lives in a fortress like facility on top of a mountain and the most current photo we have is this, taken three years ago," he said pointing to an image on the overhead projector.

"We know Samantha has multiple personalities and we believe, as many as seven. One of those personalities is an extremely dominant and aggressive male, who we believe, could have masterminded the demise of her parents. We have not been able to get remotely close to her home and therefore I can give no advice on the guarding force … Secondly, we believe, she has a large stake-holding in the world's diamond houses and might also be considering entering nuclear arms supply. The only name or semblance of a name we can help with is BB who might be a banker. Samantha Cooper has many bank accounts, as you would imagine, scattered throughout the world. One particular on the island of Sardinia, off the coast of Italy, has seen a rapid increase in the number and size of transactions over the last few months. We have tried following the money trail, but the web is too intense … Hope that helps Mister President," remarked Olsen.

"Thank you Barry," replied Forest escorting him to the door. Returning to his seat the General looked across to Wade, "Okay can you fill in the gaps from Barry's story?"

Wade stood and as he went to walk behind the President one of the Secret Service agents took a step forward and put his hand inside his jacket. Wade also noticed the two MPs tighten their grip on their rifles.

Looking down at the seated occupants, Wade took another step as the agent reached for his pistol and stepped in front of him. In one swift motion Wade grabbed the agent's pistol held hand, swung him one hundred degrees and fired a single shot into the forehead of the other agent. At the same time he wrapped his other arm around the first agent's head and snapped his neck.

Kiwi and Jacko reacted instinctively. Their Heckler & Koch 9mm pistols aimed at the two MPs before they had a chance to unsling their rifles from their respective shoulders.

Forest, Razen and Joe were half out of their seats when Wade said, "It's alright … everybody just calm down. Kiwi, Jacko put down your pistols. You two keep those rifles on your shoulders. Everybody sit down." As the sound of the pistol shot reverberated throughout the room.

"Wade, what the hell happened then?" asked Markham and Razen in unison, both looking down at the two dead agents.

Calmly sitting Wade replied, "I think you might find they're not the protection detail you expected, Mister President."

With that four men burst into the room, standard issue Secret Service weapons drawn, all dressed in black suits, white shirts, black ties and ear piece wires running up the back of their necks to their right ear.

"Down, down, down," screamed the leading agent as Markham got to his feet.

"Gentlemen, it's alright, no harm done. Could you please remove these two and find out who they are?" as he pointed at the two corpses. "And close the door on your way out," spoke the shaken President eyeing across to the blood splattered wall.

The four men looked around trying to decipher what had happened but knew better than to question the President.

As the security detail left the room Razen, looking bewildered said, "Wade how did you know?"

"Well General, I become suspicious by the way they kept looking at each other. Their demeanour was not ex-military and they didn't appear to have the typical Secret Service characteristics. I wasn't one hundred per cent certain until I started to walk behind President Markham and I saw the inverted *Opus Dei* symbol tattooed on his right wrist."

"What did they want?" asked Razen again.

"I'm not sure. I don't think their intention was to kill anybody. We'll probably find some form of recording device or microphone on them. My guess … it's Samantha Cooper."

Forest interjected and asked Wade to continue with filling in the missing or incorrect details from Barry Olsen's summation.

"Barry Olsen stated that the image was taken three years ago. Sorry I would say more likely ten or fifteen years ago. Samantha Cooper would have to be well over fifty years old. He mentioned she had seven personalities – well there are three. A young girl named Roxy, Samantha herself who is scared and a male Troy who is extremely violent, aggressive and dominant. Troy arranged the death of the father and most likely the mother. We don't need to worry about the fortress; it's destroyed along with all the guards. I believe Cooper and her psychiatrist had left before the building was blown," responded Wade.

"Also sir, Joe and I met with Professor Borgias Bart who is one of the leading scientists at the LHC Geneva. Unfortunately Mister President we know he is your son-in-law's uncle," stated Kaitlyn pausing for a response.

"I understand … go on," replied the President.

"I'm not sure I should be the one telling you this, but your son-in-law, Ryan Cotterill, was found murdered in his apartment, two days ago, along with a female who we have identified as a prostitute. We also know there has been a ninety five million dollar deposit into a bank account in his name," said Kaitlyn looking across at the glum faced president.

"Ladies and gentlemen, I appreciate your honesty and concern. We need to focus on the task at hand and I need to contact my family," replied a dejected Markham as the NSC team left the room.

16: Geneva

They discussed their options on the flight from Washington to Geneva and decided Kiwi and Jacko would try to locate the whereabouts of Cooper while Wade and Crystal would pursue Professor Bart.

Wade was the only member of the group who had spent any time in Geneva and on their arrival he took them to the Old Town part of the city. Buildings in this area are known to be over one thousand years old, but Wade was not taking them on an historical tour. Rather he was seeking out the many secret tunnels. Even though Switzerland served as a neutral country throughout most major conflicts, many of its inhabitants had ensured their safety by digging interlinking tunnels as escape routes.

Wade's association with Mossad and the Jewish community, in Israel, had enabled him to learn of the tunnels and the intricate details attached.

Tiffany Hotel was a standard level establishment that offered the group anonymity. After arriving in separate taxis and the three men certain they had not been followed, they gathered in the hotel room.

Using the secure link phone, Wade dialled Forest. "General, do we have anything on Bart or Cooper?"

"We have linked into the Geneva CCTV public surveillance system and Bart was last seen entering a building on Rue des Rois two hours ago. We have also received satellite imagery that shows helicopters leaving Cooper's Seattle home approximately three hours before you and the SEAL team arrived. We have tracked the choppers to Chicago and from there two identical private jets departed twenty minutes later. One of the jets went on an elaborate deception trail and is now on route back to Chicago. The other landed in Zurich and ten minutes later a helicopter took off for Geneva. We have not been able to get a visual, but sources confirm a middled-aged European male, a middle-aged American female and a younger Asian male were seen leaving the hanger in Geneva. Unfortunately the trail stops there," replied Kaitlyn.

"Thanks. We'll get back to you ASAP," said Wade as he disconnected the line.

"Okay guys, we have no idea what's going on and what resources they have so we stay silent unless absolutely necessary," ordered Wade as they nodded in agreeance.

Ten minutes later, as darkness came over the city and snow started to fall; Wade and Crystal dressed in fashionable black, left the rear of the hotel. A further ten minutes later Kiwi and Jacko followed suit.

17: Rue des Rois

Posing as honeymooning tourists, Wade and Crystal wandered past Rue des Rois. Hands deep into the pockets of his Armani double breasted woollen coat, collar upturned and Russian Cossack sheepskin hat low down over his face; his eyes scanned like a radar. Crystal wearing her equally fashionable long padded coat, fur hat, leather gloves had her arm linked through Wade's. The wind and snow was intensifying by the minute. The streets were deserted with the occasional shopper darting from one retail outlet to the next. After two more passes Wade was confident there were no guards or external CCTV. As they commenced to cross the street, Bart and the same Asian guard Wade had fought in Ucluelet, exited the building.

Doubling back, they followed Bart and the Asian to an apartment complex in downtown Geneva. Watching from a café across the street, Bart and the Asian returned ten minutes later. The Asian was carrying a rigid Samsonite case and was struggling with its heavy contents.

They followed them back to Rue des Rois. Wade called Kiwi and Jacko and instructed them to make their way to the apartment and do a sweep. He advised Crystal would meet them there and when finished they were all to head back to the Hotel.

Wade entered the rear of the building. He discarded his jacket and hat and made his way down the corridor, realising it was a diamond cutting house. The walls and doors were plated glass, there was vinyl floors and an exceptional high level of bright white lighting. Each room had a single fixed stainless steel table, one stool with cutting tools, large magnifying glass and a further light hanging from the ceiling.

The glass walls enabled him to check that nobody was on this level. Listening for voices he made his way deeper into the building. At the rear a set of stairs led both up and down. The lack of noise suggested underground so he headed down; three levels.

The lowest level was a storage area. Wade found a small door concealed in the lift motor room. Entering he found himself in the underground tunnel system and this time he heard voices. Following the sound he came upon a small enclave that was being used as an operations room.

Bart, the Asian, two guards and a further two suited men, of Arabic appearance, were standing around a table. The case was open and Wade saw one half contained grey uncut diamonds whilst the other had glistening, polished diamonds.

"So Professor, are you offering the uncut or polished version as your down payment?" asked one of the Arabic men, in perfect Queen's English.

"Actually Nariz, we are offering both, as a sign of good faith," replied the smiling Bart.

"Excellent Professor, we appreciate this and when do you want your first shipment?" asked the second Arabic man.

"As you are aware we lost both of our production facilities a few months back, along with Doksal, our man in charge, but Troy and I always had a contingency plan. So if you could arrange delivery to Genoa in six days, I will send through the address. It is important that the Plutonium 239 is undetectable," replied Bart.

"Understood," said Nariz as the two men and the guards were escorted, by the Asian, out of the tunnel.

Once certain that nobody was in earshot, Bart dialled his mobile phone. "Troy, it's me. Arabs are paid and we get the plutonium in six days."

Bart paused as he listened to a response and then continued, "I need two more days to finish emptying the accounts and then Li can get rid of Johansen and Staker. I have finalised the explosives for the Hadron and I was thinking we should probably blow it the day before the delivery in Genoa."

Another response from Troy and then Bart continued, "I agree and we need to disassociate ourselves from the Wolves … I'll meet you there at 11."

Trying to piece the information together Wade waited until Bart and the Asian had left the building and then went on a reconnaissance of the tunnels.

18: Bart's Apartment

Kiwi knew how much Crystal meant to Wade so he wasn't prepared to risk anything happening to her. He had her remain in a café opposite the apartment complex and watch for unexpected visitors.

Like monkeys, Kiwi and Jacko scaled the back wall as they climbed downpipes, shutters and balconies. Reaching the third floor they found an unsecured window and entered. Avoiding the cameras they used the fire stairs to the fourth floor and found the apartment.

With no apparent guards evident, Jacko removed his H+K MP5SD 9mm, sound suppressed sub-machine gun, while Kiwi had his ever reliable H+K MK23 pistol. Both men were wearing NVG's, body armour and had a second weapon, notably a Sig Sauer P226 9mm pistol tucked in their rear waistband.

Using sign language, they approached the door and within four seconds Jacko had opened the electric locking latch and they entered.

Leap frogging they made their way through the apartment, checking every room for movement or body heat detection. Convinced it was all clear they removed their goggles, and using torches, commenced searching for any relevant documentation.

Jacko was searching through boxes on the floor of the second bedroom closet while Kiwi was attempting to remove a ceiling access hatch in the hallway, when the front door burst open.

The two men lunged through the door firing rapid succession bursts of their Bullpup configured FN P90 silenced machine guns.

Kiwi took a round to the leg and one to the abdomen as he fell to the floor. The attackers had covered five of the ten metres separating Kiwi from the door when Kiwi aimed his pistol and shot the closer assailant between the eyes.

The round of the H+K MK23 instantly halted the attacker as he started to fall to his left. The second attacker realising what had happened triggered fully automatic and aimed around his falling partner. The 5.7mm rounds danced across Kiwi's body armour and one lodged in his right bicep.

With the room now in semi darkness, and as his attacker changed his empty magazine, Kiwi grabbed his dropped pistol with his left hand and fired. Unsure of whether his shots had found their mark, Kiwi felt the energy drain from his body. Jacko burst into the hallway and opened fire with his submachine gun. Certain his target was down Jacko checked outside the apartment door.

As he switched on the light he became aware of Kiwi's critical condition.

"Don't worry bro. I'll get you out of here," spluttered Jacko, trying to remain calm.

After years of being confronted with blood, guts and death; Special Forces operatives worldwide become immune to the effects but no matter how hard they try, when it's one of their own, they falter.

"How bad?" stammered Kiwi.

"You'll be rap dancing before you know it," replied Jacko, struggling to keep his composure, knowing his mate was bleeding to death.

Desperately applying compression bandages to his leg and arm whilst trying to hold a field bandage on his stomach, Jacko watched as Kiwi took his last breath.

Closing Kiwi's eyelids, Jacko knew the mission must go on. He dialled up Colonel Wine and Wade.

"Foxtrot Uniform One to Bravo and Whiskey," called Jacko.

"Bravo, go ahead," replied Wine.

"Foxtrot Uniform Two is Delta, I repeat, Foxtrot Uniform Two is Delta, over," stated Jacko knowing his voice was telling the story.

Wine knew Foxtrot Uniform One was Field Unit 1, Jackson and Field Unit 2 was Kiwi and no Commanding Officer ever wanted to hear that one of his unit was Delta, dead.

The Colonel instructed Jacko to remove Kiwi's body, ensure nothing was left behind and gave him coordinates to get to. He then rang Forest, explained the situation, upon which Forest arranged collection of Jacko, Kiwi and Crystal. The General then organised a CIA sweep team to cleanse the apartment and leave no trace of any intrusion.

19: Lake Geneva

In a heavily forested area of Hermance, Switzerland on the shore of Lake Geneva, the CIA had one of their secure locations.

Approaching midnight, Crystal looked across to Jacko, "Do you know if Wade knows yet?" she asked.

"No … we haven't made contact," he replied without lifting his head.

"He'll take this hard, won't he?"

"Yeah … he will and God knows what he'll do," replied Jacko, this time lifting his head and looking out the window into the darkness with his steely black eyes.

Crystal stood, walked over and put her arms around his neck as she said, "I love you all and I'll miss him too."

Jacko heard the approaching cars and was at the front door of the cabin before the two CIA guards had even heard a sound.

The three fully laden Suburbans passed the gate guards at the bottom of the drive and made their way along the nine hundred metre gravel road.

Each vehicle had four occupants, their packs, weapons, ammunition and all the equipment they would need for most situations. Wine sat in the front passenger seat of the lead vehicle staring straight ahead and thinking about the missions that the team and Kiwi had been through.

They had been operating for three years. Their success rate was one hundred per cent without having lost a team member. Wine knew they would all react differently and he had to ensure they were given the opportunity to mourn the loss of their friend.

As the vehicles pulled up outside the cabin and the team members saw Jacko, the reactions erupted. Some hugged and patted their mate, some looked and stared and some were angry with themselves but all offered their condolences.

"Grab and stow your gear. In the meeting room in ten," commanded Wine.

The shock of the order bought all the team members, Jacko included, back into military mode and they set about the instinctive action of mission preparation.

Jacko was reaching into the back compartment of the second Suburban, lifting out the deflated IRB (Inflatable Rescue Boat), when Wine approached and asked, "Does he know yet?"

"No sir," replied a dejected Jacko.

"I want you to explain to all of us, everything you know about what's going on and what happened with Kiwi. No one's blaming you Jacko … they're all reacting differently because he was a good friend and a great comrade and they'll all miss him in their own way," explained Wine.

Jacko nodded and dropped his head as he headed for the cabin.

Wine approached Crystal. "Are you okay?"

"I'm fine thanks Colonel," she replied looking him straight in the eyes. "How will Wade react?" she asked.

"I'm not sure ... Kiwi and Wade were exceptionally close and they've been through a lot together. Did he ever tell you that when Kiwi's grandmother died, Kiwi asked him to go to New Zealand with him to be part of a sacred burial service? Kiwi's grandmother was a Maori and his only living relative so the significance of the request developed a very strong bond between them. Therefore I hate to say this but there is a possibility he could go on a warpath of revenge," replied the Colonel looking across the lake to the lights of Geneva.

20: Hermance

It was two hours before sunrise and still snowing as Wade entered the rear door of the Tiffany Hotel. Arriving at the room he was surprised that nothing had changed and there was no warmth or noise.

Carefully searching the rooms he thought something must have gone wrong.

"Jacko, where are you?" he asked speaking into the mobile phone.

"Hi Wade," came the slow disjointed words and then the silence.

"Jacko, what's going on?" asked Wade again, this time with concern in his voice.

With still more silence Wade this time raised his voice, "Jacko, what the hell … talk to me."

"Wade its Colonel Wine, I have bad news … we lost Kiwi during the night."

The Colonel listened to the silence on the phone as he waited for Wade to respond. After nearly sixty seconds Wade asked, "He was gunned down in the apartment, right?"

"That's right."

"What happened to the shooter?"

"They're both dead," replied the Colonel trying to gauge how Wade was taking the news.

"What about Crystal?" asked Wade stepping back into military mode.

"She's here with us. Where are you, we'll come and get you?"

Wade explained and twenty minutes later a Suburban pulled up in the back alley, as Wade loaded the group's belongings.

It was snowing heavily and visibility was down to a metre as Wade exited the vehicle and crossed to the door of the CIA safe house. Standing on the porch under the shrouded single light he saw Crystal, Colonel Wine and Jacko.

Stepping out into the snow Jacko approached Wade and put his arms around his friend.

"I'm sorry … I couldn't stop the bleeding," Jacko softly said as he stepped back and watched the snow start to pile on their shoulders and heads, with their eyes fixed in a stare.

"Don't blame yourself mate … he is a great friend and we need to never forget him," replied Wade stepping forward and grabbing his friend in an overhand fist hold.

Crystal thought to herself how once again Wade had inferred that people don't leave us when they die they just enter another part of life.

With his arm around his mate Wade stepped on to the porch. He saw the tears cascading down Crystal cheeks.

"Don't cry Crystal … he wouldn't want you to," Wade said as he put his other arm around her shoulder and lead them all inside.

The team spent the next three hours talking about their friend and reliving past experiences. They laughed and at times were solemn but they all knew the profession they had chosen in life was dangerous and deadly. Every one of them knew given a second chance they would still do it a second time round and Kiwi was no different.

Wade stood in the middle of the lounge room and looked around at all the faces in front of him. He knew they were not only friends but also now more than ever determined to make Kiwi's death count.

"Alright the Colonel has arranged for Kiwi's body to be taken back to New Zealand. We're not going to bury him until we finish this and every single one of us is at his gravesite … you got that?" Wade stated, with the conviction in his voice Crystal had not heard before, "Okay, gear up, twenty minutes we're out of here."

The team went through the motions of checking their weapons, assembling their gear, discussing their tactics and dressing in the relevant clothing.

The Colonel and Wade had devised a plan that had Wine and six team members concentrate on the LHC. Jacko and three of the team would infiltrate the diamond cutting house whilst Chrissie, the only female member of the team and an ex-

Froemandskorpset (Danish Special Forces Frogmen) and Morrie, the cold and expressionless ex-KSK (German Special Forces Kommando Spezialkrafte) would concentrate on following Bart and if found, Samantha Cooper.

Forest, Kaitlyn and Joe advised they should be at the CIA Geneva station within the hour. Wade convinced Crystal that he needed her to stay with the General and try to source more information on *Opus Dei*. He believed its connection to Cooper would be the breakthrough they needed.

Wade was the first to leave. He grabbed his pack and weapon and gave Crystal a peck on the cheek. He looked at the team and without a word, walked out.

"What do you think Colonel?" asked Crystal as he closed the door.

With the rest of the team listening, Wine replied, "I don't really know Crystal … he is taking it better than I thought he would but one thing I have learnt from knowing Wade, is that when he gets that steely-eyed look, things tend to happen."

21: Capodichino

Sitting in the back seat of the CIA Suburban, Wade was trying desperately to control his emotions. With his eyes closed and his fists clenched he saw his mother and heard her telling him that vengeance was not the solution. She once again explained to him how all life was equal and the time for retribution was not for him, but for the Spirits to choose. She got him to promise that he would concentrate on his mission and leave the soul of the dead to her and his sister.

Opening his eyes, as he entered the gate of the private enclosure at Geneva International Airport, he dialled up Forest.

"General, can you organise for me to land at Naples command? I need to get onto Sardinia … silently," asked Wade.

"By the time you get to Naples, it'll be organised. Why Sardinia and why now, especially after what happened to your friend Kiwi?"

"Difficult question, short answer. I need to finish this for him and something tells me Sardinia is where it will start," replied Wade as he disconnected the line.

The CIA private jet landed on the busy runway at the US Naval Base, Capodichino, Naples. The jet taxied to the assigned hangar at the furthest end of the base. Wade exited as a young naval seaman, stepped forward, "Sir, you must come with me," motioned the seaman pointing to the black windowed Lincoln parked behind him.

After a short drive to an abandoned looking warehouse, they got out and entered a rear door. Leading Wade, through a maze of empty offices, pallets stacked to the roof and surplus shrink wrapped military equipment; the seaman stopped and knocked on a very insignificant door.

"Come in," said a disinterested female voice.

Wade entered to see an immaculately presented female Lieutenant Commander seated behind a small desk and working under a single desk light. Upon seeing Wade, she stood up, put out her hand across the desk and welcomed him.

"Good afternoon, Mister Ross. Lieutenant Commander Price. How are you?" she asked in her strong Georgia accent.

"Fine thank you Commander," replied Wade still trying to gauge why he was here.

"Please have a seat. You are probably wondering why you have been brought to me and why here?"

Nodding, he replied, "I guess it has something to do with my request and the less who know the better."

"Correct. The Admiral thought it best I get whatever you want and get you to the carrier."

Wade explained the equipment he required and asked to leave as soon as possible.

22: USS Harry S. Truman

Two hours later he was on a Seahawk helicopter bound for the aircraft carrier USS Harry S. Truman, currently deployed with the US Sixth Fleet stationed in the Mediterranean Sea.

Admiral Sandy (Tank) Boston sat in his chair high up in the Flag Bridge watching his pilots and crew go through their drills. A plane was launching or landing every fifty seconds and Tank loved the buzz it caused on the carrier deck.

"Admiral we have to delay landings. We have an incoming Seahawk from Naples command," reported the Air Boss through the closed address system, two levels above.

Tank knew even he could not override the Air Boss when it involved planes around or on the carrier.

"Blast … who the bloody hell is this pain in the arse?" retorted Tank swinging his chair around to watch the incoming helicopter.

"Captain, get that bloody pest from the Seahawk up to me straight away. He better have a flaming good reason for interrupting these exercises," blasted Tank.

Tank watched as a black-clad, dark-skinned male carrying two oversized black carry bags, jumped out of the Seahawk. He watched him walk across the deck and could tell by the way he carried himself he was definitely military. He noticed how he seemed to float on the balls of his feet, jungle cat like, and his head and eyes were continually scanning.

The knock came at the door as his visitor entered.

"Admiral Sandy Boston, and who do I have here?" he stated in his big booming Irish American voice.

Noticing the admiral didn't get out of his chair, Wade replied nonchalantly, "Wade Ross."

Standing up and walking around his desk the Admiral stood nose to nose with Wade and bellowed, "Well Mister Wade Ross you might want to remember who you are addressing and you will salute me."

Wade not budging, infuriated the Admiral even more as he further bellowed, "Son, I don't know or care, who you are but this is my fleet and everybody does as I say. You have just crossed the line and I intend to have you written up. Do you understand?"

"Admiral, you might want to shut the hell up, sit down and get the Chairman of the Joint Chiefs on the line," calmly replied Wade.

Tank could not believe his ears. "What are you talking about?"

"I assume as an Admiral you know who the chairman is?" Wade calmly replied again.

"Why the hell would the CJCS need to talk to you?"

"I think you might want to ask General Razen that question, not me," Wade replied as he lowered his bags and sat in the vacant chair at the desk opposite the Admiral.

Conceding, Tank sat down and got his aide to get the CJCS on the line. The air in the Admiral's office was so tense you could cut it with a knife as the two men sat in silence.

Two minutes later the red phone on the Admirals desk lit up and a voice came on the line.

"Who do we have?" emanated out of the phone.

"Mister President, it's Wade and I'm here with Admiral Boston."

"Well hello Wade, you sure do get around. I've got General Razen, Charlotte Bysmith and somebody I don't believe you have met Admiral Paul James. Admiral James is the Director of National Intelligence and we felt could be beneficial with this mission."

"Thanks, but I've called to get General Razen to authorise Admiral Boston to get me in the air."

Admiral Boston was completely dumbfounded as he sat and listened to this most unlikely person, with the Australian accent, talking to the three most powerful people in Washington, as if they were his best friends.

"Admiral Boston, can you hear me?" asked Razen.

"Sorry sir, yes I can hear you," replied Tank.

"Good, so you will ensure Mister Ross gets whatever he wants … am I clear on that Admiral," stated Razen.

"Yes sir, very clear," replied Tank as the line went dead.

Sweating profusely and trying to stay calm, Tank looked at Wade and said, "I'm sorry for what I said before Mister Ross."

"Admiral, don't worry about it. I'm not part of your military, so call me Wade … I need you to get me to 30,000 feet at one hour after sunset. I'll give the pilot the coordinates once I'm in the air."

"What do you intend to do once you get there?" asked the Admiral with astonishment written across his face.

"HALO jump."

23: Geneva

The Geneva CIA office was typical of all CIA offices around the world. The rooms were small catering for no more than three people, a front reception that was indistinguishable and a secure, soundproofed meeting room.

Forest needed everybody to be in the secure room. A room that would normally cater for a table, chairs and six people was now occupied by Kaitlyn, Joe, Crystal, the General, two analysts, a communications controller and four aides plus all their respective equipment.

"Okay people, I know it's squashed but what've we got?" asked Forest. "You all know what it's like with Wade. We're not going to get ahead of him, but we should at least be able to keep up."

"Sir, we have uncovered the name Barkers and even though we can't cross match, it's interesting that Barkers are a diamond cutting tool company that has its main facility on the island of Sardinia. They operate out of a small warehouse in the town of Porto Cervo. We've been able to intercept some product coming off the island and it appears to be high grade steel cutting gear. We believe it's destined for the banks of Switzerland, as they are one of the few countries that use this quality steel.

The main problem we have with our deduction is the equipment needed to operate these cutting tools is quite large and cumbersome and highly unlikely to be dragged into a bank vault during a robbery," said Kaitlyn.

"Sir, we have also had information back from the lab at Langley and they have been able to find traces of Tungsten carbide in the indentation of the inverted *Opus Dei* symbol in the desk. Tungsten carbide is a product normally associated with encasing Plutonium 239," stated one of the aides.

"Do we know where this Tungsten carbide comes from?" asked Forest.

"It's quite a common product and the small sample we obtained would make tracing it virtually impossible," replied the aide again.

A second aide went on to explain the production process of Plutonium 239 and the potential consequences associated with its manufacture as she flashed images of the process on the overhead screen.

"What are you thinking Joe?" asked Forest as he watched him screw his face up in concentration.

"I'm not sure sir, but I get the feeling this has something to do with nuclear production and a new form of weapon."

"Kaitlyn we know Wade is on the USS Harry S. Truman and headed for Sardinia, so can you get this information to him. Joe can you relay about the cutting tool equipment to Colonel Wine so his team in the tunnels can keep a lookout?" ordered the General.

"General, do we know how Wade is getting back?" asked Crystal.

"Depending on what happens on the island; he was hoping to enter mainland Italy at Portofino and we would pick him up … why Crystal?"

"Sir, I'd like to surprise him there … please!" she asked with pleading eyes that Forest couldn't resist.

"Okay," replied the General with a smile on his face. "I didn't realise the CIA had become a dating service."

The rest of the group immediately stopped what they were doing and looked at the General in surprise. No-one had ever heard him speak in this tone, let alone make a joking remark.

24: Sardinia

Wade explained to Admiral Boston that he needed to be at 30000 feet to avoid the elaborate radar detection that operated around the western end of the Mediterranean. The plane needed to be able to operate in stealth or radar blocking mode. The height of the parachute jump plus rapid descent and low opening reduced the likelihood of detection.

The Admiral mentioned that no matter how low he opened his chute the ground radar would still pick him up.

"I intend to land in the water."

"That would be suicide. To avoid detection you would need to be six thousand metres from land and at that distance either the currents, shipping traffic or sharks will get you," stated the Admiral, looking across to the other man in the room, Captain Mike Sover who nodded in agreeance.

Sover had control of the carrier and was a veteran of thirty five years naval service with most of that in the Mediterranean or Middle East. He had seen and heard most of the daring and ridiculous ideas that individuals and Naval Command had dreamt up and he felt this was just as ludicrous.

"Thanks for your concern and help gentlemen but I leave in ten," said Wade as he stood and left the Flag Bridge.

"He is either crazy or some type of super SEAL," remarked Sover.

Fifty minutes later as the V22 Osprey approached the coordinates that Wade had provided; the pilot advised that they were two minutes from the jump point. The jump door opened and the air buffeted the inside of the aircraft escape hatch. Wade checked his altimeter, oxygen, parachute, tightened all his straps and looked out into the darkness as he waited for the green light to appear.

He started to think of why he was here. Was he making any difference every time he put his life on the line? Closing his eyes, he thought of Kiwi and his wasted loss of life. The vision of him and his mate sitting in the sunshine as they drank their beers and talked about anything that popped into their heads, made Wade smile. Continuing to imagine these thoughts the vision faded to Kiwi lying dead on a table and everything getting darker. Trying desperately to stop the images and open his eyes, the vision disappeared as quickly as it had appeared.

As he stood there with his helmet on, hearing the sound of the oxygen and the roaring of the air forcing its way through the small opening; he saw the elders appear before him.

Wade had great respect for the aboriginal elders and he watched and listened as he heard them say 'You must accept who you are and what you are expected to do whilst always remembering where you came from. You are not being judged but merely part of the life cycle. Just as the kangaroo will struggle to find food in the desert and the field mouse will endeavour to avoid the clutches of the hawk, you must continue to fulfil your obligations no matter how difficult.'

The wisdom of the elders always made Wade feel better as he stood and concentrated on the green light.

To keep radar detection to a minimum the Osprey needed to continue, at least, at its cruising speed. At four hundred kilometres an hour Wade's exit was never going to be easy. The light went green as he dived into the darkness and the turbulence generated by the large three-bladed prop rotor threw him into a vicious continual barrel roll.

Finally able to contain the rolling he clamped his arms to his body and adopted the head first dive to help maximise speed. Opening his chute at two thousand four hundred feet he had slowed just enough as he released himself from the harness and fell the last ten feet into the water.

Bobbing on the surface he removed his helmet, checked his dive oxygen was operational, put on his flippers, took his bearings and dived underwater.

He was at forty feet and had got himself into a rhythm of kicking and stroking, checking his handheld sonar detector and GPS every two to three minutes, when he saw the screen on his right wrist suddenly flash red. It was a ship and the draft was far deeper than his current forty feet.

With the ship closing on him at fifteen kilometres an hour he knew he had less than sixty seconds to get to a minimum of ninety feet. Frantically kicking and stroking he dived down as he felt the water turbulence, of the supertanker, start to increase. Keeping himself directed into the ocean current he kicked as hard as he could to fight the suction.

The lactic acid in his legs had reached a crescendo. He was using up valuable oxygen as he forced his legs to keep pushing him down. Eventually he felt the water turbulence change from an upward sucking affect to a scattered washing machine motion, indicating the rear propellers were passing over.

When certain the ship had passed he started the slow ascent. Coming to the surface and by now approaching exhaustion he checked his tank and saw it was at ten percent. The swell had increased to six feet and he was still two kilometres from the shore.

Accepting the tank was of no use; he ditched it and started swimming. The current running in the same direction aided him but the wind was increasing the height and intensity of the swell.

Wade could tell from the pain in his arms and legs and the double vision that he was fatigued and starting to lapse into a semi-conscious state. He tried to stop to get his bearings but the ever increasing swell only served to crash waves over his head. Desperately treading water he caught a glimpse of light and estimated he was two hundred metres from the shore.

The handheld sonar tracking device lit up again. Bringing the unit to his face and attempting to decipher what was happening he never saw the bow of the boat as it came over the crest of the wave and slammed into his shoulder. The force of the impact, and the speed with which the boat fell down the face of the wave, pushed Wade under the boat and knocked him unconscious.

"What was that?" screamed Luigi to his brother as they both looked out into the blackness of the violent sea and dangerous waves.

The small fishing boat had reached the bottom of the swell and was about to head up the next wave when Luigi and Pepi were thrown off their feet. Grabbing for the gunnels they saw the fishing net had broken the surface and something large was caught in it.

These poor Sardinian fishermen depended on their daily catch for survival. They had been out in their small twenty foot fishing boat for thirty two hours and nothing to show for their efforts. They had held off heading back to shore, hoping their luck would change. Waiting too long they got caught in the storm.

"We need to cut the net," shouted Pepi, trying to find the knife.

"No, we can't. How will we catch anything," shouted Luigi. "Come on, let's try and pull it in," he said as he grabbed one of the ropes leading out to the net that was now starting to pull them under the next wave.

Both men, using all their remaining strength, dragged at the net. The next wave swamped over their boat. Luigi being closer to the face of the wave took the full brunt smashing into the floor. Pepi who had the rope wrapped around his arm was thrown into the ocean. The wave had turned the boat across the direction of the swell and the small inboard motor was screaming to compensate for the extra water in the boat and the added tow weight.

Pepi's head hit the side of the boat. He lost consciousness as the rope pulled tight and he was flung on top of Wade. The impact of Pepi into his chest jolted him. Trying to decipher what was happening, Wade pulled himself against the net to free his legs and get his head above water.

Using all his strength he lifted himself onto the net. With his knife he cut his legs free and pulled himself to the edge of the boat. Another wave crashed over him.

With each wave, came more water into the boat, which aided to steady the rocking. Dragging himself aboard, Wade lifted Luigi into a sitting position. Pulling on the rope, he was able to grab Pepi's arm before the next wave engulfed the three men.

The blackness of the night had worsened as the intensity of the rain increased. Wade knew he had to find a way to shore. The engine stalled as Luigi coughed and opened his eyes.

"Who are you?" asked Luigi, in Italian, trying to focus on what was happening.

"The name's Wade. We need to get out of here. Do you have a life raft?" responded Wade in fluent Italian.

Luigi moved towards his brother who was propped against the bulkhead, as the next wave crashed over their heads.

Wade knew they only had about one or two more waves before the boat would sink. Feeling around the bulkhead he found two life jackets. Sliding one over Pepi's head and handing the other to Luigi, he cut the net rope and started to tie it around their waists. The boat started to rise over the next wave; Wade grabbed the two men and jumped into the water.

Having determined the direction to shore and struggling to keep Pepi's head above water, Wade started swimming and dragging the two men.

After a further twenty minutes, the rain had increased but the waves had stopped breaking. Still contending with the swell and dragging the two men backwards, he finally felt the rocks and heard the sound of shore breakers.

Helping Luigi, and carrying Pepi, all three crawled up the shore and collapsed at the tree line. Removing the vests and rope, Wade tore off Pepi's shirt and used it as a bandage for his arm.

Getting to his feet, Luigi helped Wade carry Pepi as they headed for their home.

"Thank you for helping us," shouted Luigi, over the wind, rain and surf as they staggered along the foreshore road.

Arriving at a small, clean and tidy home, Luigi's wife Maria met them at the door. She grabbed hold of Pepi and assisted Wade to get him onto the bed. Wade applied a proper bandage to his arm and left him to sleep.

Wade looked around the small fisherman's cottage and saw the tattered lounge chairs, the faded picture frames, and the walls that had not been painted for years. The bare timber floors were worn and scratched and the thin curtains would provide no protection against the hot summer sun. He saw the dried fruits and vegetables hanging above the kitchen sink. The tiny two room building was in urgent need of repair but Wade was amazed at how well this incredibly poor Italian couple looked after their property.

"I'm sorry for the loss of your boat … and I hope you are both okay," said Wade watching as Maria, shaking, sat down.

"What will we do," whispered Maria crying into her hands.

Watching this poor middle aged lady in the worn clothes trying desperately to keep her composure; Wade started to feel overcome with emotion.

"I know it might be hard to believe but I will arrange for some help for you. Thank you and I hope we meet again." He put out his hand to Luigi.

"Where will you go? What will you do at this time of night?" asked the devastated and exhausted Luigi as they shook hands.

Wade explained he had a job to do in Porto Cervo and then he would head back to Switzerland. Omitting to give any details, he turned to open the door as Luigi said, "Please take our truck; it is a long walk to Porto Cervo."

Wade, knowing that they clearly could not afford to lose it, suddenly felt an emotion rise up through his back. An emotion he had never felt before, nor could explain.

He was a trained killer. He had seen the worst in people and felt the loss of his family and as the tears of emotion overcame him; he dropped his head in embarrassment.

"Thank you, your offer is truly humble. I genuinely appreciate it. But I really don't need it and I promise I will return." Hugging them both, picking up his pack, he turned and left.

25: Porto Cervo

Three hours later, jogging through unrelenting rain and in complete darkness, Wade arrived at the warehouse facility of Barker Tool Company. The building was a standard, corrugated iron construction on the western side of town. In the distance was the luxurious Yacht Club Harbour, frequently visited by the rich and famous.

Skirting the perimeter, checking for detection devices, Wade scaled the eight foot fence, framed in barbed wire. Using pallets stacked beside the main roller door, he was able to access a small upper level window. The internal layout had multiple offices facing the front road. There was a small packaging warehouse at the rear. Searching the offices, he found the one he considered to be for the person in charge. Activating his computer key he waited for the company's information to be uploaded to Kaitlyn.

Whilst waiting for the upload, he noticed a photo that resembled somebody familiar. Putting the photo in his pack, removing the key, he set about placing C4 throughout the building.

It was early morning, the sun starting to crest the horizon as the water taxi from Portofino approached.

Wade took his seat on the luxury cruiser. As it departed he activated the remote detonation, destroying all evidence of the Barker Tool Company facility.

26: Portofino

Wade tried to sleep, without success, the entire six hour trip from Sardinia to the Italian Riviera, small coastal town of Portofino. Arriving in the quaint fishing village, renowned as a destination for the wealthy, he made his way through the arrivals lounge to be met by Crystal.

"Hello gorgeous," he said as Crystal threw her arms around his neck and started kissing him passionately.

After minutes of standing in the same place, kissing, looking around, kissing again – passengers trying to avoid them in the middle of the thoroughfare, Wade put back his head and said, "Well this is a very nice welcome."

With her arms tightly wrapped around his one free arm, Crystal led him out into the midday sun.

"I've booked a room for us at the Hotel Splendido," remarked Crystal trying to emphasise the name with some Italian flair.

"That's wonderful but don't we need to get back to Geneva?" asked Wade continually checking the surroundings.

"I teed it up with General Forest and Colonel Wine," replied Crystal, trying to keep the huge smile off her face.

They spent the remainder of the afternoon exploring the sights of Portofino, sitting in luxurious bars overlooking the magnificent harbour, as they talked, laughed and enjoyed feeling carefree.

With the sunset reflecting off the water Crystal looked across and said she was going to take a shower. She reminded him of the dinner she had booked and the clothes she had arranged for him were on the bed.

After she had left, Wade headed back to the jewellery shop he had seen as they were wandering around the marina.

He was dressed, ready and had been waiting in the lounge as Crystal walked from the bedroom. Wade could not believe how beautiful she looked. Dressed in a one-shoulder, white, skin-hugging, mid-length dress that the crystalline green waters of the harbour behind her accentuated. Standing, as she approached the couch, he held her at arm's length. He gazed into her gleaming green eyes and saw her purse her lips in embarrassment.

"Stunning ... absolutely beautiful," he said softly kissing her.

"You don't look too bad yourself, Mister Ross," she replied wrapping her arms around his neck.

Wade had met and slept with numerous women throughout his life but for the first time it felt different. He knew he had fallen in love.

He squeezed her body against him as he ran his hands up and down her back, while continuing to kiss her lips and neck. The feel of the dress and her body was electrifying and as he reached her bottom, she suddenly tensed and pushed harder against him. Wade realised she was naked under the dress and was becoming extremely excited. He felt her erect nipples against his thin linen shirt as he became more and more aroused.

They were both in a frenzy of arousal when Crystal suddenly stopped and pushed him away.

"Mister Wade Ross, I love you and want you now more than any woman could possibly want a man but we have a dinner we are going to first and then … you can ravish me to your heart's content," she said with a huge smile as she pulled her dress back into shape.

Wade gently grabbed her hand and they started for the door. "I'm not sure you'll be safe walking in public in a dress like that," he remarked gently tapping her behind.

Walking through the streets, of Portofino, on the balmy evening they looked like movie stars dressed in their beautiful white Italian clothes, with their rich olive skin, arm in arm and very much in love.

The owner thought that the couple that had just entered his restaurant must be very important or famous so he organised the best table with magnificent views of the harbour.

110

Italians are renowned for their love and fascination of all things beautiful. Wade and Crystal, sitting at their table attracted a lot of attention. Passer-by's stopped and looked, men complemented Crystal on her beauty and tourists tried to get the courage to ask for an autograph.

They had finished their dessert and the second bottle of Chianti when the lights went dim as the waiter approached carrying a single lit candle.

Crystal looked around, trying to figure out what was happening. She saw all the faces of the restaurant patrons, the staff and passers-by, looking directly at her. Wade stood and came around to her side of the table. Bending down on one knee, he removed the small velvet box from under the gold dome that had been on their table the whole evening.

"Crystal Carters … the most beautiful and caring woman I have ever met … will you marry me?"

Crystal was stunned as she looked at Wade. She looked at all those watching, looked at the beautiful diamond engagement ring and tried so hard to say yes, but nothing came out.

Watching her, Wade realised what was happening as he stood and helped her to her feet. Once standing and now slightly more composed, she replied, "Yes, yes … my God yes," as they kissed and the crowd cheered.

With the lights back on and after much congratulating and celebrating, Wade and Crystal left.

Crystal could not take her eyes off the ring as they strolled along the walkway with the cruisers and yachts to their left and the exclusive shops and fashion designer outlets to their right. The full moon was directly overhead as Crystal asked, "Thank you for asking me to marry you, but why now?"

Staring at the moon, Wade explained the unusual emotions and feelings he had been getting since arriving in Italy. Crystal knew Wade was a person who had a strong belief in these thoughts and feelings and wanted to talk to him about it. She also noticed he had that faraway look and this was not the right time to discuss it.

Arriving at the room, he scooped her up and carried her to the bedroom. Placing her down he kissed her and ran his hands up and down her electrifying dress. Crystal wanted him to love her his way and lay there as he slid her dress up her thighs, over her waist and then off her arms. Wade began unbuttoning his shirt and removing his pants as he kept kissing her body and her aroused nipples. Naked, they rolled, hugged, kissed and caressed until Crystal, squirming and bucking her body in desire, could take it no more.

"Please love me now, before I go insane," she pleaded trying to force him into her.

Wade made love with her passionately, forcefully and gently through the night until they both collapsed in exhaustion and fell asleep in each other's arms.

The sun was starting to break through the gap in the curtains as Wade stirred and sat up. Leaning against the bed headrest he watched as Crystal, in her naked state, lay asleep. He truly felt lucky to have met such a beautiful woman. He thought at that moment that he should get out of this business so they could start a new life together.

Standing and walking to the curtain, as he separated them he heard her stir.

"Good morning."

With her eyes only half open and still in a sleepy state, she looked at him as she asked, "This is all real. I didn't dream it … did I?"

"No you didn't dream it … it's real," he replied walking back to the bed and kissing her.

After making love again, Wade, stood, got dressed and said, "I'll get us a coffee."

Nodding, Crystal smiled as she headed for the bathroom. Wade thought her smile was odd, but ignored the thought and headed for the coffee shop.

Wade felt so alive and exhilarated as he walked with the early morning shoppers and traffic. He met people who remembered him from the previous evening and congratulated him again. After finding their coffees and as he approached the gate, leading into their apartment, he saw the car parked across the entrance.

Wade was not a rich man, but over the years and through astute investment, he had developed quite a substantial portfolio of property and reserves. Coming from a poor upbringing he did not consider himself a materialistic person, but he still appreciated the nice things in life. A silver-grey Aston Martin DB9 convertible was definitely something that attracted his attention. After walking around the car numerous times and then realising the coffees would be getting cold, he made his way back to the apartment.

As he entered he noticed Crystal had a glow that would light up a room. Handing her the coffee she smiled and started drinking.

"Okay, what's up?" he asked.

"Nothing," she replied still smiling. "How was your walk?"

"Very nice thanks. I met some people we saw last night who congratulated us again and I was checking out this really neat car parked outside our front gate."

"Really," said Crystal still smiling.

"Alright, I give up. What's the joke?" he asked, grabbing her around the waist and starting to tickle her.

Unable to handle being tickled, Crystal succumbed and replied, "Okay, okay … you might need these," as she threw him a set of keys.

"What are these for?" asked a surprised Wade, noticing the Aston Martin logo.

"I got us a vehicle to get back to Geneva, and I know an Aston Martin is your favourite car," she replied with a huge smile as she hugged him.

"Well that's very nice but how did you know?"

"Colonel Wine and Jacko told me," she said pressing her body against him.

This pressing action only caused them both to become aroused and it took another hour for them to leave the apartment.

27: Hermance

An Aston Martin DB9 has a top speed of three hundred kilometres an hour and a vehicle that can travel at that speed needs to have a lot of power. Cruising down the Autostrade of Italy, Wade enjoyed the exhilaration. Stopping for lunch at the French ski resort Chamonix, they crossed back into Geneva, Switzerland late in the afternoon.

Wade climbed out of the car, and looked across at his beautiful fiancée. He knew there and then he had to protect her even if it meant lying to her.

"Well hello, you pair of movie stars," remarked Sammy the ex-Reeces, South African Special Forces Commando, as he stepped on the porch.

Looking around the snow covered area of the CIA secure location house, in the forested area of Hermance; Wade felt he probably was like a movie star arriving in the luxury sports car with the beautiful woman.

"Yeah, does seem like that," he replied shaking hands with his friend, the huge six foot seven, two hundred and sixty pound black African.

Helping Crystal from the car all three entered the house and Wade immediately called a meeting. Looking around at the faces, of this elite group, helped remind him of why he was here.

"Alright, what've we got?" asked Wade.

Chrissie spoke first and detailed how she and Morrie had followed Bart and the Asian to various places throughout Geneva, but nothing fruitful came of it. She also mentioned they had not seen nor heard of Samantha Cooper.

The four man team, that included Jacko, gave a comprehensive analysis of the people and the various groups using the tunnels.

Wine explained how he believed if anything were to happen at the LHC, then it would have to come from within.

Once everybody had finished and Wade had explained what happened in Sardinia, Kaitlyn stood up. All the members of Colonel Wine's team knew of Kaitlyn's reputation and her association with Wade. Nobody in the team trusted her, but they accepted her because of Wade.

"I see Crystal has an engagement ring," remarked Kaitlyn in a perfunctory manner.

All eyes in the room instantly went to Crystal's left hand as she slowly raised it.

"Well, my boy. You're getting married," said the Colonel in his best English aristocratic speech. "Congratulations," as he shook Wade's hand and gently kissed Crystal.

"Thank you Colonel," replied Wade as the group all gathered around.

Chrissie was the first to ask the obvious question. "Does that mean you're leaving us now?"

Wade looked from Chrissie to the Colonel and then at the rest of the group. Focusing on Crystal, he said, "We've not had a chance to talk about that yet. I'd rather we focus on finishing what we've started, and then give Kiwi the burial he deserves."

Everybody agreed in unison as Kaitlyn interrupted. "I think we've discovered a meeting that involves Cooper. It's in two days time in Cortona, Italy. We know from the information Wade obtained in Sardinia that Cooper definitely has established a cult that operates under the guise of Ied Supo and the inverted *Opus Dei* symbol. We're still going through data but it appears that the senior members of the cult have been called to a castle. We don't know who or how many."

"Do we know where this castle is?" asked Wade.

"Not really. Only that it's near Cortona and is on a hill with a three hundred sixty degree view."

"Well I guess that means Cortona, here we come. Joe, Kaitlyn can you arrange a flight to Florence for everybody and we'll all meet in Cortona 0700 tomorrow morning. Throb this is your old stomping ground; whereabouts in Cortona should we meet?" asked Wade.

Throb, the Egyptian, ex-Russian trained Spetnaz Special Forces, who spoke fluent Italian had spent many months training and living in the Umbria area of Italy.

"As you enter the main square, from the south side, there is a church on your left. Behind the church are three old stables that we converted into a command centre for our exercises. The locals won't go near it, so it will work perfectly," replied Throb, swinging his arms everywhere as if emulating the actions of Italians talking with their hands.

The group burst into laughter. Throb was the team joker and could always be depended upon to raise everybody's spirit with his humour.

"Excellent. Thanks Throb. No one arrives in groups bigger than three and we're all there by seven … let's go," ordered Wade.

28: Cortona

Wade was definitely enjoying Crystal's present as they rocketed along the Milan to Florence Autostrade, at two hundred kilometres an hour. The Aston Martin DB9 is the leader of the pack when it comes to luxury super sports cars. He could feel the incredible grip as it cornered and how there was no vibration through the body or the steering wheel.

Enjoying the sensation, he had not noticed the fast approaching, two black seven series BMW's. Being in the fast lane, of the four lane motorway, he went to move across as they boxed him in. Gradually increasing their speed and getting closer, Wade knew they were not just two idiots skylarking.

"Hang on," he said as he planted the accelerator, and the five hundred and ten horsepower, six litre V12 motor instantly responded.

The rapid acceleration surprised the BMW's who had lost about two hundred metres before they responded. Wade knew the Aston could outrun the BMW's but he wasn't sure how much clear road he had ahead or whether he should take an exit and try his luck on the country roads. By now approaching two hundred and seventy kilometres an hour, with Crystal gripping the door handles, he needed to decide fast.

Whizzing past the cars and trucks he saw the exit sign stating four kilometres ahead. At this speed they would be there in fifty seconds. They rounded the sweeping left hand bend and the decision was made for him with traffic blocking the two exit lanes. Checking his rear view mirror he could not see the BMW's as the sign stating Autostrade toll point, two kilometres, flashed past.

Decelerating and gently touching the brakes he passed under the automatic toll scanner at one hundred and thirty kilometres an hour. The slowing down enabled the two BMW's to catch him as they passed under the scanner at one hundred and eighty kilometres an hour.

The Italian Polizia are fairly accepting of speed but the BMW's had crossed the acceptance line. The two Polizia pale blue Lamborghini Aventador's appeared from behind the traffic control building.

Realizing their predicament the BMW's raced passed Wade and Crystal with the Polizia in pursuit.

"What was that all about?" asked Crystal still gripping the handles.

"I'm not sure but I think we need to get away from here as quickly as possible," he replied turning his attention to the city of Florence as they exited the motorway.

The remainder of the journey was uneventful and they arrived in the hillside town of Cortona at midnight. Leaving the vehicle parked outside the train station, ringing through its location to the hire company, they made the three kilometre walk up the steep hill to the designated rendezvous.

Arriving first they were sitting enjoying a glass of the local wine as Wine, Throb and Chrissie entered.

"Well look at you two being the married couple," jokingly remarked the Colonel.

The eight hundred year old stables were built in an era when people were generally shorter. Crystal noticed how most of the men had to keep ducking to avoid the large beams that supported the roof. The Spetnaz had done a good job of cleaning, lining, rewiring, painting and generally making good the inside of the buildings. They had knocked out doorways linking the buildings, added meeting and comms rooms and brought in furniture.

Wine checked they had a communications link with Washington and to their supporting satellites. The others collected the team's equipment and weapons from the van Wine, Throb and Chrissie had arrived in.

Over the next four hours the remainder of the team, including Joe and Kaitlyn arrived.

At 0700, after everybody had eaten, slept, checked and rechecked their equipment, Colonel Wine and his team headed out in their tourist garb.

Sitting at the meeting table Wade, Crystal, Joe and Kaitlyn waited for the link to connect with Forest.

"Crystal, I envy you. He's a special man and I love him like a brother. I can tell he loves you very much, so I hope you have a wonderful life together," said Kaitlyn in a very soft and sincere tone.

"Thank you Kaitlyn. I appreciate that," replied Crystal.

"Thanks Kia," said Wade.

"General Forest here team. What've we got?" asked the bellowing voice of the General through the secure link hands free phone.

"Hi General. We're here in Cortona, Italy. It's 0700 and Colonel Wine and his team have just left on a reconnaissance. I have Wade, Joe and Crystal with me," replied Kaitlyn.

"General, I feel we're missing something. I know we'll probably catch-up with Samantha Cooper here but something about what Bart said that makes me believe this is only half the story. Remember I mentioned overhearing him talk about a delivery in Genoa, the explosives for the Hadron and emptying accounts. I think we can probably piece all that together. He also mentioned that he and Troy had a contingency plan and needed to dissociate themselves from the Wolves." Pausing Wade continued, "Colonel Wine said nothing peculiar was happening at the Hadron and an attack would need to come from within. So I think we should get Joe and some CIA operatives to start making enquiries and set up a surveillance in Genoa. Kaitlyn should head back and using your resources, access all the Swiss bank accounts to watch for any movement and we need to get somebody inside the Hadron. Your team, there in Washington, should concentrate on finding this long-lost brother, Thomas Cooper. While we worry about what happens here," said Wade with determination in his voice.

"Very good. We have just received word that Samantha Cooper, a person matching the description of the doctor and an Asian have arrived at the Le Richemond Hotel in Geneva. Kaitlyn if you and Joe could check this out first," said the General.

"Will do," replied Kaitlyn.

As the line went dead, Wade looked across to Crystal, put her hand in his and said, "You need to go back to Washington with Kaitlyn. We've just heard your Dad has got worse."

Crystal looked at Joe and Kaitlyn and then turned to Wade. "I know you love me and are only trying to protect me, but I rang the hospital last night, when we were in Florence, and they said he was unchanged," said Crystal leaning across and kissing him. "If you really want me out of here I'll go but I would prefer to stay with you."

"I do like you being with me but it's not safe."

"And it's any safer in Washington, after what happened?"

"Alright … alright. You win."

29: Geneva

The room was a picture of opulence as Troy sat looking out the window at Lake Geneva below. The penthouse suite had magnificent views of Brunswick Garden and the lake but Troy was not interested in the views. He was trying to gather his thoughts on the latest occurrence of events.

The waiter had just left a bottle of 1951 Grange Hermitage and a tray of beautifully presented tapas but even this could not sway his thoughts. Turning to his Asian confidant, Li, Troy said, "Get Bart on the phone. We all need to talk."

Two minutes later, with the phone on speaker, "Bart what's your take on what happened in Porto Cervo?" asked Troy.

"I have no idea who's behind this but it could be an agency. Maybe CIA, MI5 or Mossad."

"Why would an agency suddenly be interested in us and how would they have known about Barkers?' asked Troy becoming agitated. "Could it be that blasted soldier again?"

"I don't think so," replied Li. "He took a fair beating in Ucluelet and survived but there would have been no way he got off Mount Walker. He was still inside the compound when we detonated. I'd say he's definitely out of the picture."

"Well Bart, why do you say an agency?" asked Troy again.

"When I returned after meeting with the Arabs and yourself, I felt as if somebody had been in the apartment. I couldn't find anything out of place but I saw two fine burn marks to the carpet in the hallway, the access hatch had been moved and the carpets had been cleaned. I also found what looked like three bullet holes that had been neatly patched on the ceiling … then two days later Barkers gets blown. I find that a little too coincidental."

"It could be one of the members," stated Li.

Referring to the eight members that along with Troy made up the controlling faction of Ied Supo. The group consisted of a billionaire industrialist, a merchant banker, dictator, ore miner, media baron, art collector, drug lord and oil oligarch. These men collectively controlled seventy percent of the world's private wealth.

"Good point Li. Which one do we think would be the most likely?" asked Troy.

"Well, if I had to pick one I'd say Rubenstein," replied Bart.

Joseph Rubenstein, the Bahamas based merchant banker who had always been a thorn in Troy's side. The common denominator, with the cult, was their interest in sacrifices. All members had partaken in various sacrifices but as they had gotten older they now preferred to watch. Troy had been able to provide the entertainment as often as they wished and this in turn enabled him to form the group. Rubenstein had struggled with Troy being in a woman's body and was always questioning his motives.

Troy agreed and decided he wanted all eight members and their families watched, their phones tapped, computers hacked and anything out of the ordinary reported to him immediately. He decided that a meeting would be held at the Cortona castle in two days and all members must attend.

Li was to arrange maximum security at the castle. Bart was to ensure they were ready to empty the accounts from the Swiss banking system.

It was after midnight when Li knocked on the penthouse door. Even though Samantha Cooper was a fifty six year old woman, the adrenaline drive that Troy provided meant she was limited to two hours sleep each night. Li knew Troy would be awake as he waited for the answer.

"Enter," came the savage female command through the door intercom.

"Sir, Rubenstein is moving funds," shouted Li as he entered the room.

The luxury penthouse covered over six hundred square metres and Li needed to walk thirty metres to get from the front door to where Troy was seated. With his back to the window and sitting at the large mahogany desk with five screens in front of him; Troy looked up.

"Thanks Li, but I already know. I've sent in a team to finish him. I've instructed them to make it look like a CIA hit. As soon as it's done, can you get messages to the other members that they must have no communication, don't do anything to raise attention and they need to get to the castle," ordered Troy. "I want us ready to leave at sunrise."

30: Bahamas

Life in the Bahamas had been wonderful for Joseph. Living on his own three hundred square kilometre island, he had developed a fortress. The sprawling forty four bedroom mansion, with the two attached workers villas and the thirty car garage were testament to his wealth. Along with the nine hole golf course, Olympic size swimming pool, hangers for his luxury jets and helicopters; he had also established the head office of his Bank.

J.R. Banking Corp was the world's largest private bank with branches in every country. Joseph was earning over one billion dollars a month and needed an army of workers to control and supervise this. He had left his offices in Manhattan to escape being around people. As an extreme introvert, his island hideaway was perfect but as a control freak, he needed to know what was happening at all times. He had installed the latest high tech communications and computer linkages, which operated along with his two private satellites. His eight most loyal and trusted workers lived and worked on the island and would spend their day scrolling and checking proceedings within the bank.

The island had the capacity to cater for four hundred people, but Joseph lived alone with his staff of cooks, cleaners, gardeners, technicians, pilot, aides and thirty two security personnel.

Joseph had never trusted Troy and his Ied Supo group, but his desire for sacrifices, especially young girls, and Troy's ability to be able to provide them, kept him coming back.

He had done his own checks on Cooper and knew she was an extremely wealthy individual. His fears that Troy had formed the group to get at their money seemed to diminish with time but Joseph was the eternal banker and when the message arrived it rang alarm bells.

As a billionaire he had access to vast amounts of funds but very rarely did people in his position have cash instantly available. He had made sure he could move his wealth, on short notice, by depositing large quantities of untraceable bonds in Swiss bank accounts. The numerous accounts were protected by an elaborate electronic numerical security system that was updated every three seconds.

When the message of the Cortona meeting arrived, he immediately activated the movement of ten billion in bonds and one and a half billion in cash to new accounts.

Feeling satisfied with his actions he advised his security detail and staff to be ready for an early departure the next morning. The frenzy of activity had nobody on the island notice the black clad figures that dropped from the sky and cross the beaches at eleven that evening. All fifty plus people on the island were executed, laptops and data enabling equipment were gathered and any signs of the attackers were covered or removed.

31: Cortona

"Wade we have just returned from the Le Richemond Hotel. Cooper, the Asian and the doctor were definitely there. They left early this morning. We tracked their plane to Florence and then their helicopter to a castle. The castle is located six kilometres north east of Montecchio, on a hill overlooking Lake Trasimeno. It is a walled fortress surrounded by olive tree plantations. Sorry no more details."

"Thanks Kaitlyn," replied Wade. "Do we know of any security details?"

"The castle is built in a typical circular configuration with all the buildings at the south end facing the lake and there are four turrets around the perimeter. Satellite imagery has detected a guard in each turret. Otherwise nothing else."

"Excellent," replied Wade as he cut the connection.

Wine and his team had returned from a very unsuccessful day of reconnaissance.

Wade arranged for Bart, Sammy, Stewie and Bassa to check out the castle. Chrissie and Throb to find suitable surveillance posts and watch for all incoming and outgoing traffic. Forest to provide continuous satellite coverage of the castle.

Crystal, Wade and Wine were watching live satellite imagery and discussing the castle when the Colonel turned and looked at Wade.

"I've known you for a long time and I initially thought it was Crystal that was making you appear at odds with yourself but I'm now not so sure," he said. "Are you okay?" he asked with genuine concern in his voice.

Pausing and looking from Crystal to Wine, "I'm fine thanks Colonel … I've just been getting strange feelings since I've been in Italy … but it's all good. Don't worry."

Wine knew this was a very unusual response from Wade but he also knew it was a discussion that needed to be had at a later date.

"I love you," said Crystal, grabbing his hand and looking directly into his eyes.

"I love you too," replied Wade, "but I think I need to go for a run to clear my head a bit." He removed his hand, stood, kissed Crystal on the cheek and left the room.

Looking across to Wine, Crystal asked, "Is he alright?"

Nodding, as he looked back at the screen the Colonel replied, "I think so … or at least I hope so."

Wade had decided a good five to ten kilometre run would be all he needed. After running for an hour and finding he had covered fifteen kilometres he felt good and continued.

It was approaching midnight and he had been running for four hours as he entered the northern side of Cortona. Sweating profusely, having removed his shirt and wearing only his shorts and runners, he saw the commotion.

Four men of bulky Middle Eastern appearance were manhandling and threatening a young local man and his wife. The man closest to him was standing beside a black van and Wade saw the flick-knife in his right hand. The second had hold of the distressed, scared, beaten man with the third punching him in the stomach and face. The fourth had the woman pinned against the wall of their house as he tried to grope her.

Not normally wanting to get involved in domestic issues he became hell bent on protecting the woman. He approached the group with the man beside the van stepping forward.

"Piss off wog. Not your problem," he shouted in Italian, as he stuck out his chest and held up his left hand in a fist.

Wade continued to approach as the man flicked the knife open and thrust it out. Watching the other three men, Wade leapt the final two metres. He smashed his fist down on the attacker's right arm, twisted to his left and crashed his elbow into his face, breaking his jaw and nose. Continuing the twist he thrust his knee into his assailant's midriff, breaking three ribs and finished the attack with an uppercut under his chin.

The punching man turned to be met with a decisive punch to the side of his head, instantly knocking him out. The second man had only been able to release his captive, who fell to his knees, as Wade unleashed a flurry of kicks to his head and torso.

Controlling his furry he ran across the twenty metres separating the fourth attacker. The woman, whose dress had been torn off, was standing in her underwear as the man was roughly squeezing her breasts and trying to rip off her panties. He was the largest and definitely the leader of the gang as Wade tore him off the woman. Falling to the ground the attacker reached into his jacket and attempted to remove a snub nose 9mm pistol. As he brought it into a shooting direction, Wade slammed his foot into his throat, killing him instantly.

Upon seeing Wade and what had happened, the woman became shocked and fainted. Wade carried her inside, placed her on a bed and covered her. He helped her husband inside and called Forest to arrange removal of the attackers. He searched the house for something to help the battered and bruised husband and was bandaging his arm when the wife reappeared.

"Thank you for helping us," said the redressed, shaking young wife.

Speaking in Italian Wade replied, "No problem. I think your husband will be okay … and don't worry about those four out front, they won't be bothering you again."

"Who are you and why are you helping us?" asked the stammering woman standing in the doorway trying to keep her balance as she became more and more pale.

"My name is Wade and it's not important why I helped but you definitely need to sit down."

Helping her sit beside her husband, who was now trying to open his swollen eyes, Wade asked, "Why were those men doing this?"

Lowering her head, shaking, she grabbed her husband's hand as she replied, "We have a small grocery business, in town and we get our produce from the markets in Florence. Those men are standover goons who extort protection money from everybody at the market. We pay the money to get our goods but they keep putting up the amount. Last week they doubled the figure and we only had until today to pay. We don't have any more so they had come to beat my husband and then probably kill him. They would have raped me and burnt our house and shop to the ground. They do this to make an example and we can't go to the Polizia as they won't intervene."

"What're your names?"

"Alessandro and Sofia Rossi."

"Sofia. I can guarantee you'll never have any more trouble from these men or anybody associated with them."

"How can you say that? You don't know what they're like," she said as tears cascaded down her scared face. "There will only be more of them tomorrow."

Before Wade could reply a knock came at the door and three huge men walked in. Upon seeing them Sofia went to scream as Wade gently grabbed her arm.

"It's okay Sofia … they're with me," Wade replied as he got to his feet.

Sammy the huge South African spoke first. "I thought you were going for a run, not a demolition derby," he exclaimed with a big smile on his face.

"Yeah Wade, how come you get all the action while the rest of us miss out?" asked Bassa, the tough east Londoner, ex British SAS. Bassa was renowned within the group as the fighter. He had no hesitation in challenging anybody, except Wade and he respected nobody, including the Colonel, as much as he respected Wade.

"What are you three doing here? I thought I said to go to the castle?" questioned Wade.

"We were on our way back when the message came through from the Colonel," replied Stewie, the tall, sinewy, softly spoken, French Foreign Legion trained Canadian.

"Alright. Clean up that lot outside," ordered Wade.

As the three men left he turned to Sofia and once again, speaking Italian, asked her to give him details of where he could locate the attackers.

Opening the door, he turned. "Good luck to you both. You will never see us again and you will not have any more trouble at the markets or from these men."

32: Florence

Two hours after Wade's first contact with the Rossi's and their attackers; Wade and his team arrived in Florence. Having arranged prior, with Forest, they dropped the goons at a CIA warehouse.

The address given by Sofia was a seven storey abandoned hotel on the banks of the Arno River.

"How're we doing this?" asked Bassa.

Studying the surrounding area and checking for detection equipment Wade replied, "We don't have enough time to stake out this joint so we go in with mikes. C4 on each corner of each floor. Stewie they probably have a basement so can you blow a hole to the river. If we find any comms equipment we leave a message. Something like anymore threatening at the produce market then next time no one survives."

They donned their night vision goggles (NVG), body protection armour, checked their weapons and ensured the throat mikes were active.

They swept the first five floors and had planted their explosives. They had not met or seen anybody when the door at the top of the stairs, slowly opened. Bart fired a single silenced head shot. The propulsion pushed the victim back into the door and the consequential noise alerted the other occupants.

Bursting through the door Bart and Sammy became pinned down with enemy cross fire.

Wade and Bassa had entered from the opposite end of the building, whilst Stewie was finalizing in the basement.

"Sammy, Bart. I want one of you to put down cover fire and the other get into the stairwell. Then repeat. You need to head to the car double time. Stewie you need to get out now," ordered Wade.

"What's the plan?" whispered Bassa.

"Once Bart and Sammy are in the stairwell I'll provide the cover fire while you get a rope out that window," replied Wade pointing to a shattered window that looked out over the river.

Bassa watched as Wade removed two C4 packages from his pack and fixed them to the wall that ran along the corridor. The sound of automatic AK47 gunfire had ceased and had been replaced with the distinctive sounds of H&K assault rifles. Twenty seconds later the AK47's commenced again and Wade knew Bart and Sammy were out. Signalling to Bassa he switched his H&K to semi automatic and opened up with sporadic fire. Watching from his peripheral vision he saw Bassa connected to the rappelling rope, standing on the outside edge of the window sill. As Bassa opened with cover fire Wade hit the thirty second timer to activate all the C4 detonators and charged for the window.

Bassa continued to fire as Wade hooked his carabineer on to his pre tied waist rope. Wade turned and lobbed a grenade as he threw himself out the window. He hoped the rope support would hold. Bassa was already in the water as Wade let the rope free travel through his hands. Not knowing or having time to ascertain where he was, he needed to depend on his wits to determine when to stop. He locked the rope behind his leg as he felt it cut into his gloved hands. Having only momentarily started to slow he crashed, back first, into the water. Bassa grabbed him and they both dived underwater.

The sound of the explosions was deafening as both men struggled to stay under. They narrowly avoided a large section of brick wall that smashed into the water and grazed along Bassa's back.

Dragging themselves up the steep, boulder lined, slime covered banks of the river they were thankful as Sammy and Stewie reached over and lifted them onto the road.

Rocks and debris littered the road and surrounding area as the dust started to settle. Lights were appearing throughout the immediate area and the sound of sirens was ever increasing as Wade ordered, "Let's go."

In the vehicle Wade arranged for Kaitlyn to get a message through to the goons that their market racket was finished and if there was ever a need for them to return; then next time it would be more than just their building.

33: Castle

Troy, Li and Bart had arrived at sunrise and over the next five hours the balance of the Ied Supo group arrived in their respective helicopters.

All seven men were seated at the huge mahogany King George IV dining table in the expansive dining room. Troy and Li entered followed by seven large Chechen guards brandishing AK47s.

"Troy, what the hell is this all about?" demanded Claude the German billionaire industrialist.

"Give us some bloody answers ... now!" screamed Jose, the Columbian drug lord as he went to stand.

With a guard positioned behind each seated member, a hand clamped on Jose's shoulder and held him down.

Standing at the head of the table Troy looked at the seven seated men and replied.

"Firstly, I would recommend that none of you attempt to stand from your seat. A sensor activated explosive has now been set and if you stand you will die and most likely those beside you. You are all now my prisoners and you will do as I say. Do not try to contact anybody with your phones or hidden communication devices as I have disabled all communication in and out of the castle.

Secondly, all your guards and travel personnel have been eliminated so don't expect any help. Finally, we are going to have a meal, watch a show and then I decide your fate," stated a smiling Troy.

"How the hell do you expect to get away with this? My men will hunt you to the end of the earth," screamed Jose as his dark brown eyes glared at Troy and he slammed his fists on the table.

Without warning a guard reached over Jose's shoulder and drove the rifle butt into Jose's hands smashing the bones. As he screamed in agony the guard thrust the butt into his face knocking him unconscious. With blood pouring from his face the guard slammed Jose's head face first onto the table.

"I have loyal men on all corners of the world. You will regret the day you came up with this ludicrous idea," barked Omar, the Russian oil oligarch.

"Shut up you lot," yelled Troy. "You have all became so lost in your own power you do not even realise that I already have control of all your men. Do you think for one moment I would have started all this without having pre-empted your actions. All your closest allies have either been killed or I have bought their loyalty. So I would suggest you stay sitting and enjoy the show."

"What about Joseph? Where is he?" asked Winston, the American media baron and the most controlled member of their group.

"Didn't want to play by the rules," replied Troy as he smiled, stood and left the room. Passing Li who wheeled in a machine, not dissimilar to a heart monitor.

"Each one of you will place his hand flat on the glass and look directly into the eye socket until I tell you to stop," ordered Li.

Walking behind Claude and grabbing his left hand Li continued, "I suggest you don't make this difficult. If you don't cooperate we will cut off your hand and remove your eyeball. So either way we get what we want."

In a gesture of German defiance Claude snatched his hand away. Without warning the Chechen guard reached over and grabbed Claude's arm at the wrist and bicep and in one smooth motion broke his elbow. Claude screamed out in agony as Li reached behind his back and swung a razor sharp machete, slicing Claude's hand off at the wrist.

With blood gushing all over the table the guard pushed Claude back into his seat as Li continued his swing and decapitated him.

Casually placing the blood engorged hand and head onto the trolley, Li turned to the remaining members as he said, "Who else wants to resist?"

Five minutes later the members had given over their identification as Li left the room and handed the data to Professor Bart.

"How long will you need to empty the accounts?" asked Troy.

"Now that we have both forms of identification we should be able to clean out an account each hour," replied Bart.

"Excellent … Li how are we going with the show?" asked Troy again.

"It will be ready to start by this evening. We have found two in the town and we pick them up at four this afternoon."

"As always Li, well done. Bart can you get started on the accounts. Li can you bring the doctor in … I want you to stay this time. If he doesn't do as I ask, I want him finished," ordered Troy as Li nodded in acknowledgement and left the room.

34: Cortona

"Wade, we have received word from our operatives in Cortona that two men are asking around and offering a lot of money for a male and female to perform in a show at a castle tomorrow night. They're driving a white Mercedes van with blackened windows and Swiss plates. The men are speaking Italian with a French accent," said Kaitlyn over the encrypted phone.

"When and where were they last sighted?"

"We're tracking the van and it's currently parked in Piazza Pescaia and the two men were last sighted entering a brothel on Vicolo Maria Rina Pierazzi."

"That's on the other side of town. Let us know if the van moves. We're leaving now."

Wade explained to the team the latest developments. They gathered their gear and headed for their vehicles.

The team had split into various groups and were searching the Cortona shopping precinct when Wade and Crystal happened upon two fair skinned men, dressed in black suits who were talking to a group of young adult females.

Eavesdropping they listened. The two men asked if the women were interested or knew anybody who would be interested in earning some quick easy money. They explained that they were looking for a man and a woman to dress and parade in various costumes to some wealthy businessmen at one of the local castles the next evening. They advised how their boss was quite specific in who he was looking for.

Ensuring they were not noticed Wade and Crystal followed the two men until they were sure they had identified the two people the men had decided to offer the job to. Photographing the selected two, they split up and tracked them to their respective addresses. Once confirmed they returned to their base.

The sun had started to set and the evening was closing in as the last of the team returned.

"Crystal and I have identified the two people who will be going to the castle tomorrow night. Here are photos of them and they are to be picked up at 1600 hours from the Piazza della Repubblica outside La Grotta," said Wade handing around the mobile phone.

"These two would pass for you and Crystal," said Chrissie as she looked across to Wade.

As each team member looked at the photos they all agreed.

"Unfortunately that's not going to help as the Asian has already seen my face," replied Wade.

"What about Throb?" asked Stewie looking at the photo.

"Could work," said Wade. "Throb is probably four inches taller but otherwise would pass … but how can we solve the female problem? Chrissie has blond hair and fair skin and the woman selected is dark haired and olive skinned?"

"Why can't I do it?" asked Crystal.

"Well … we have no idea what to expect when we get in there and how or what we'll need to do to get out. You have no experience or training in this and I won't be letting you do anything that could get you hurt," replied Wade with a stern expression.

The group discussed options for the next thirty minutes until Wade stopped the conversations.

"It seems our only option is to kidnap those two and Throb and Crystal take their place. When we get to the pickup point I need to somehow ensure I'm in that van when it leaves. The Colonel will monitor things from here and the rest of you will need to be at the castle. Bart, Sammy, Stewie, Bassa we need details on the castle and as much of the layout as you can. You all need to be in position by 1630 hours," ordered Wade.

Pausing and looking around the group he continued, "Okay let's go and pickup these two. Remember we don't hurt them and they don't see your face."

They found and extracted the two Italians. No noise was made. They were overpowered with no resistance. Bundled into the respective vans and

150

taken back to the team's base. The chloroform used to knock them unconscious gave Crystal and Throb the opportunity to study their prey to help emulate the role they needed to play.

During the night Wine had organized for Stewie to establish a surveillance post overlooking the castle.

As the morning progressed Stewie reported in the arrival of helicopters. Landing within the castle walls he was unable to identify the passengers. Forest had arranged for satellites and radars to track the helicopters as they left the castle and upon their landing a CIA team was waiting.

By 1100 hours Stewie had estimated twenty four people had arrived in the helicopters with an unknown number of Cooper's guards already present. Wade and the Colonel discussed the information and decided that Cooper would have between ten and fifteen guards.

Addressing the team and using a whiteboard Wade explained the predicament they were in.

"We have a castle with walls eleven metres high. There is one drive through gate, which is the only entrance, as the pedestrian gate appears boarded up. There are four turrets, which have a guard in each, and they're all brandishing a sniper rifle. One thing in our favour is the olive groves that are growing only four metres from the walls and we should be able to utilise these for cover. As you have heard we could expect up to forty people in there and there will be only eight of us. Plus we have a priority of protecting Crystal and Throb. Satellite imagery shows a helicopter in the grounds and that will be our most likely form of escape. Chrissie can you concentrate on the pilot and ensure the choppers are ready to go? We have no idea of the layout inside the castle so I'll concentrate on keeping with Crystal and Throb. Sammy, Jacko and Stewie will focus on the charges throughout the buildings and I would take particular interest in the largest of the three buildings, first. Bassa, Bart and Morrie need to get rid of the turret guards. If you get a chance I want you to check out the smallest shed. I can't explain why but I feel there is something about it … Crystal and Throb get picked up at 1600 hours so be at the castle by 1700. It's dark by 1730 so we need to have control of the castle by 1800. One of the major problems is if Crystal is forced to speak. She knows no Italian and the American accent will blow our cover. If that happens I'll advise what we'll do but I'd imagine a firefight … any questions?"

"Are we to bring anyone back?" asked Sammy.

"If we can keep Cooper alive that would help," replied the Colonel. "Otherwise I leave it up to your initiative."

"We take as much firepower as we can carry," ordered Wade.

The team members all nodded in agreement as they stood to prepare their gear.

"You appear worried," asked Wine.

"Yeah … I am. I'm just not convinced Crystal going into this is such a smart move. You should have seen what they were going to do to this young girl in Ucluelet. They're a bunch of weirdos and they get off watching sacrifices," replied an extremely concerned Wade.

"Do you want to look at alternatives?"

"No … we'll do this. But the split second something isn't right I'll bring the whole thing down on top of them," he replied sternly.

35: La Grotta

By 1500 hours the team had Piazza della Repubblica surrounded with all access points under observation. Throb and Crystal were sitting in the outside chairs of the Trattoria La Grotta and Wade was inside the van parked alongside.

Wade watched as Crystal sitting in her designer jeans, tee shirt and leather jacket tried desperately not to appear nervous. He saw how she kept touching her hair and face and was constantly looking around the square.

It was 1550 hours, and still ten minutes until the van would arrive, when two men approached her and attempted to strike up a conversation. Realizing the problem Wade was about to leap from the van when Throb came to her rescue. After some discussion and threats, from Throb, the two men left as the van arrived.

Parking their van directly in front of Wade's, two men got out and approached. Ensuring they were the same two men from the day before, Wade called through his throat mike to confirm 'all clear'. The group had already decided that Crystal would act as if she had laryngitis and Throb would do all the talking. Stalling for time Throb kept watching and talking to the men until he was certain Wade was in the van.

They each pocketed the ten thousand US dollars as the men helped them into the van. Throb noticed how Wade had lain under the bench seat, running the full length of the rear compartment, and had used a worn tarp to cover himself.

With the two Frenchmen in the front seats the van entered the gate of the castle at 1715 hours.

The sun had already dropped behind the mountains. The two men helped Crystal and Throb from the van and led them into the largest building.

Waiting two minutes, Wade opened the rear door and silently entered the same building. It was a rear entrance to a long corridor. Searching for CCTV or any detection devices he approached the last door of the corridor. About to turn the handle he heard the screams. Bursting through the door he was confronted with three sets of stone steps leading down into basements.

The scream came again and he charged down the one to the left taking four steps at a time. Rounding a corner he stopped. He saw Throb and Crystal being coerced, at gunpoint, to strip naked and put on a long flowing robe. Halting himself he waited to see what would eventuate next.

Crystal was forced to put on a white robe and Throb a black. With the robes on, one of the Frenchmen activated a lever that lowered two platforms. Each platform had two ankle shackles bolted to the floor half a metre apart and swinging above was a two metre bar with a length of chain and a shackle on each end.

The two gunmen and the second Frenchmen shoved them onto the platforms and shackled their ankles. They spread their arms, shackled their wrists and had them standing in a crucifix pose. Lifting the hoods of the robes they covered their heads as the four men turned off the lights and left the room.

By now convinced there was no surveillance Wade approached and removed the hoods.

"I'll try and find something to undo these shackles but we need it to look like they are still locked," whispered Wade.

"On the table near the stairs. I saw one of them put down something that could've been the key," whispered Throb.

After fumbling around in the dark until his night vision returned Wade found the key. Undoing the shackles he applied tape, which he placed across the openings as Crystal and Throb resumed their pose.

"Wade you said you were going to use the money, they gave us, for something. It's in the pockets of our clothes," said Throb.

Once again fumbling around he found the clothes, pocketed the money and approached Crystal.

"I know this is going to be hard but you'll need to hang onto the chains with all your strength. If you let go the tape will break and the shackles will fall off," said Wade whispering into her ear.

Nodding in acknowledgement Wade knew she was extremely scared as he touched her arm.

"I imagine these platforms will take you up to whatever is going to happen," said Wade as he replaced the hoods. "I'll be there when you get there so stay focused."

36: Castle

"Good afternoon Doctor Eberharter. Please have a seat," instructed Troy.

"Good afternoon Troy," he replied as he took a seat on the club lounge sitting directly opposite Troy. Li took up position directly behind the doctor.

"Have you bought me here for a session?" asked Eberharter.

"I have."

"Very good. What about Mister Li?" as he tried to turn toward Li.

"Li will stay for this session," replied Troy as he calmly looked around the room at the paintings on the wall.

"Is that wise, Troy?" questioned the doctor. Suddenly feeling something was amiss.

Slowly rising from his chair, and still not making eye contact with Eberharter, Troy walked toward the computer terminal. Bending over he hit a key and slowly turned the screen to face the doctor. On the screen were the names Roxy and Samantha.

"Now doctor this is your last chance. You either get rid of these two, once and for all or you don't leave here alive. Li will make sure of that … am I clear?" yelled Troy.

Nervously looking around Eberharter replied, "Troy you know I can't just stop them. We have to work a way through somehow controlling them. This is in your head and it's not controlled by a switch."

"Wrong answer, doctor," said Troy as he started for the door.

"What … what … what," stammered Eberharter. Li produced his razor sharp machete and in one fluid action separated the doctor's head from his body.

Standing at the door Troy looked back at the blood flooding onto the floor. He turned to Li, "As soon as Bart has finished get rid of Johansen and Staker and bring Bart to me. Once the show starts finish those two idiot Frenchmen and the kitchen staff."

Nodding in agreement Li went to walk past Troy as Troy touched him on the shoulder and said, "Remember only you, me and the pilot leave here."

37: Castle

Wade had left the basement and was making his way back to the courtyard when he saw Li exit a door at the end of the long corridor. Hurrying to the door, he slowly opened it as Li entered an archway, six metres along the wall.

Darkness had engulfed the castle and Wade saw that the only light was coming from the three small windows on the first and second floor. The four turret guards were obviously not expecting any company, with each smoking as they leant back against the wall or moving about stretching. The burning tip of the cigarette was the perfect target the others could use.

He saw a sliver of light coming from under the door of the small shed and it confirmed his suspicions.

Keeping hard against the stone walls and using the shadows; he followed Li through the arch and up the stairs. The further the stone enclosed stairwell went the narrower it became. After circling around he arrived at the fourth and top floor. The thick oak door had been left ajar and Wade heard Swiss voices.

Entering he saw one large open room off to the left that was empty except for a laser guided, tripod mounted missile launcher. The first room to the right had three males sitting facing computer screens and discussing numbers. Wade recognized the one on the left as Bart and Li was leaning over his shoulder.

"How much longer?" asked Li.

Looking across to the other two men and their screens Bart replied, "We're on to the last one now so should be about ten to fifteen minutes."

"Mister Troy wants to get the party started so you two come with me," ordered Li as he pointed at the two Swiss men. "We'll be in the main hall when you're finished," he said looking towards Bart.

Wade darted into the second room and noticed the stacked boxes of missiles. Removing a C4 block from his pack he attached it to the blind side of the boxes and activated the remote detonator.

Approaching the first door he heard Bart speaking on the phone. "Troy has a show planned for them and then we're going to blow the whole castle. We have missiles targeted for six different European and Middle East locations which will cover our tracks." There was a pause in his voice as he listened and then continued, "Troy, myself, Li and the pilot." Pause. "We should be gone in less than an hour." As Wade heard the phone replaced on its cradle.

Wade stepped out from behind the door and in one leap wrapped his right arm around Bart's neck and grabbed his left shoulder. With his left hand he grabbed Bart's head and snapped his neck. Dropping the body to the floor, he found and pocketed the external USB sticks of all three computers. Smashing the hard drives and closing down the online connections he left the room. Passing the first room he deactivated the missile.

Taking the stairs three at a time he came out from under the arch just as he heard the distinctive sound of silenced rifle shots. Looking up he saw the four turret guard's drop into the turret wells and knew the team were coming up the walls.

Darting back into the corridor he leapt to avoid two bodies lying dead on the stone floor. Without hesitating he knew they were the two Swiss computer operators. Back down the left side set of stairs he came into the basement to see the platforms had risen to the floor above.

Pausing, he set two remote detonated C4 explosives within the room and then started for the door the four men had previously exited from.

Behind the door was a tunnel that wove under the castle and led to the four turrets. The tunnels were dimly lit with a single hanging globe every forty metres. Wade knew the castle and tunnels were over one thousand years old. He was hoping this would aid in its destruction as he placed explosives along the tunnel route. Arriving at a fork, he deducted that the two passages off to either side led to the turrets.

Directly ahead was a hidden opening with a very small steep set of stone steps leading up. Climbing the pitch black circular stairwell he became disoriented as to how far he had climbed when he crashed into a small solid timber door. Squatting down he opened the door to find he was in a bedroom on the top floor.

Creeping through the room he saw a faint light from under a pile of papers. Removing the papers he found a small laptop. On the screen was the letters PTAFE all written in disjointed fonts. Unsure of the significance he slowly opened the door to see Li coming from a room, two doors along the corridor.

Wade watched as Li, with his machete hanging in his right hand and blood dripping from its tip, made his way to the next door.

Li repeated the entering and leaving of rooms, three more times, and then replaced the machete in its scabbard and headed down the stairs.

Wade checked each room to find Li had beheaded all the occupants. As he was leaving the last room he noticed the shirt on one of the male victims had been torn open. With blood flooding all over the man's body he was just able to distinguish the inverted *Opus Dei* symbol squashed into his chest. The symbol caused him to remember the significance of the acronym in the first room: PTAFE, 'Punishment To All For Eternity'.

Standing on the landing at the top of the stairs, hidden behind the balustrading, he relayed the information to Kaitlyn. Checking on the various locations of the team he advised Jacko to activate the explosives in ten minutes.

Using the stair balustrading as cover he started down the stairwell. Having gone only eight steps and halfway to the first landing, the building became engulfed with the ear piercing sound of screams, followed by two gunshots.

Wade checked over the side of the stairwell. Certain it was all clear; he leapt to the floor, four metres below and darted to the huge oak door, six metres to his front.

Slowly pushing the door open he was thrown back by the explosion that erupted two metres inside. Gathering his composure he again crept forward to see Cooper holding her hands in the air and telling everybody to calm down and not move.

38: Castle – Sacrifice

Troy nodded and the Chechen guards slammed the butt of their rifles into the backs of the remaining four seated members. As they started to fall forward the guards grabbed them by either the hair or shoulders and held them back into their respective chairs.

"I told you what would happen if you left your seat," casually said Troy slowly looking around the group. "If you want to be the next Delani, by all means. I won't stop you." He nodded and the guards released their grip.

Delani, the overweight Indian billionaire ore miner from Mumbai, whose body parts were grossly splattered throughout the room.

"I think it's time we start the show," said Troy. "Li will you do the honours?"

All those in the room looked away from Troy and to the opposite end of the room. A large, heavy black screen covered the entire wall. Li walked to the furthest left hand side, reached behind the screen and pulled a lever.

The screen rose to reveal a hooded Throb and Crystal standing in a crucifix pose. They were atop platforms that were a metre above the floor level.

Two extremely powerful floodlights beamed at them.

The seated members were drooling at the mouth in anticipation of what was to come.

Li produced a razor sharp fillet knife with a blade that had been resting over a flame and was glowing. He walked to the black robe. As the tip of the knife touched the robe it melted as if dipped in acid. He ran the knife from the floor to the hood. Using his other hand Li reached across and ripped the robe off.

Throb was trying to adjust to the intense light whilst concentrating on not losing his grip and breaking the tape. Opening and closing his eyes he saw as Li touched the knife to his chest. In a fluid, effortless motion, that a surgeon would be proud of, Li sliced Throb, on his right side, from chest to waist.

Throb tried desperately hard not to shout out or react as he felt his skin peel open.

Li, just as casually, took four steps and stood in front of Crystal. Touching the glowing knife to her white robe, he went through the same motion and ripped her robe off.

The four seated members, and Troy, were screaming and clapping as Throb's skin continued to peel open and the blood started to pour down his body.

The Chechen guards were dumbstruck at the site of Crystal's naked body. They had either lowered their guns to the floor or pushed them on the slings behind their backs.

Wade had removed his automatic H&K pistols. He lay on the floor with his blowpipe in his right hand, poison darts in his left and the pistols directly to his front.

Years of practice had enabled him to master the art of using the deadly blowpipe. He had an accuracy rate of ninety eight percent and could continually send a dart through the air in less than two seconds. Ten seconds later all seven guards were either dead or falling to the ground.

Troy looked across to the door and seeing Wade yelled to Li. Li spun to the sound as Wade got off two shots from his pistol. The trained Special Forces take down shooting style of a double tap had the first shot at Li's head.

The first round passed across Li's forehead, tearing an arc from eyebrow to eyebrow. The impact of the round and his turning motion knocked him to the floor. As he fell he slid under the platform and crashed to the level below. The second shot missed, as Li spun, and went through Crystal's right thigh.

In the confusion and chaos Omar, the Russian oil oligarch, Winston, the American media magnate and Paul, the French art collector, sprung from their chairs. The ensuing explosions also killed Munga, the Kenyan dictator.

Wade rolled behind two of the Chechen guards. Five seconds later he scanned the room to see all dead. Throb and Crystal lay on the floor covered in shrapnel and body parts and Cooper was gone.

"I have two down. Repeat two down. Second floor main building. Cooper at large," yelled Wade into his throat mike.

"Copy that," came the replies from the respective teams.

Wade raced around the table and scooped up the white robe. Ripping into lengths he applied a tourniquet and bandage to Crystal's leg. He was thankful she was in shock and had lapsed into unconsciousness as he went to lay her back down.

The smell of disintegrated body parts, human excrement, blood, explosions and shattered glass made the scene intoxicating as Wade worked feverishly to control the situation.

Throb had lapsed into a blood loss state of shock. A piece of timber, from one of the chairs, had lodged into his right shoulder and Wade could tell his right knee was shattered. Trying desperately to stem the blood flow down the full length of Throb's upper body, Wade heard somebody behind him.

Sammy was already removing his field bandages as Jacko and Bassa lifted Throb up. Thirty seconds later and looking like an Egyptian mummy, Sammy picked him up. With Wade carrying Crystal the group charged down the darkened stairwell and out into the forecourt.

Smoke and the smell of cordite filled the air. Wade saw the remainder of the team had cleared and secured the castle. They had circled the helicopter. Chrissie was in the pilot's seat as the blades started their revolutions. The team squashed into the back with Crystal lying on the floor wrapped in a field blanket. Stewie was removing his jacket to cover the convulsing Throb. Bassa had a knife to Cooper's throat and pinned against the side wall.

Wade was last to climb aboard. He jumped into the front passenger's seat and swirled his right index finger in the air, indicating for Chrissie to go. The Eurocopter X3 luxury helicopter lunged forward as Chrissie tried to familiarize herself with the controls.

Starting to rise Wade saw the smallest building door was open.

Clearing the walls of the castle Wade removed his headset, turned to Chrissie, "Florence hospital. Get them on the blower and tell them two incoming. One a gunshot to the leg, the other knife cut neck to navel."

Leaning over the back, "How are they?" screamed Wade.

Before they could answer the helicopter lurched to the left and threw everybody against each other. The force of the blast from the castle explosions had been tremendous and Chrissie fought with the cyclic and collective to bring the helicopter back level. Wade looked back to see the castle had been blown to oblivion and the top of the mountain was gone.

"Hell, Jacko. How much HE did you put down?" Wade asked still watching as the smoke dissipated.

"Wasn't me Wade. I haven't even activated."

Wade turned in his seat, looked at Cooper and realized the activation was on her body.

"Bassa. Zip her hands and keep a bloody good eye on her," said Wade. "How're Crystal and Throb?" he asked again.

"Crystal's still unconscious but she seems okay," replied Bart, holding her head and trying to protect her leg from anyone falling on it.

"He's not good," said Sammy. "The blood won't stop and he's seriously pale."

Stewie grabbed a syringe from the team medic pack and thrust the adrenaline needle into Throb's arm.

"How long Chrissie?" asked Wade.

"Eight minutes and they said they'd be ready for us."

"Alright. Listen up. Anybody who leaves the chopper I want no weapons on you in the hospital.

Bassa you keep her hidden and she isn't to make a sound. Chrissie keep the blades going. As soon as the hospital staff take Crystal and Throb we're out of there … got it?" ordered Wade.

Even though Chrissie was an accomplished helicopter pilot, the controls and feel of the Eurocopter were different to anything she had previously worked with. She needed to land in the centre of the helicopter landing pad atop the Florence hospital. Misjudging her distances the force of the impact once again threw the team. Getting their balance Wade, Sammy and Stewie bolted out. Fighting against the down draft of the fully powered blades, they dragged out Crystal and Throb and rushed to the waiting trolleys and hospital staff.

The emergency doctor upon seeing this raggedy dressed group, covered in cam cream, blood and carrying two bodies as if they were sacks of potatoes – baulked.

"I'm sorry but who are you?" asked the doctor in Italian.

"We're American military and our people have been injured," replied Wade, in Italian, as he handed a blood splattered card. "If you call the person on this card he'll explain."

Looking at the name on the card and the wild looking men in front of him the doctor nodded and instructed his people to get them to the operating rooms.

39: Cortona

"Where to … Wade?" asked Chrissie.

"Back to Cortona. Get Forest to call the hospital. Find out what he wants done with Cooper. Have we got a vehicle that'll get us back to base? Geez I hope there alright," rattled off Wade.

"Slow done buddy. It's alright. They'll be fine," said Jacko as he put his hand on Wade's shoulder.

Looking at Jacko, then Chrissie, then the others, Wade knew he was right.

"Sorry."

"Don't be sorry. You deserve someone special like her. We know you don't want to lose anybody else after Kiwi," said Sammy. "Chrissie get the Colonel to pick us up at the reserve we were at yesterday. It's about ten klicks north of the castle at the top of the town."

The helicopter landed in the wooded reserve twenty minutes later. Bassa dragged Cooper from the cabin and lay her face down on the harsh rocks and thistles. The rest of the team removed all their gear and anything of use from the helicopter. Jacko set a remote detonator in a fist size lump of C4 under the fuel tanks.

"I demand to be let up. I'm a middle aged lady and under the Geneva Convention you cannot treat me like this," screamed Cooper.

"Shut up bitch," yelled Bassa, putting his boot on her back.

"I've done nothing wrong. You can't treat me like a common criminal. Do you people not know who I am," she screamed again.

Wade stormed over. Grabbed her by the hair and dragged her to her feet. She struggled to stay balanced with her wrists zip tied behind her back and Wade reefing her up.

"You are no fucking lady, man or even a half decent human being. You're lucky I don't slit your throat and leave you here for the dogs. So shut your mouth … if I hear one more word, he," pointing at Bassa, "will have you dead before you get to the second word. Am I clear?" Wade yelled, dropping her back on the ground.

Ten minutes passed and the Colonel arrived. They bundled their gear and Cooper in to the back of the van. Fifteen hundred metres down the hill Jacko activated the remote and the night sky was lit up in a huge blue and white fire ball.

Nobody said a word on the drive back and the Colonel could sense something was wrong. Arriving at the Cortona stables; Wade leapt from the van and rushed to the van's rear door. Jacko and

Sammy instantly knew what was up as they saw Wade drag Cooper across the van's floor.

Sammy grabbed Wade's arms as Jacko stepped in front of him.

"Mate, it's alright," said Jacko. "You go with the Colonel. We'll look after this. I promise."

"Wade, come with me," said the Colonel, grabbing him by the bicep and leading him away from the team.

"Talk to me. What's happened?" asked the Colonel.

"I don't know," he whispered.

With his head in his hands, Wade slowly slid down the wall he was leaning against.

"I'm scared Colonel … I don't think I've been scared before."

Sitting next to him the Colonel paused for a moment. Looking straight ahead and speaking in a soft tone. "There's something I haven't told you about me. When I was your age I met a woman. She was the most beautiful person I could have imagined ever lived. I fell in love with her and asked her to marry me. She said yes and we were to be married on my return from staff training college. Three days before my return she was walking past a chemist shop when two African teenagers, who had robbed the store, ran out. One of them had a knife. As he ran past he lashed out and cut her across the throat. No one came and she bled to death in a dirty, stinking rotten gutter."

By now the Colonel had Wade's full attention.

"I'm sorry."

"It was a long time ago but I still miss her … my point is you're not scared. You're in love. You don't want to lose her and you're not able to control what's happening. So go and be with her. Do whatever it is you need to do. We'll still be here," said the Colonel with a smile on his face.

Getting to their feet, Chrissie approached.

"Apparently they're going to be okay. Crystal won't be walking for a while but all good. Throb will be in ICU for a few days, mainly because of blood loss. No internal damage. One hundred and twenty two stitches, a dislocated knee and a shoulder that won't be lifting weights for a while. The doctor said we can see them in the morning."

"Thanks Chrissie," said Wade grabbing her in one of his bear hugs. "By the way. What was in that small building?"

"Props, costumes, photos and sacrificial robes."

40: Florence

It was 0600, still one hour until sunrise and the team had only been able to get three hours sleep when the squawk of the Sat phone startled everybody. Forest spoke with Wine and advised that a CIA jet was ready to take them back to Washington.

The team had a round table meeting and it was decided that Wade and Jacko would call the jet to Florence, pick up Crystal and take her and Cooper back to Washington DC. Stewie and Bassa would leave for Genoa and undertake surveillance. Sammy and Bart would head to Syria. Kaitlyn had discovered the two Arabic men, who had been in discussion with Professor Bart, had arrived in Latakia, the coastal port city of Syria. The remainder of the team would head back to northern England.

Wade handed the twenty thousand dollars cash to the Colonel and asked that it get to Luigi and Pepi. He wanted the Colonel to ensure it be delivered anonymously.

Cleaning and packing their gear, showering and changing into their civilian clothes, the team wiped the stables clean and drifted off in various directions in the early morning traffic.

The black CIA Gulfstream had been setup to take Crystal on her bed with all the medical equipment that the accompanying nurse might require in an emergency. The ambulance pulled alongside the jet's door. As it opened and Crystal came into view, Wade struggled to control his emotions.

"Hello gorgeous man," said Crystal in her half drugged state.

Wade fought his way between all the tubes and wires and stopped the ambulance staff and the trolley in its tracks. He bent down gently grabbed her face and kissed her. Crystal saw the tears slowly trickling down his cheeks.

"What's wrong?"

"I nearly killed you … I can't believe I did that," he replied as his hands started to tremble.

"Hey … it's okay. You didn't and you did save my live for the third time. I love you Wade Ross but I'm not sure I want to keep doing this."

"I promise. Never again will anyone hurt you."

They boarded the plane. Crystal was sedated. Cooper was taken to the rear, secured to her seat and placed under the guard of two CIA field agents. Wade and Jacko tried to resist the temptation to sleep but the luxurious chairs with the soft pillows were too much and they were asleep before they reached the end of the tarmac.

The trip was uneventful. Cooper and the agents headed to the Warehouse. Wade, Jacko, Crystal and the nurse went by ambulance to the same hospital as her father. When Wade was convinced Crystal was comfortable and safe he and Jacko were picked up and taken back to the Warehouse.

41: Washington DC

Kaitlyn, Joe and the CIA interrogation specialist had been interrogating Cooper for an hour as Wade approached the soundproofed, one way glass of the interrogation room.

Wade, Jacko and Forest looked in as Wade asked, "How's it going?"

"We don't seem to be getting very far. She's not saying anything of any substance," replied the General.

Wade looked in at the middle aged woman sitting on the raw steel chair bolted to the bare concrete floor. Her hands shackled to the steel table top and feet shackled to the floor. Her shoes and any jewellery had been removed. Her expensive designer clothes were ripped and filthy. Her hair was singed, hanging over her face and littered with day old pieces of body parts. Her arms were covered in cuts, bruises and blood. He saw how she had bitten her lip and dried blood had hardened down the side of her mouth. He noticed her eyes were extremely wide open, blood shot and the time between blinks seemed excessive.

"Cooper we have no intention of playing games here with you and your personalities. I don't care whether it's Samantha, Troy or Roxy. You either

180

cooperate with us or we leave you here and let you rot. We have all the time in the world," pausing for effect. "And we don't answer to anybody so don't expect any outside help," said the interrogation specialist as they stood to leave.

Entering back behind the one way viewing glass all six stood and watched. Cooper could only raise her hands ten centimetres above the table and the shackles stopped her hands coming together. Banging her fists on the table she screamed and threw her head around until she became exhausted.

"I think we need a new tactic to handle this," said the interrogation specialist looking toward Forest.

"Any thoughts?" asked the General to the group.

"Is this filmed or recorded?" asked Wade.

"Well yes it is. Why?" asked the General, confused.

"Turn off the filming and lights. Jacko and I'll have a go."

"Ok," replied the General. "But I don't particularly want her dead."

"Can't guarantee that," said Wade as they headed for the door.

They opened the door and Cooper caught a glimpse of her new interrogators as the lights went out. Wade and Jacko stood at the door and let their night vision adjust. Two minutes later Wade walked behind Cooper, grabbed her hair and pushed his right index finger into a pressure point at the base of her neck. With her screaming in agony, Wade kept pressing for twenty seconds and then backed away behind her.

Wade knew by the tone of her voice that Troy was the current dominate personality. He waited sixty seconds until her breathing had started to calm down and the shaking had slowed. He approached from behind grabbed her hair and applied pressure to a different pressure point. She screamed in agony, thrashing against her restraints until Wade stopped twenty seconds later. Wade kept up this tactic for a further ten minutes until he could tell her body was about to crash. Her breathing had reached the point of asphyxiation and her limbs were convulsing.

Standing behind her, in the complete darkness, he spoke.

"Cooper you have once chance to talk or we do this until you die. Personally I would rather kill you now. But there are others, out there, who think you deserve a chance. So now is your chance."

"Who are you? What sort of a deranged creature are you?" she pleaded between gasps of breath.

"Last chance. Answer the questions."

With no reply and only sobs, Wade stepped around Cooper and smashed his fist down on her right fingers. Shattering three of her fingers she screamed out in agony as Wade stepped around and shattered three on her left hand. He then grabbed her hair again and stuck his right thumb in her left eye socket. Pushing harder and harder, he could feel the socket starting to loosen, as the eyeball was about to pop out.

"Please, please stop," she screamed.

Wade could tell that Samantha was now the dominate personality.

"Turn on the lights," said Wade.

As the lights came on and they were adjusting to the brightness Wade took a seat opposite Cooper. With tears streaming down her face and trying desperately to get her breath under control, she looked up. Her eye was bruised and engulfed in blood. Shaking from the onset of shock she tried to speak.

"I don't control all this," she said in a disjointed splattering of words.

"I know," said Wade. "But who does?"

"I have no idea who he is. I receive all my correspondence by secure email. There is no communication back from me. Every time an instruction comes through it is always as he says it will be. If I don't follow his instructions to the letter something happens or someone dies."

"What was Bart doing with the bank accounts?"

"We were to empty the accounts and transfer the money to account numbers that kept appearing on the screen."

"How do we contact this person?"

"You don't. He contacts you."

"How?" demanded Wade.

"You type PTAFE into a browser and a password appears. The current password is 'Crystal' and then information will come through."

"Did you say 'Crystal'?"

"Yes. But it changes every time I receive a communication."

"What was the last password?"

"I think it was 'Joe'."

"What about before that?" asked Wade becoming extremely concerned.

"I can't remember exactly but it was either 'Kia' or 'Wine' or something," Cooper replied as she started to sway and her head fell forward crashing on the table.

Wade abruptly stood from his chair, nodded to Jacko and they left the room.

Forest, Kaitlyn and Joe met them outside the door as the interrogation specialist and a doctor rushed into the room.

"What do you make of all that? And why did you say you knew she was not in control?" asked Joe looking at Wade.

"Whoever is the mastermind of all this, knows who we are and must be getting their information from here," he replied heading for the closest Suburban.

"Wade, wait," said Kaitlyn walking with him. "I meant to tell you earlier but forgot. Remember the Secret Service agent you shot when we were with the President? Well, we found a recording device built into a button on his coat. We traced the link and got as far as a Midwest state before it was severed."

"Thanks," he replied.

"Where are you going?" she asked. "We have work to do."

"I'm going to make sure nothing happens to Crystal," said Wade more as a command than a reply.

Wade and Jacko leapt in the vehicle and with a squeal of the wheels, on the highly polished concrete, raced out the drop down opening.

"Sir. What do you want to do now?" asked Kaitlyn.

Turning back the stunned General replied, "I'll never get used to that guy … but I'll admit he does get results."

Kaitlyn ordered a technician to access a browser and go through what Cooper had said. The password was typed and the moment he hit the enter button, pages of encrypted data flashed on the screen and then the browser crashed.

With all eyes focused on the screen, the General asked the obvious. "What the hell was that?"

The technician explained that whoever had set up the program had built in protection that caused the system to collapse if the access wasn't initiated from a certain location. He went on to explain that the elaborate process had many firewalls and could have commenced anywhere in the world. There was nothing further they could do.

"Great. We're back at square one," said an exasperated Forest.

42: Inova Fairfax Hospital – Washington

They had been sitting in the private room of the Inova Fairfax hospital for an hour. Jacko had been watching Wade and all his various facial expressions. Being such close friends whenever they were together there was always non-stop chatter. The quietness made Jacko realise Wade was going over the mission, in his head, to the absolute detail.

Wade had been calling on the spirits for advice. He remembered an elder saying 'the snake does not watch and wait for its prey to move but watches it's prey's eyes; as the eyes move before the brain activates the muscles'. He concentrated and concentrated trying to decipher how this could help him.

"Hey buddy, do you want to talk about it?" asked Jacko.

Wade looked across at his mate, thought for a moment, then proceeded to explain the chain of events that led from his walkabout to the current hospital room.

Two hours had past. Doctors and nurses had come and checked Crystal's vitals, charts and all the equipment hanging around her. Cleaners had done the floors and attached bathroom. Crystal had slept through it all.

When Wade was finished, Jacko asked him what he felt; not what he thought.

"Interesting you should ask me that," replied Wade. "I've been going over this Professor Faux End and I feel he is not who he tells us he is."

"Why do you say that?"

"When he came into the meeting room, with the General, he wasn't nervous. The place and all the activity overawe most people. Instead he kept looking at everything like he was searching for something specific. Then he said to go to the Vatican for answers. Then he mentions only the senior members utter these certain words. Finally his word of caution was said with almost glee."

"I think we need to pay this professor a visit."

"Yeah, you're probably right but I'm not leaving Crystal."

"That's nice. But I'm sure I'll be fine in this hospital," said Crystal in her half sleep state.

Turning in his chair, standing and fighting his way through the tangle of tubes and wires, Wade was thrilled to see her smiling face awake.

"You won't remember but I promised you that no one will ever hurt you again. So here I stay until you're ready to leave," he said kissing her hand.

Crystal smiled and was about to reply when Jacko said, "How about we get Crystal moved up with her dad and I watch them both. You then won't need to worry … and we both know you need to finish this for Kiwi."

Wade looked at his mate, nodded, gave Crystal a peck on the cheek and left without a word.

43: The George Washington University

"Kaitlyn, what can you tell me about Professor Faux End and the Academy of the Study of Religious Developments?" asked Wade.

Four minutes ticked by until she returned to the phone.

"You're not going to believe this. We've checked all the data bases and known websites. Nothing, all gone. It's like it never existed."

"You need to get the General to understand that the Warehouse is compromised. He needs to either sweep it or get out. We're having no more contact until it's clean," declared Wade as he disconnected.

The Academy of the Study of Religious Developments is housed in a pre-Civil war building, in the furthest reaches of The George Washington University. Used as a hospital staff building during the Civil War it now stands as a memorial. The academy operates from two rear rooms and has no distinguishing signage. The current Dean of the Columbian College of Arts and Sciences, the body responsible for the building, was aware of the academy. One of the few faculties to not be continually seeking funding he never saw a need to investigate or query its operations.

Wade parked the Suburban in the carpark and made his way behind the academy building. It was approaching 1600 hours on a dark, cloudy afternoon. Most of the students had finished for the day. Wade had arrived at the rear doors without having met anybody.

Knocking, checking for lights and confirming the building was deserted, he used his KaBar knife to pry the old oak door open. Waiting the standard thirty seconds, for alarms, he entered.

The first office had a desk in the centre of the room with four chairs set around it. A starfish conference call phone was on top and a coffee table was off to the left. There were no papers or anything of assistance.

The second room was Faux End's office. A standard table, chairs, laptop docking station, lamp and single drawer filing cabinet. The walls were bare and the old timber floor was heavily scratched. The desk had all the normal paraphernalia of a working office.

The filing cabinet was scattered with newspaper and magazine clippings. Moving the table and filing cabinet still produced nothing. Wade had placed the small pencil drawer on the wheeled chair and as he brushed past, it fell. Stuck to the bottom was a card. Scribbled on it was the name of a park that was located within the university grounds.

Assuring everything was back where he had found things. Patching the splintered door jamb as well as he could. Ten minutes after his arrival, he left.

The university covers thirty six acres and the park was at the opposite end, so Wade drove. The lights of the university had started to appear. Even though sunset was twenty five minutes away, the lack of street lighting made the park and its surroundings obscured.

Wade noticed there were only three other cars in the carpark. Starting to feel he was at a dead end, he saw the professor walking toward the sports pavilion in the middle of the lacrosse ovals.

The stooped figure looked out of place walking into the changing rooms of a sports area. Wade waited. Four minutes later a fit looking, thirty plus, blond male, carrying a sports bag walked out. Wade watched him walk to the old, battered Toyota Supra and drive out of the carpark.

He waited a further five minutes then decided to check out the professor. The toilet block and change rooms were deserted and all the lights were off. After going through the entire building a second time, he realised the young guy was the professor in disguise.

Annoyed at himself, for being conned so easily, he drove back to the Warehouse.

Entering the drop down entrance door, he leapt from the Suburban and walked toward Forest, Kaitlyn, Joe and General Razen.

As Forest was about to speak Wade threw his hands in the air to signify no sound. Signalling to the four to follow him: they all climbed into the Suburban and Wade drove back out followed by Razen's protection detail.

Keeping everybody quite Wade drove through the deserted streets of West Washington until he found a fire hydrant. Stopping in the deserted, dark, rubbish splattered street he motioned to the protection detail to remain one hundred metres further back. Leaving the vehicle Wade got everybody to remove his or her shoes, coats, belts, mobile phones, jewellery, wallets, etc. With all the items left in the vehicle, the unusual looking quintet approached the hydrant as Wade opened it to its maximum.

Standing on the cold bitumen with the spray of the hydrant drifting over them, light rain starting to fall and the wind lashing their faces like a whip; Razen spoke. "Wade what's this all about?" he said through chattering teeth.

"I know you might think this a bit odd but somehow our foe always seems to have the upper hand. I believe we are being bugged. So I'm trying to mask the sound with the hydrant and wind, and visual with the darkness and rain. The whole purpose of removing your clothing parts was in case they had somehow got to our possessions."

"I assume you have something in mind?" asked Forest.

Wade explained about Professor Faux End and what happened at the university. He explained the minimal description, he could remember, of the younger guy and the car he drove.

Five minutes later the group had devised a plan. Kaitlyn and two technicians would plant bugs at the academy. An around the clock surveillance would commence. Reluctantly Forest agreed to empty the Warehouse, sweep the entire facility and check all their software. He explained they would be off the air for approximately thirty hours. Joe and the CIA interrogation specialist would persevere with Cooper in a makeshift facility. Wade would check in and report on his team's findings in Syria.

Razen looked at the faces of the four cold individuals standing in front of him.

"The President and I would like to commend you all on your results but it is imperative you understand the significance of what we are up against. If our intelligence is correct, whomever Cooper is talking about has now accessed the bank accounts of most of the world's wealthiest individuals. The combined power would enable them to crash or control any financial market. So forget about weapons, diamonds, terrorists, nuclear or and any other concerns. We are to focus on finding these people and recovering these accounts. Am I clear on this?"

Nodding in agreement, they all raced for the warmth of the vehicle.

44: Syria

Wade passed on the USB external drives; he had recovered from the castle, to Kaitlyn for analysis. She had already decided to return to Israel and utilise the state of the art equipment that Mossad had available, while Wade caught up with Sammy and Bart.

The commercial international flight from Cypress had been uneventful but incredibly crowded and noisy as it landed at Damascus International Airport.

The sun was at is greatest intensity as the time approached 1400 hours. The thermometer topped forty two degrees Celsius. Syrians knew better than to be out in the peak of the summer sun as Wade stepped from the taxi. Surveying the scene, to his right, he saw the two undercover secret service agents trying to remain hidden in the beat up old Datsun. Further down the street he saw an old lady scavenging through a pile of boxes that had been left outside a butcher shop. As she bent over he noticed the outline of a gun under her Burkha. Glancing to his left he caught the flash of glass, indicating a riflescope, from the second floor of the dilapidated hotel window.

After pretending to tie his shoelace, he picked up his backpack, walked up the eight stair entrance and, without knocking, entered. He heard Bart and Sammy leap to their feet and adopt the defensive pose in the second room.

"All right you two, ten seconds we're out of here," ordered Wade as they both looked into the hallway.

Grabbing their prepared packs they started following Wade to the back of the building.

"You've got company out the front. So how do we get out the back unnoticed?" asked Wade.

"Follow me," said Bart as he led them to the back kitchen.

Sliding the fridge aside he hooked his fingers into the wallboards and lifted out a panel. The three men dropped down the makeshift shaft and crawled along the two foot high tunnel. Slowly pushing the sheet, of burning hot corrugated iron, aside they exited into an old car-park. The weeds and shrubs were over four feet high. The bombed concrete hardstand was littered with car bodies, rubbish, household products and blown out containers. Before replacing the sheet Sammy added a small tripwire and C4 explosive to bring the tunnel down on anyone following.

Crossing the car-park and hiding in one of the blown containers Wade asked how their surveillance was progressing.

"We've been unable to locate or get anything on anyone. Latakia was a complete dead end," replied Sammy.

Wade explained about Cooper and Professor Faux End. They were deciding what to do next when his watch scanner beeped. Turning on his secure mobile phone he answered on the first ring.

"Wade, we've found an address in Damascus of somebody enquiring about Plutonium 239. I'll send it through now," said Kaitlyn as Wade disconnected the call without responding.

Wade gave Sammy and Bart an address on the eastern side of the city and told them to be there by midnight. All three men had very good knowledge of Damascus. They checked their street clothes and ensured the shemaghs covered their faces as they stepped out into the brutal afternoon sun. Convinced they were not being followed; they split up.

The address was an old church that had been converted into a nightclub. It was a men's only club and Wade knew the rear entrance would be filled with prostitutes. The three men watched from their vantage point as Wade explained.

"Kia has found an address, here in Damascus, of somebody making enquires about Plutonium 239. Unfortunately we'd never get near that area so I've decided we grab one or two of these prostitutes, as they're finished for the night and we pay them to make us look like a group on a night out."

Nodding in agreement, they waited. It was after 0200 when a short haired brunette Turkish girl and a taller blond both wearing leather jackets walked from the rear alley. Approaching Wade asked, offered them money and the girls agreed.

Walking through the narrow, dimly lit streets, Bart with his arm around the shoulders of the blond and Sammy joking with the brunette as Wade continually scanned for onlookers.

The address in question was on the side of a gentle sloping hill. The entrance gate was set back from the road. Wade had already explained to the girls that they were to keep walking no matter what happened. Having received their money they were not interested in being involved and agreed wholeheartedly. As the group approached, the two half asleep guards took no notice and continued leaning back on the corner posts. Having already dropped back three steps Wade waited until Sammy was beside the second guard. With both men in position they lashed out with their right hands and smashed into the guards faces. They then spun them around grabbed the guards from behind and snapped their necks. Opening the gate and dragging the two bodies inside Bart had already ushered the girls along as the three men checked their weapons and snuck around the building.

After circling the building, checking for surveillance cameras and certain there were no more guards they entered a rear door into a corridor. The building was surprisingly small considering the more affluent area it was located in. Two doors off to the right were bedrooms, the first on the left was a bathroom and the second area was an open kitchen. After checking there were no further occupants Sammy and Bart burst into the room and dragged the startled Arab from his bed. With the house still in darkness they zip tied him to a kitchen chair.

"I know you can speak English. I don't care who you are, what you're doing or what you're involved in but you better start talking about Plutonium 239 and why you're making enquiries," quietly and calmly spoke Wade.

With no response Sammy stepped in front and put his head down inches from the Arab's face. The Arab spat into Sammy's eyes as Sammy retaliated with a lightning fast right hook to his head. The punch knocked the Arab, and his chair, over and he banged his head on the cupboards. Sammy wiped the spit from his eyes, bent over, righted the chair and the Arab and hit him again. This time the Arab's jaw was smashed; nose broken and blood gushed everywhere. Not waiting for any response he used his left hand and hit him again. Teeth flew across the floor as further sounds of crushed bones emanated within the deathly quiet room.

Wade cut the bindings and the Arab fell forward onto the table.

Wade grabbed his hair and smashed his face into the table top.

"Last chance," whispered Wade as Bart walked into the room with a laptop under his arm.

Opening the lid the letters PTAFE flashed on the screen. Wade turned the laptop so the Arab could watch. With Sammy holding his head Wade typed in the password box 'Crystal'. The page opened and another Arabs face appeared. Seeing that Wade had gained access the Arab leapt from his chair as he pulled a carving knife from under the table. The knife sliced through Wade's left sleeve and cut a three inch slit across his forearm. Bart put a silenced single shot into the side of the Arabs head.

Whilst Wade attended to his arm Sammy searched the laptop and found an address for the second Arab.

After destroying the laptop and dragging the guards bodies inside, they set a time-delayed explosive and left via the rear neighbours roof.

The second address was located on the outskirts of the city. After stealing a car the three men arrived at 0430. They knew they only had another thirty minutes of darkness as they crept around the building. After finding no guards or surveillance they entered the rear door. Wade and Bart were hard against the corridor walls, weapons drawn when suddenly the lights came on. Automatic gunfire sprayed all about them and they hit the floor. Rounds whistled above their heads and tore at the floor and walls whilst they both strained to keep themselves as low as possible.

As the shooting stopped a heavily Arab accented voice yelled, "If you move … you die. Drop your weapons. Hands behind your head."

Both men realising the fruitlessness of resistance, obeyed. With their heads on the floor and hands behind their heads they heard the footsteps of six men approaching. They were then kicked, punched, hit with the butt of rifles, hands tied behind their back and whipped. With only their pants and boots remaining a hood was placed over their heads and they were thrown into a room.

As Wade and Bart had entered the back entrance Sammy had headed for the front. Unaware of further attackers the Arabs had not pursued and Sammy slunk away. Sammy knew the sounds of the automatic gunfire would bring others so he found the vehicle and headed back into Damascus.

45: Syrian Desert

After being moved from building to building throughout the morning Wade and Bart were dragged and thrown into the back of a pickup truck. It was late morning and the temperature was already approaching forty degrees Celsius. Still only wearing pants, boots and hoods their backs were burnt on the scorching tray of the truck as their captors unleashed more hitting, kicking and rifle butting.

Wade estimated they had been driving for two hours when the truck stopped and they were dragged out on to the ground. One of the guards removed their hoods. After their sight had refocused they realised they were in the desert. The second guard had gone off to relieve himself whilst the first barked orders in Arabic.

Wade was not fluent in Arabic but could say and understand enough to be convincing. Pleading with the guard he offered to show he would help by shooting his mate. Continually talking and trying to persuade him the guard suddenly thought this would be very interesting to have one of his captors, who spoke in an unusual English dialect, shoot another Englishman.

Walking behind Wade he dropped the rifle in front of him.

"Any tricks and you die," said the guard as he bent down and cut the bindings.

With the razor sharp knife against Wade's throat the guard motioned for him to pick up the rifle and shoot. As he slowly leant forward the guard followed suit. When Wade was sure he was off balance, he distracted him by using his right hand to grab the weapon and his left to grab the guard's wrist. In one motion holding the knife away from himself he spun around and as he smashed his forehead onto the bridge of the guards nose, he snapped the guards knife holding wrist. The guard was about to scream out as Wade slammed his fist into his throat, cutting off all sound and killing him instantly.

Cutting Bart's bindings he handed him the rifle and told him to take care of the second guard. Unsure of who was following or what predicament they were in, Wade punctured and drained the fuel tank and smashed up the engine. Taking the guards rifles, knifes and shirts they set off. Wade could tell they had been taken southwest from Damascus and were in the mountainous region of Mount Hermon, very close to the border of Lebanon.

Both men were highly trained and skilled in survival as they battled their way through a very sparsely populated and difficult terrain. They had been running, climbing and stopping only for drinks, for the last nine hours, when they came upon an Israel border control point.

"What now?" asked a completely exhausted Bart.

"Get rid of all weapons and take off your shirt," instructed Wade as he watched the border guards.

Checking Bart had done as he ordered. Wade said, "Follow me and don't say a word."

It was 2100 and darkness had set in as the two shirtless men walked down the dirt road leading to the border patrol. One hundred metres out suddenly two large spotlights lit up the area.

"Halt. State your purpose," came the voice over the loudspeaker as three highly armed border police stepped from the side covers.

Speaking in Hebrew Wade asked to be taken to Mossad headquarters and in particular to speak with either operative Kian or Director Harel. He also asked that they mention his name, Wundurra, when contacting Mossad.

Remaining held at gunpoint for ten minutes they were then led into the commanding guards office.

"Mister Wundurra. A helicopter will be here to pick you up in twenty minutes. My officers will escort you. Please put on these shirts and jackets and thank you for your services to our nation," stated the Captain as he got to his feet and saluted.

"*Al-Lo-Davar*," replied Wade nodding to him as they left.

The helicopter landed on the roof of Mossad headquarters after a brief forty minute flight. Kaitlyn and a heavily armed squad of soldiers were there to meet them. With the blades of the helicopter not slowing and the pilot and crew anxious to depart they jumped from the rails.

Once they were clear and the chopper had started its accent Kaitlyn stepped forward and gently kissed Wade on both cheeks as she said, "*Ma Nishma.*"

"*Tov, toda* … How about you? I'm guessing glad to be home."

Nodding Kaitlyn led them into one of the most secure buildings on earth.

As they entered the fortress like structure Bart noticed how no two sets of doors were ever open at the same time. He saw people sitting in front of computer screens, others were working with explosives, some appeared to be preparing for missions and he saw four men practising the Israeli combat self-defence art of Krav Maga. All eyes watched as the party walked through the building. The elevator took them down five levels into the deepest bowels and as the doors opened a short, immaculately dressed, middle aged man, with a receding hairline and flanked by two heavily armed black clad guards; stepped forward.

"*Shalom* Wundurra … it is so good to see you," said Director Ben Harel as he and Wade hugged. "What brings you here?"

Wade proceeded to explain what had happened and was about to ask Kaitlyn if she had been able to obtain any information, from the USB stick, when an aide approached.

"Sir, excuse me," she said as she then noticed Wade and Bart. "Sorry sir," she stated as she turned to walk away.

"No, it is alright. What do you have?" asked the director.

Nervously glancing at the two filthy, unshaven, battle scarred men; she looked to her boss.

"Sir, we have received word that the Mexican economy is about to enter a financial free fall. Somebody or some organization has withdrawn seventy five percent of the governments trading bonds and is attempting to cash them in at highly deflated rates. The value of the Peso is falling by the minute and with the sale of these bonds it will crash. Unless something is done to stem the flow we estimate that within six days the government will be insolvent and unable to operate."

"Thank you," replied Director Harel as the aide handed a wad of pages detailing the situation.

Leading Wade, Bart and Kaitlyn into his office, with the two guards stationed outside his door, Harel asked to be connected with his American counterpart, General Forest. Secure lines were established, pleasantries completed and Harel explained who was present.

"General as you are no doubt aware the Mexican financial market is in trouble and our computer generated models indicate that within seventy two hours, as a worst case scenario, the Mexican populace will start to withdraw their money on mass. A further twenty four hours and the economy will start to falter and we could expect anarchy to commence. I appreciate this situation will have a far greater impact on the US economy than Israel's but our concern, as advised by Wundurra, and what happened in Italy is that of a global collapse."

With silence from the other end of the line, all ears waited for Forest to respond.

Twenty seconds later. "Do you have any suggestions?" asked Forest.

"Our president has suggested that your president call a world summit Telco and discuss possible options to slow down the withdrawal," replied Harel looking across at Wade.

"Wundurra … you looked puzzled and in deep thought. I know from experience that when you are like this we should listen," said Harel.

Pausing for a moment and looking around the table, Wade spoke. "I'm not sure but my spirits are telling me Samantha Cooper is the key."

Director Harel is a very religious man who follows and practises Judaism (the religion and philosophy of the Jewish people) and would never normally consider the spiritual beliefs of others.

Wade had proven, beyond doubt that his thoughts and beliefs were to be taken seriously.

"What do you want to do?" asked Harel and Forest in unison.

"General can you arrange to get her and anything we know of her to Tel Aviv as soon as possible. We'll check out more on the Plutonium and the Arab."

The group agreed and Forest advised that Cooper and a CIA detail would be in Tel Aviv within ten hours.

Harel had arranged quarters within the building for Wade and Bart. After showering, eating and a short nap Wade, Bart and Kaitlyn were gathered in the large conference room. They had been discussing options, analysing data from the USB stick Wade had taken from the castle and listening to Harel's advisors when the large screen, at the end of the room, lit up.

An Israeli male was looking directly at the screen as he spoke in hushed tones and explained the Brazilian financial market was crashing. He explained that over thirty percent of the market's value had been lost in dead trading in the last two hours, since the market closed. Government bonds were being sold at ridiculously low rates and major overseas investors were liquidating their positions. At the current decline the economy would struggle to be able to match their debts by the time the market opened in fifteen hours.

Harel burst into the room and was about to speak as Wade stood and said, "I'm going for a run to clear my head."

Stunned by the statement Harel finally said, "I'll organise a protection detail."

Wade smiled and shook his head, "No thanks Ben. They'll slow me down."

Springing to their feet Bart and Kaitlyn advised they were coming.

46: Israeli Desert

Outside of the populated areas much of the remaining country, of Israel, is hot, dry, mountainous and rocky.

As a three and a half minute per kilometre runner Bart had always been able to lead or at least keep with most runners. The first hour, through the populated areas, had been hard and Bart had been breathing like an oxygen depleted heavy smoker but he had matched Wade and Kaitlyn.

Upon entering the baking hot, barren areas his breathing had become more and more difficult with each passing kilometre. Bart knew that as an elite Special Forces soldier he had endured the worst conditions and punishment that anybody could throw at him but he could not believe the furnace like, oxygen deficient terrain he was now in. What made it worse was how easily Wade and Kaitlyn seemed to glide along in their Zen like states.

They had been running solid for three hours when Wade unexpectedly stopped at an oasis. Bart doubled over to try and get his breath back and take the pain out of his legs.

The group collapsed at the water's edge and had been splashing the cool water over themselves, with Bart spread eagled on his back, when Wade sprang to his feet, pulled out his knife and raced into the reeds surrounding the spring.

Kaitlyn and Bart now standing, Wade parted the reeds and led a young Arab girl out. Half lifting and half dragging her he had one hand around her upper arm and the other holding a rusty Janbiya, an Arabic dagger. Forcing her to sit on the ground Wade looked into her fiery brown eyes and saw total despair and hatred.

"Why did you try to attack us?" asked Wade.

"I want to kill all Jews," screamed the girl as she tried to stand and grab the dagger from Wade's hand.

Holding her back on the ground and waiting until she had slightly calmed down, Wade leaned his face close into the girl's and whispered, "We are not Jews or Israeli and do not even come from this country. So calm down and tell us why you want to do this."

Seeing genuine kindness in his eyes, but showing caution towards Kaitlyn, the young girl lowered her head. Whispering and with tears cascading down her cheeks, she tried to speak.

Kaitlyn stepped forward and put her arm around the girl's shoulder. "What's your name?"

"Hayat," replied the young girl who was by now scared and shaking.

"Hayat … please tell us so we can help," calmly said Kaitlyn.

With her hands trembling, "My older brother double crossed our family by selling information to the Jews and the soldiers retaliated by killing my father, mother and two sisters." Pausing with her entire body shaking. "I was getting water and by the time I had returned they had burnt our home, and everything we had, to the ground. A neighbour told me what had happened and helped me get out of the village … I must find and kill my brother and avenge my family's death by killing as many Jews as possible," stammered Hayat.

Raising her head and looking into her eyes Wade asked, "Are you sure about what your brother has done?"

"Of course I'm sure. They killed my family."

Wade looked across at Bart and Kaitlyn, nodded and returned his gaze to Hayat. "Okay you're coming with us and we'll find your brother."

With a stunned expression Hayat got to her feet as Kaitlyn remarked, "Are you sure we have time for this?"

Ignoring Kaitlyn's comment, Wade called for a vehicle to pick them up and take them to an undisclosed location in the Or Yehuda district of Tel Aviv, just north of Ben Gurion Airport, Israel's main international terminal.

The drive was very subdued with the only sounds being the continual banter on the driver's radio. Wade sat in the rear of the vehicle, beside Hayat, and he noticed how she was forcing her fingers backwards, nearly to the point of breaking. He watched the expression on her face and he realised she was in so much emotional pain she wasn't even feeling her hands.

They arrived at the house that had no distinguishable features. Was in a dead end street and all the windows were covered.

The group entered the single level, four room building and were met by a huge, six foot five, two hundred and forty pound man with long, curly, unkempt jet black hair. His eyes were blood red and as he smiled the missing front teeth gave a very discomforting appearance.

Stepping around Bart and Hayat, Wade grabbed the huge man in a bear hug.

"It's good to see you Jamshid," said Wade.

"You also, Wundurra," replied Jamshid looking around at the others. "Who are these people and what do you want from me?"

"I want you to talk with Hayat," as Wade motioned her forward, "to see if we can locate her brother. Kai will help and arrange anything you need. I have to get back and talk with Director Harel. Let me know as soon as you have something."

Bart, Wade and the driver, left the house and as they entered the car Bart asked, "Who's that guy? He's one scary looking unit."

214

Casually leaning back in his seat, Wade smiled as he replied, "Jamshid is an interrogator for Mossad … he was a Kidon but lost the use of both legs in a failed Palestinian ambush. Now unable to operate as a Kidon he specialises in getting information out of people."

"Surely he's not going to force it out of that young girl?" asked an amazed Bart.

"On the contrary. He doesn't use force. He is incredibly quick-witted and very intelligent so he utilises his psychological skills … I guess his demeanour half scares people, which can help."

"What is this Kidon you're talking about?"

"It's a very secretive arm of Mossad that specializes in assassinations."

"Really!" responded a surprised Bart. "How come after all these years mixed up in the Special Forces world I wouldn't have heard of them?"

"I'm not surprised. Not a lot is known and less is said about them. Israel is one of the most guarded countries on earth and Mossad one of the most secretive organizations. So I'm sure their most secretive department is going to be fairly hard to get information on."

"Have you worked with these Kidon?"

Smiling Wade looked out the blackened window at the suburbs zipping past. "Yeah, I have but I'd rather not talk about it; all the same."

Bart nodded in acknowledgement as he too looked out the window and thought 'how much more is there to this guy that we don't know about'. Bart's admiration for Wade seemed to grow every time they spoke.

47: Mossad HQ

Director Harel is an extremely busy individual who is responsible for a staff of thousands. He answers only to the Israeli Prime Minister and must deal with the continual conflicts at their borders and around the world.

Bart had been asked to wait outside the office as Wade sat opposite Harel and watched the comings and goings of staff, telephone calls and messages.

With a mobile phone in his left hand, listening to his assistant through the desk phone and watching the two seventeen inch screens mounted on his desk; the director casually looked up, "So Wundurra. What now?"

"Jamshid is trying to get some information on an Arab girl's brother. Samantha Cooper should arrive in about four hours and Kian is still analysing data from the USB we got from Cooper's castle. It appears this will only give us bank accounts and the details of the transactions."

"I understand the significance of Cooper and interrogating her but why a young Arab girl and chasing after her brother?" asked Harel with a stunned expression.

"Let's just wait and see."

Wade and Harel engaged in continued talk about past experiences and events, in between interruptions. Harel enjoyed his time with Wade and was always interested in Wade's thoughts on Israel and the actions of Mossad. An hour had passed when an aide entered and advised Hayat's brother had been located.

Her brother was a sleeper operating in rural Syria who was in Tel Aviv on a post mission briefing and would be at Or Yehuda within the hour.

Wade, Bart and Harel headed back to the safe house and arrived as the brother was being escorted from an unmarked white van.

Upon seeing her brother Hayat leapt from the chair and charged towards him. Screaming and yelling she banged her fists on his chest as her brother wrapped his arms around her shaking shoulders.

"Hayat it's okay," softly spoke her brother trying to calm her down.

"How can you say that Lais? Omy, Aby, Alea and Safi are all dead … you killed them. Why did you do this?" pleaded Hayat.

"Please Hayat, sit down and I will explain."

As Hayat and Lais sat on the small tattered couch Wade motioned for everybody to leave the room.

"Please stay," asked Hayat looking at Wade.

Accepting Wade took a seat opposite the two siblings.

"Omy (their father) had a secret and a wish that he only ever told me about and I promised on my eighteenth birthday that I would fulfil this wish." Pausing he grabbed hold of her hands. "You need to be strong to hear this Hayat," said Lais looking into her bloodshot eyes.

Nodding Hayat watched her brother intently as he spoke.

"Our father is a Jew," said Lais waiting for the impact of the statement to fully sink in. "He decided that he loved our mother so much he was going to live his life as an Arab in Syria but the plight of the Jews was always in the back of his mind. Three years ago he found out his brother and his brother's wife had been murdered by Arab extremists, as they were shopping at a market in the border town of Mehola. They were buying food for the upcoming Passover festival, a celebration of the freedom of the Israelites from slavery, when the extremists stabbed them in an open market. From that day forth he was determined to do anything he could to help the Jewish people but he was torn for his love of our mother and her Arabic beliefs … I promised to fulfil Omy's wishes and spend my life helping the Jewish people in any way I could."

With tears running down both their cheeks Hayat and Lais hugged.

"I'm sorry … I thought you had betrayed us," said Hayat. "Does this mean we are not truly Arabic or

Jewish … where do we belong?" asked a confused Hayat looking at her brother and then toward Wade.

"The Jewish people have been very kind and have welcomed me with open arms, so I believe we will now call here home," replied Lais looking toward Wade.

"I know they will," said Wade as he stood. "Good luck to you both."

As Wade left the room it was as if a light bulb had suddenly lit up.

"We've been doing this all wrong. It's not Samantha Cooper's association with this Opus Dei or Ied Supo that we should be pursuing, it's her younger brother," he said out loud to himself as he charged from the safe house with Bart and the director in pursuit.

48: Mossad – Interrogation Room

Samantha Cooper sat on the steel chair that was bolted to the floor with her head collapsed on her chin and her bandaged hands in her lap. The CIA had made no attempt to clean her up. She had been kept awake since her capture. Offered only minimal amounts of food and water. She was approaching a state of collapsing as Wade, Bart and Jamshid entered the room. Upon seeing Wade she bolted upright and wrapped her arms across her chest.

"What more do you want from me?" she stammered nervously looking at the three imposing figures.

"Information on your brother," quietly answered Wade.

"He's dead."

"Other brother," replied Wade.

"I don't have another brother."

"Don't lie to me," yelled Wade as he slammed his fist on the table and Cooper starting shaking. Bart grabbed her shoulders to stop her falling off the chair.

"I haven't seen or heard from Thomas for over twenty five years … so as far as I'm concerned he doesn't even exist."

Stepping forward Jamshid asked, "That maybe the case but tell us everything that you can remember up to the last time you saw him."

Wade and Bart left the room as Jamshid listened to Cooper explain that Thomas had been an unusual child who had always been very distant and despising of his parents. How he hated the family wealth and would do anything to show disrespect toward it. Would only wear second hand clothing and never accepted gifts from anybody who was wealthy. How he would always eat alone. Had an obsession with soldier games and the American Red Indians. Had no friends and spent no time with anyone except for the family gardener Julius. She told how he ran away from home at fourteen.

When asked where he might be, Cooper replied she had no knowledge but would not be surprised if he was with the Indians.

The twenty plus year old description she gave of Julius would probably be a dead end but Wade insisted Kaitlyn pursue anyway.

Mossad agents used their information technology hacking skills to access all the relevant US departments.

An hour had passed. Jamshid was still persevering with Cooper. Kaitlyn had discovered that Julius had died nine years earlier of natural causes. Wade was on the phone to Jacko and Crystal.

"How's things in Israel?' asked Jacko from the hands free speaker phone in Crystal and her dad's room.

"Actually I'm a bit stumped," replied Wade who went on to explain his thoughts on Thomas Cooper.

Sitting quietly listening to Wade and Jacko discussing options, Crystal sat up in her bed and asked, "What's the professor's full name?"

"No idea … why?" asked Wade.

"I have the suspicion that his first names start with the letters T and A and that would make the PTAFE his initials. I would also not be surprised if Thomas Cooper's middle name is the same letter A."

"That's brilliant," replied Wade. "I'll call back as soon as I can," he hastily stated as he disconnected the call and dialled Kaitlyn.

Ten minutes later Kaitlyn called Wade back to advise him that the professor's first names are Tomas and Andre and Thomas Cooper's middle name is Alexander. She went on to explain that these are the French conversion of Cooper's name.

"Okay, we've established that Thomas Cooper and Professor Faux End are one of the same. Now we need to find him. How are we progressing with the Indian search?" asked Wade.

"Absolutely nothing," replied Kaitlyn. "The Indian people have kept so few records that the likelihood of locating someone is very slim, so to confirm it would be next to impossible. We have widened the search to include the FBI and local police department records targeting missing persons, vagrants, small crimes, etc … this is definitely a long shot Wade."

"I know," he said coming down from the exuberance of the small gain in linking the names. "Bart and I are leaving on the next flight. Can you ensure this stays between you, me and the Colonel?"

Director Harel had come to farewell Wade as his personal assistant approached.

"Sir, we have another economy that has been hit. This time it's South Africa at the Johannesburg Stock Exchange. There is a slight difference in that this market has been flooded with dummy bonds aimed at the resources sector. Their coal values have plummeted and their major oil supplier, Saudi Arabia, is threatening to take up the option of cancelling out of their contract. Indications are by the time the market opens they will have no ability to trade on the world stage. We have also received unconfirmed reports that four major electricity producing facilities, in the north east of the country, have been taken over by unknown identities and these identities have planted explosives."

Nodding acknowledgement Harel turned to Wade. "I spoke with Asimov (Israel Prime Minister) and he agreed we need to get ahead of this. Any thoughts?"

"Do you think you could convince Forest and Spencer (British MI6 chief) to talk to your respective Presidents and Prime Ministers and somehow get them to sell a story to the world's media that we have figured out where these attacks are coming from?"

"How and for what reason could I do that?" asked a surprised but smiling Harel.

"It seems to me that whoever is doing this is focusing on emerging or mid-range economies that have extremely high levels of poverty within their respective countries. So we get the experts to focus on other similar markets and maybe we can stop or slow down further collapses. But it could also be the catalyst we need for Cooper to make a mistake or show his hand."

"I'll give it a try. Always a pleasure to see you Wundurra. *Shalom.*"

49: Inova Fairfax Hospital – Washington

After eleven hours of bouncing around on the cargo harnesses, drinking warm water, freezing cold and the unrelenting sound of rushing air; the unmarked Israeli postal freight flight landed at Dulles International airport.

Wade and Bart were glad to be off the Boeing 747-400 and were also pleased to have returned undetected. They separated, with Bart heading back to the team.

It was 2300 hours and the Inova Fairfax Hospital had entered the wind down stage of its day. The night staff had arrived. Had checked their respective patients and were sitting at the nurses stations. Reading magazines, texting friends, watching television; they were into their nightly routine. The lights had been dimmed with only enough in the hallways to aid in an emergency.

As he pushed the emergency stairwell door open on the fifth floor, Wade stopped and listened. The sound of patients snoring, medical equipment beeping and oxygen being pumped emanated from the ward.

Keeping to the shadows he crept down the hallway and entered the private room.

Jacko, a highly trained Delta Forces operative spun around to the sound behind him but lucky for him it was Wade. Startled he whispered, "How the hell do you do that? You're like a snake the way you sneak around."

"Thanks for looking after them," said Wade as Crystal stirred and woke.

After many hugs and kisses they decided to put Crystal in a wheelchair and go down to the first floor cafeteria.

The cafeteria was deserted except for the friendly young guy serving behind the counter who was more interested in getting back to his university assignment.

Crystal and Jacko watched as Wade ate two full meals and drank three cups of strong black coffee. They talked for two hours about what had happened in Israel, about Trent's condition and had got onto menial subjects when the lights browned down and then lit back up.

Wade wondered why this would happen in a hospital that has an emergency backup generator, so he led the group to the elevator. The lift doors opened at the fifth floor reception and they were confronted with screams, the sound of smashing glass and objects clanging together.

227

"Jacko, kill the power and lights. Crystal, I want you down to the ground floor and out of the building. We'll get your dad," commanded Wade as he hit the lift button and he and Jacko leapt through the closing doors.

Pressing the single digit direct dial number on his mobile phone and keeping against the wall; he raced to Trent's room. Jacko headed in the opposite direction.

With staff frantically racing from room to room, patients who were capable staggering into the corridor and all the lights blazing Wade tried to relay to Kaitlyn what was happening.

"I'm at the hospital on the fifth floor. I've sent Crystal to the ground floor and out of the building," screamed Wade as the sound of automatic gunfire rang through the ward.

Diving to the highly polished linoleum floor; the rounds continued shattering glass and ricocheting off beds, doors and the walls. Wade estimated five shooters. They appeared to be spaced at strategic points. He could tell they were highly trained. They covered each other's arcs of fire and alternated with reloading and the continuous firing of two round bursts.

As quickly as the shooting had started, it stopped, with the entire floor plunged into darkness as black as a cave. Even the emergency lights and fire evacuation signs did not activate. Only the street lighting from five floors below and the LED lift floor indicator was evident.

The sound of people screaming and crashing into things aided Wade as he raced down the corridor. Each second ticked by and his night vision improved.

Arriving at the door to Trent's room he lent around the door jamb and saw a man, through muzzle flash, dressed in surgeon's greens, pumping rounds from a silenced Uzi 9mm sub machine gun into Trent's bed.

Removing the razor sharp garrotte from his pocket he raced into the room but not toward the shooter rather to the wall behind him. The shooter, realizing somebody was behind him, spun around and started firing. This was the advantage Wade needed as he utilized his Parkour skills and jumped five feet up the wall, pushed off and came in behind the shooter. With the garrotte now around his neck the shooter aided Wade by attempting to spin further and sliced his own throat.

Dropping the body Wade reefed the blanket off the bed to find three bullet ridden pillows.

With a quick dial to Jacko he explained the shooters were probably dressed as staff, if not surgeons and Trent was gone.

They coordinated their plan and started sweeping the floor, whilst leaving their mobiles connected.

"Wade we've a problem. There's a huge lump of C4 in the cleaners room and we've only got forty seconds," yelled Jacko.

"To the stairs. Go," screamed Wade.

Trying to avoid the patients and staff he rounded a corner and crashed into an upturned trolley. Clambering to his feet the rounds punched the walls beside him as he dived into the opened doorway. Bouncing out of his parachute roll he wasn't expecting the mop handle that crashed down across his shoulders knocking him back on the floor. Wary of another blow he rolled to the side as he caught a glimpse of his attacker.

"Trent! It's me Wade," he yelled avoiding the second blow and grabbing hold of the mop.

"Hell Wade. What's going on?" stammered Trent as Wade grabbed hold to stop him toppling over.

"We need to get you out of here. The whole floor's going to blow," yelled Wade over the gunfire.

Grabbing his mobile phone. "Jacko we're in the laundry room behind the reception. I've got Trent and two tangos have us pinned," screamed Wade.

"Coming."

Five seconds later Wade heard the distinctive sound of a Delta Force weapon of choice, the Glock 22 and its double tap pistol fire.

Charging into the room Jacko yelled, "We've got ten seconds."

"Down here," yelled Wade as he grabbed Trent and dived, feet first into the laundry chute.

The chute led to the first floor laundry area and had been designed with no bends. Years of linen sliding down the stainless steel walls had rendered them smooth as glass. Wade struggled to hold Trent as he used his boots and back to slow their fall. The last two metres had a ninety degree sweeping bend and the three men got spat out into a large overflowing steel bin. Fighting their way through the bursting laundry bags they heard and felt the explosion.

With Wade carrying Trent on his shoulders, the two men raced down the emergency stairs and out into the rear courtyard, facing the emergency department.

"Wade we have a chopper landing for you just south of the emergency department. I can see you on the hospital CCTV. Turn right and you should see it coming down now," said Kaitlyn on the mobile phone. "We've got a team on route, ETA four minutes and they'll look after the loose ends."

"Where's Crystal?" said Wade frantically searching.

"I'll explain in a moment. Just get on the chopper. The areas getting too hot. If you don't get out of there now, there's going to be a lot of explaining … Wade you need to move," yelled Kaitlyn.

Realizing the seriousness in Kaitlyn's voice they charged for the hovering unmarked helicopter. The hospital had become engulfed with emergency personnel and the sky was filling with media and police helicopters.

Laying the unconscious Trent on the floor, Jacko checked for further injuries and Wade scrambled to redial Kaitlyn.

"Where is she?" he asked.

"Street CCTV shows an ambulance with two men who grabbed her at the front entrance and headed south down Wellness Boulevard. That was three minutes ago and we're still trying to locate the ambulance."

"Kaitlyn, I want you to stay on this line. I want to know what's happening at all times. Clear," ordered Wade.

"Sure," came the frustrated reply.

Turning to the pilot Wade ordered him to Bethesda Hospital and he instructed Kaitlyn to get guards to Trent's room.

The helicopter landed on the roof mounted platform. As the medical team headed into the building, Wade and Jacko made a beeline for the fire stairs. Using the cover of darkness they made their way through the city. They stole a pickup truck, parked outside a liquor store, and drove back to The George Washington University. Ensuring there was no surveillance on the Academy of the

Study of Religious Developments, they entered the rear door. Jacko stumbled on a FedEx parcel and upon opening they found a small wooden box. It contained three dice stuck to the bottom with the number eight facing up on all the dice.

Wade relayed the information and parcel details to Kaitlyn and asked if there had been further developments on Crystal.

"I promise, I will call the moment something comes to light," she said.

50: Montana

"Wade, we're on our way. We should be at the Site by 0900," said Wine through the secure encrypted phone line.

"Thanks Colonel. We're going to check out a possible lead in Havre, Montana. Then we'll meet you at the Site."

Site 180 is a secure operations location hidden in the South Dakota mountains. Developed as a storage silo for ICBM's (Intercontinental Ballistic Missiles) during the Cold War, it had been decommissioned by the US Army. Through some cleverly planned paperwork all the relevant departments, that had access to the site, were led to believe that a different department was now in control. Its remote location, one metre thick concrete walls, completely self sufficient and undetectable from the air; made it the perfect hideaway for the Colonel and his team to train and regroup whenever in the States.

The President and the Chairman of the Joint Chiefs of Staff were the only two people who if they wanted could ever find out about Site 180. There had been a further three presidents, since President Slater had first made the facility available to Wine as gratitude for the Colonel's help in saving the life of the President's wife.

A helicopter would land on an unmarked pad that appeared from the air as a large rock outcrop. Once secured, the helicopter and pad would rise up out of the rock and be winched into the cliff. Access to the site was through a labyrinth of corridors protected by state of the art security. Each entry point included a full body scan, retina check and voice activation. All team members knew that if the system failed to recognize them, they were to stand completely still until deactivation was secured. Not complying would release 'Jumping Jack' landmines behind them.

'Jumping Jack', also known as a 'Bouncing Betty', an anti-personnel mine that upon activation leaps three to four feet in the air and sprays fragmentation in all directions up to twenty five metres. The confines of the concrete enclosed Site 180 corridors makes survival impossible. If not killed by the fragmentation the sonic boom of the explosion shatters the eardrum and ruptures the brain.

The small twin engine Cessna landed at Havre County Airport as the hire car booth opened. Wade and Jacko fought desperately to control their frustration when after drinking her coffee, firing up the computer and rechecking her makeup, for the fourth time, she asked if she could help.

Using an alias credit card they secured a pickup, loaded their gear and headed for town. Five minutes later they were standing outside the local police station. The sheriff stepped from his car. Eyeing the two dark skinned individuals standing in front of him and thinking they represented trouble, the sheriff stepped forward.

"I hope you two boys are looking for the way out of here as you pass through," he asked unclipping his pistol holder and ensuring they saw.

"We're not looking for any trouble sheriff. Just want to enquire about an arrest that was made at this station twenty five years ago," said Wade.

"And who the hell might you two be wanting to know that?" boomed the sheriff as two deputies exited the station and came up behind him.

"Like I said sheriff we're not wanting any trouble. Just two citizens making an enquiry under the Freedom of Information Act about a Thomas Cooper," calmly replied Wade noticing the reaction from the larger of the two deputies at the mention of Cooper's name.

"Don't know and never heard of any Thomas Cooper. So you might as well keep moving."

"Well sorry to disagree sheriff but he was arrested here twenty five years ago and we would like to see the arrest paperwork."

"I've had enough of this shit. Cuff'em boys," ordered the sheriff as the deputies stepped around him.

"I wouldn't do this sheriff," replied Wade as he and Jacko adopted a defensive stance.

With that the deputies lunged. Wade and Jacko leapt into the air and drove their knees into the deputy's midriffs. The first deputy went to the ground as Jacko prepared to finish his attack. The second and larger deputy doubled up but was still standing as Wade saw the sheriff pull his pistol. Instinctively diving he rolled toward the sheriff and kicked his legs out from under him. As he fell Wade snapped his wrist knocking the pistol clear. The sheriff was a large man and it took a further twenty seconds for Wade to pin him to the ground and use the sheriff's handcuffs to lock his hands behind his back. Looking across he saw Jacko had done the same to the now unconscious deputy.

Springing to their feet they saw and heard the police cruiser, with the larger deputy at the wheel, squeal its tyres and race from the station car-park, north down Third Avenue. Yelling to Jacko they charged to their pickup and headed off in pursuit. The cruiser turned west at First Street on to Highway 2, the road out of town. To elude the sheriff, or whoever else was watching from the police station, Wade turned at Second Street, the road running parallel with Highway 2.

"What do you think of all that?" casually asked Jacko.

"I'm not sure this deputy will help us that much but there's a chance he could lead us to somebody who will."

After joining back onto Highway 2 they caught up with the cruiser and followed at a safe visual distance. About to enter the small roadside town of Kremlin the cruiser swung off the road, careened in the dirt and with a bloom of dust came to a halt at the back of a roadside tavern. Frantically leaping from the car the deputy looked like a sideshow alley clown with his head continually swinging from side to side. He removed his police clothes and dressed in ripped jeans, a hunting jacket and a baseball cap. He entered the backdoor.

Wade and Jacko were easily able to watch from the rear kitchen window. With his cap pulled tightly down over his face, he sat at the first bar stool and looked up trying to catch the bartender's attention. After sending away the first two barmen a large, bald heavily tattooed American Indian approached. The Indian listened without looking at the deputy and then sent him away. When sure the deputy was gone and nobody was within eavesdropping distance he picked up the phone and dialled. After talking and listening he too was in an extremely agitated state with his head pivoting from side to side. Approaching another Indian of equal size, they

238

spoke; he reached under the counter and slid a 44 magnum into his rear waistband.

Wade and Jacko watched and followed as he climbed into his vehicle and headed back towards Havre. After following him through the town, south down Highway 87 and up into the mountains; he turned into an overgrown dirt forest track.

Wade knew that following him any longer would be extremely dangerous and a lot easier to be detected. Driving the pickup into a large clump of densely overgrown vines, they grabbed their gear and set off on foot.

The clouds had rolled in. The dense forest had further darkened as the heavens opened and the rain belted down. The wind picked up slashing the rain into their faces. Trudging up the track with the ever increasing stream of water, they were soaked through as they climbed higher and the temperature dropped lower.

Highly trained Special Forces operatives, they were used to these types of conditions as they fought to block out the cold and focus on anything unusual. Keeping to the side of the track they crested a rise and caught a flicker of light. Dropping into the growth and mud Wade signalled they should split up and circle.

Two hours later exhausted, cold and wet they came back together.

"What'd you get?" whispered Wade.

"A house that doesn't seem to be very occupied. A barn that I guess has about six to eight but I'm not sure. Three two man roving patrols with dogs and a front gate with no idea how many. They all seem to be carrying H&K 417's … fairly serious firepower for out here so they're definitely guarding something. It's a fully fenced compound and possibly electrified but I couldn't get close enough to check. What about you?"

"Same but the guardhouse has three. I found two movement and heat sensors at the fence line which I deactivated and it is electrified."

"How do you want to handle this?"

Looking around at the now pitch black environment, the rain still pelting down and both men fighting off the first signs of fatigue.

"I don't think we should try a flank assault and we don't have the time for a decent reconnaissance. We're not dressed for the conditions and we don't know what other early warning devices they might have set up. We definitely don't want to have to try and out run those dogs; the way we are at the moment," replied Wade pausing. "We'll go silent and through the front gate."

Years of working together had made Wade and Jacko into a formidable team and enabled them to know what each was thinking. Separating to either side of the track, with their weapons over their backs, they slid along the mud; crab style. Eighty metres from the small shed, which acted as the front gate guardhouse, Jacko set up in sniper profile. Wade continued and came alongside the wall of the guardhouse that had the small viewing opening cut in the side.

Completely covered in mud Wade had blended into the ground so well even Jacko was having trouble seeing him through the high velocity night scope. Wade slipped the garrotte out and had it wrapped around his palms as the first guard walked from behind the shed. On guard duty for the last month and not seeing anything more than a wild cat he was completely disinterested and only focused on lighting his cigarette. Wade easily slipped the razor sharp thin wire around his neck. As he lowered the body the second guard came round the corner. With his back to the second guard Wade heard the distinctive silenced thud sound. He turned and saw the single shot bullet hole through the bridge of the guard's nose as he fell face first into the mud.

Still as rocks the two men waited. Five minutes lapsed when suddenly two huge floodlights lit up the surrounding area. Wade instinctively closed and covered his eyes and put his head towards the ground, trying desperately to save his night vision and goggles. Jacko aware of what Wade would do, took aim and shot out the two globes.

With darkness returned the third guard charged from the shed leading with his weapon. The barrel came into view and Wade grabbed the end with his left hand. He pulled it forward at the same time thrusting down with his right hand. The action caught the guard off balance and he let go of the rifle. Wade reversed the direction and face planted the rifle butt up into the guard's nose; killing him instantly.

Checking no further occupants, he disabled all the early warning devices and waited as Jacko stumbled up the road.

"How're you?" asked Wade.

"I'll be glad when I can see. This is bloody horrible," he mumbled.

Smiling Wade asked, "Well tell me when you're right to go … and thanks for that."

A further three minutes past until Jacko was comfortable with his vision. They had sent a message of events to Wine, hidden the bodies and destroyed the incoming comms line.

The house and barn were a thousand metres up the hill. They had covered half the distance when Wade smelt the dogs. Inside the fenced compound the forest was not as dense so they adopted sniper pose keeping as low as possible in the mud. With their night vision scopes they saw the two roving patrols coming towards the track from opposite directions. Being downwind the dogs had not picked up the

242

scent and the slightly abating rain was muffling any noise. With silenced weapons and the two patrols at fifty metres they shot the dogs. Wade and Jacko knew that the falling of the dog would temporarily pull the handler off balance so they swung their rifles to the respective second guards and shot off a double tap. Wade's first shot on the handler was directly between the eyes but Jacko shots missed. Taking aim for their second shot neither man had heard the dog approach from behind.

With teeth bared and growling the huge Rottweiler bit into Jacko's left forearm. Calmly Wade took his second shot and hit the second handler through the neck. Using his left hand, he grabbed his doubled bladed knife and plunged it between the dog's eyes. With his right hand still wrapped around the rifle stock he swung it around searching for the remaining two guards.

The guards had heard the dog's growl but the darkness had stopped them from properly determining the location. Wade saw them forty metres away running perpendicular to where they should be and he picked them off with single shots. Finishing Jacko's targets he dropped his weapon.

Pushing off the dog, he ripped the field bandage open and wrapped Jacko's forearm as quickly and tightly as possible. The wound was severe, the dog having bitten to the bone and lacerating a large section of the forearm muscle.

"How do you feel?" asked Wade listening for any further sounds.

"I'm fine. Feel a bit lightheaded but otherwise okay."

"This should help," he whispered as he stabbed the amphetamine laden needle into his shoulder.

"Come on. We need to get out of here." He grabbed Jacko by the upper arm and lifted him to his feet.

Noise of the commotion had alerted the other guards. They poured from the two buildings as angry as wasps with their nest under attack. Dropping to their knees Wade and Jacko were able to pick them off with their night scopes. Advancing further up the hill they would drop to their knees and repeat. This went on until they had reached the side of the barn and sixteen guards and two more dogs were dead.

Trying desperately to focus on the surroundings neither man saw the thin laser beam, at ankle height, which triggered the explosion behind them. The force threw them both into the barn wall. Climbing to their feet slightly concussed, fragmentation cuts to their backs and heads and their ears ringing; Wade noticed how Jacko was swaying.

Pushing him back against the wall he motioned as he said, "You wait here. Cover me. I'm going to have a look behind the house."

Jacko nodded in acknowledgement as he bought his rifle up to covering fire. Wade turned and raced across the thirty metres separating the house and barn.

The house was a typical log cabin construction that had been added on to many times. A four metre wide veranda ran down both sides and there was one small fixed window on each end. Wade stood against the end wall listening for any movement. He heard a television from one room and the sound of weapons being loaded and cocked. The voices were distinctively American Indian and sounded as if they had just woken. Placing the large lump of C4 under the floorboards and setting the timer he darted back to Jacko.

Using the rear of the barn as protection they crept on all fours. The explosion was immense and obliterated everything within a thirty metre radius. Parts of the barn walls were disintegrated and the two large front doors collapsed off their hinges. The inside of the barn looked like a scattered jigsaw with horse stalls half collapsed, equipment lying everywhere, broken beams sagging from the roof and hay sprayed throughout.

Arriving at the opposite end of the incredibly large barn they watched and waited. The increasing lightning strikes across the sky gave a clear view of the surroundings. With Jacko propped against the corner wall Wade scouted to confirm the all clear.

Still cautious and convinced they had missed something, ten metres to their front the hay moved. A trap door was raised and two men climbed out. The first was the large Indian from the tavern who had a 44 Magnum in one hand and an M16 in the other. A shorter, younger, geeky looking, spectacled teenager clasping a laptop closely followed him.

Light flooded out of the underground basement. Wade and Jacko were able to get a very good look at them. They closed the hatch, spread back the hay, turned on a torch and crept across the strewn floor. As the Indian stepped over the collapsed front doors Jacko took him out with a clean double tap. Wade grabbed the teenager from behind, grabbed the laptop and threw him face first into the mud.

With his hands zip-tied behind his back, coughing and spluttering mud from his mouth and nose and his glasses lost in the mud; Wade lifted and carried him back to the trapdoor. Pushing the hay aside he thrust the teenagers face into the locking dial that secured the steel door.

"The code?" ordered Wade.

With no response Wade viciously slapped his hands onto the teenagers ears.

Screaming in agony and blood gushing out of his nose Wade asked the teenager again.

"The code? Now," he yelled.

Spluttering, tears running down his face and shaking uncontrollably Wade put his pistol to his head.

"Last chance."

"888 then pause. 888 again," he replied as Wade realised he had shit and pissed his pants.

Dropping to the floor Jacko pulled him aside. Wade punched in the code and lifted the door.

"You first," ordered Wade with his hand around the teenager's skinny little neck.

"No, no, no," he screamed trying desperately not to be forced down the ladder.

"That's not the right code is it?" said Wade tightening the grip on his throat.

Gasping for air he replied, "Yes … yes it is."

"Then why won't you go?" asked Wade, this time releasing his grip.

"I gave you the code. What more do you want?" he replied between gasps as he tried to back away.

"Wrong answer." Wade grabbed him and threw him head first down the hole, diving to the side taking Jacko with him.

The explosion was a dull thud as the toxic gas started to rise out of the opening. Holding his breath Wade reached in and stuck the C4 on to the bunker roof. Grabbing Jacko under the arm and retrieving the laptop they ran for the track. One hundred metres down the track slipping and sliding Wade hit the remote as the barn erupted in a fireball.

The concrete bunker had suppressed the gases from the explosion and caused a fire torch effect to burst out of the small opening. The heat and intensity of the fire destroyed the toxic gas and either melted or disintegrated everything inside the bunker.

Back in their vehicle Wade checked and rebandaged Jacko's arm and called the Colonel.

51: Big Sandy Montana

A deserted area ten kilometres from Big Sandy, Montana, at 0200 the highly modified black unlit Westland Wildcat landed. Chrissie as the pilot and Wine beside her; Bart, Stewie, Bassa and Sammy leapt from the rear. They helped Jacko aboard and Stewie prepared the flight medical equipment and tended to his wounds.

Chrissie powered down the chopper as Wade handed the laptop to the Colonel.

"It appears to be associated with the Chippewa-Cree Indians and more particularly the Rocky Boy Indian Reservation … I think I'll pay the reservation a visit. Bart can come with me and Sammy can take watch," said Wade.

"Are you sure? You look like you could use some rest," stated Wine with Chrissie nodding in agreeance. "We can look after it and we'll meet you back at the site."

"Sorry Colonel but I'm finishing this … I owe it to Kiwi," he said turning and gesturing to Sammy and Bart.

0300 Wade and Bart left Sammy parked on the small hill overlooking the tribal administration buildings that had been mentioned on the laptop. The complex was quite nondescript consisting of three interconnecting single storey buildings. Twenty minutes of searching they found the main office. Wade inserted the CIA upload device and called Kaitlyn. The upload was timed for nine minutes.

Still wearing their NVP-60 night vision monocular's they snuck around the various offices and administration areas. Entering a children's retreat area Bart found a pile of files, neatly stacked under a child's iPad.

"You need to see this," he whispered into the throat mike.

Entering the room Bart handed him the green A4 manila folder with the name Chief Big Oak and the letters PTAFE hand scribbled on the spine.

Finding a windowless room, Wade removed his night vision goggles and turned on the light. Reading the file he saw that it outlined hundreds of bank accounts, thousands of transactions and millions of dollars. The accounts were all scattered throughout the mid west and each appeared to be associated with the Indian reservations. Chief Big Oak was mentioned as a tribal elder.

Pocketing the file, iPad and upload device, they reset the alarms.

"Take these," said Wade handing over their find. "Get back to Sammy and I'll meet you both down the road. I'm going to have a quick look out back."

Bart watched as Wade slunk along the front wall and vanished around the corner.

The overnight storms had passed but the ground was saturated. Creeping back into the forest, that was further up the hill behind the buildings, he sensed somebody was nearby. Avoiding tracks, overhanging branches and using the great Aspen trees as cover he wound his way across the leaf covered terrain. As one of the world's best hunter/trackers he caught the reflection of water droplets on the single strand razor wire that was at ankle height, just above the leaves, slung between the two trees. Further on he saw the vine hanging against the tree trunk that would have activated the mountain lion snare suspended in the branches.

Stepping to avoid the snare he didn't see the bear trap until too late. Built with sloping sides and mud from the rain his weight caused the fern-covered top to collapse and he fell into the poison spear-lined walls. Grabbing for the sides the spear tips cut into his hands and chest as he crashed into the pit which was filled with mud. The poison, used to sedate bears, was quick acting as Wade felt his arms and legs become like jelly and his vision blur.

52: Montana Forest

No matter how hard he tried his eyelids would not open; they felt like they had been weighted shut. Slowly moving his head from side to side he could feel the effects of the drug starting to wear off but not a muscle in his body wanted to work. His body was in a state of clonic spasm.

It was exceedingly hot and Wade could feel himself sweating profusely when suddenly hundreds of litres of freezing water crashed on to his body. Coughing and spluttering he got his composure as he opened his eyes. The first image he saw was a blur of a bald American Indian whose face was extremely scarred and covered in bold red and black tattoos. The man was bending over with his face twenty centimetres from Wade's. He smiled and showed a mouth full of perfect teeth with a front one missing and drool running out the side.

As he turned away, Wade could hear chanting and felt the intensity of the heat. The room was a cave that had been carved in to the mountain. Located one hundred metres from the surface it was twelve metres wide by eight metres deep and three metres high. A fire was roaring inside a furnace beside the small one metre wide by two metre high entrance point. Three men and two women, were dancing and chanting near the fire whilst a fourth man stood off to the side. There was no lighting except for the fire.

The man returned with a glowing red hot, star shaped branding iron. The man was huge, sweating profusely and smiling as he used both hands and plunged the iron into Wade's abdomen just below his ribcage. Continuing to push the Indian laughed as the remaining Indians danced and chanted around the table Wade lay on. He could smell the burning skin but could not feel any pain as he passed out.

Trying desperately to get away from the burning sensation in his nose Wade opened his eyes. A highly tanned white man was leaning over him and removing the smelling salts he had used to revive him.

Still unable to move any muscles he realised he was naked on the table but not restrained in any way.

"Well Mister Ross," said the white man in eloquently spoken upper crust English. "Haven't you been a pain in the arse."

The chanting had abated but the crowd was in a dancing frenzy as the white man spoke again "I know all about you and your little group of problem makers and now it is time for you all to come to an end. I think as you have gone to so much trouble and as I'm going to kill you anyway. You probably deserve to know what's going on and how close you got," he said casually smiling.

"My name's Thomas Cooper and, yes, I am Samantha and Daniel's younger brother. You were nearly on the right track but the thing you got wrong was that my motivation is not money. That's my partner's agenda. I want to make those who have the money … pay for their sins, just like my parents did."

Wade noticed how Thomas Cooper was an extremely good-looking man, in his late thirties, well-dressed and groomed even though he was in this heat asphyxiating cave. The only distinguishable feature was his different coloured eyes. His left eye was as blue as the Mediterranean Sea whilst his right was as black as night.

"I know about your spiritual beliefs and the Australian Aboriginal Dreamtime. I know how it seems to be some form of strength for you and how it helps you in your time of most need. Well unfortunately this time you're right out of luck. The potion that was on the spears is enough to knock out a bear so your muscles won't be moving for a long time and by then you'll be dead," he said pausing for effect.

"My friend, Megedagik will continue to burn your Solar Plexus until your soul and any attachment to your Dreamtime has gone," he whispered with his mouth beside Wade's ear.

Standing up he looked at Wade and said, "Time for me to go and pay your friend Crystal a visit and get a couple of Minuteman on that secret Site 180 you all think I don't know about. You lot are so stupid. I know everything you're going to do before you even start … see you in hell Ross; you won't be getting out this time," he shouted as he walked through the small opening.

Megedagik approached again with a glowing red-hot, small-tipped iron as the others recommenced their chanting and dancing. Pushing the iron into Wade's shoulder they all screamed as the skin burnt. Removing the iron Wade watched as they each took turns in prodding each other and screaming out in pain.

The cave stunk of burning skin as one of the female Indians placed the iron back in the fire and the remainder continued to scream in pain. Four minutes later the screaming had stopped but the chanting and dancing was building to a crescendo as Megedagik once again removed the iron.

The group had donned headgear of bears, feathers and skulls. They were naked from the waist up, sweating and nearly all their upper body was scarred in some way. The dancing had stirred up the dust and combined with the fire they were gasping for air as they continued in their drugged fazed state.

Forcing the iron into Wade's other shoulder the Indian became annoyed that Wade was not screaming out in pain as he yelled to one of the female Indians. "Tahki, give him some of that oil."

Tahki, the larger and more heavily scarred of the two women, grabbed a small bottle. She reached over, forced Wade's mouth open and poured a small amount on to his tongue.

Instantly Wade felt his nerve endings and the pain spread across is abdomen and both shoulders. He also noticed that he had movement in his fingers, hands and feet. Realising this was some form of antidote to the poison he remained motionless as Megedagik approached and plunged the iron in to his thigh. Using all the will-power he could muster and calling on the spirits he remained motionless.

The lack of response further agitated Megedagik as he ordered Tahki to apply more drops to Wade's tongue. After three more burns and three more doses of the drops Wade could feel all his muscles and senses had reignited. Each time they burned Wade, they went through the ritual of burning and scarring themselves. One of the males and one of the females had passed out from pain and the remaining trio were on their last legs as Wade spun off the table, grabbed the poker from the unsuspecting Megedagik and cracked it across his skull. As the big Indian fell Wade spun and hit the second male in the same way. Tahki screamed as she charged but Wade deflected her assault and pushed her into the dirt.

The pain in his abdomen was excruciating as Wade grabbed her hair and forced her face toward his.

"Answers? Now," he ordered as she attempted to spit in to his face.

Dropping the iron and using the back of his free hand he slapped her across the face.

"Last chance. Where are we? What's going on here and who are you?"

Tahki laughed as she grabbed the iron and attempted to swing it. Wade rolled with the swing and still hanging on to her hair dragged her over and face planted her into the ground. With his free hand he reached across and applied a pressure point to the back of her neck as she collapsed in to an unconscious state. Checking the other two he also applied pressure points.

Finding his pants, boots, knife and shirt he dressed as well as he could and headed out of the cave.

Bouncing off the walls and continually needing to stop as he doubled up in pain, he arrived at the cave mouth. Trying to get his bearings he started down the mountain. He was making more noise than a freight train as he crashed into trees, stumbled over branches, fell through shrubs and occasionally slid down slopes.

Sammy and Bart had no trouble finding him as the big South African lifted him on his shoulder and Bart gave him a morphine shot.

53: Site 180

"You must have more lives than a cat," said Wine as Wade opened his eyes. "How're you feeling?"

"Not so great," he replied slowly swinging his legs off the bed and looking down at Chrissie's handiwork.

"Chrissie seems to think you'll be okay but you might want to get that burn to your abdomen checked out. It went pretty deep."

"Sure," replied Wade nodding in acknowledgement as he felt the bandages on both shoulders, his thigh and around his chest.

"How long have I been here?"

"Sammy and Bart found you about eight hundred metres up the hill from the Indian Reservation Administration block. You appeared to be coming down. So from when they got to you to now would be about three hours."

The rest of the team had gathered as Wade commenced explaining what had happened. "It was Thomas Cooper in the cave. The description we have is fairly accurate but he has a sky blue left eyeball and a black right one. He talks like English aristocracy and he mentioned he had a partner. Apparently the partner wants money whilst he wants revenge. But the alarming part is he knows all about us, about here, Site 180 and everything we are ever going to do before we even start. He also mentioned organising a Minuteman for here and his next stop was Crystal."

"Stewie and Bassa, we'll drop you at Malmstrom. Sammy and Bart, I want you at Fort Bragg and you need to get a team ready to deploy. I would suggest at least three teams. I believe Joe Carr and Seal Team 6 are on exercise there so Wade will call him. Morrie and Juan at Bethesda. Bud, I want you to stay here with the rest of the team and concentrate on the reservations. We leave in ten," ordered Wine as the team scattered in all directions.

"You two need to slow down, you'll be no use to anyone at this rate," said Wine as he looked across at Wade and Jacko sitting on the bed nursing their wounds.

Ignoring the Colonel, Wade said, "Cooper is no idiot but he does seem to follow a routine. I'm thinking this partner, he mentioned, is probably the name Chief Big Oak we found on that file at the reservation admin building and my guess is he's not Indian."

"Why do you say that?" asked the Colonel.

"Cooper mentioned his partners agenda is money and those records show millions of dollars."

"Actually it's billions," interrupted Wine.

"Really!" exclaimed Wade.

"Close to seventy billion to be precise."

"Well that makes my idea even more believable. There is no way Cooper could access all these financial markets around the world and have the capability of intercepting our data without help from somebody incredibly high up the chain of command."

"Any ideas?" asked the Colonel.

"Let's pay General Razen a visit. Someone in the White House, or at least associated with it, knows what's going on and we need to find them; sooner than later," replied Wade as he stood and headed to the chopper that Chrissie was getting ready for take-off.

Standing next to the mechanical opening device that enabled the helicopter to be moved outside, he dialled Kaitlyn.

"Any word on Crystal?"

"We haven't seen her yet but we've located the ambulance she was taken in. An extraction team is on route ETA forty minutes and we have an eye in the sky," replied Kaitlyn.

"Thanks Kia. Let me know what happens."

The team departed exactly ten minutes from when the Colonel said they would leave. First stop Malmstrom Air Base, Great Falls Montana. Malmstrom is one of three bases on US soil that operates the Minuteman III InterContinental Ballistic Missiles. Wine had already gained approval from General Razen, for Stewie and Bassa to search the facility with a team the base commanding officer had on standby. Their orders were to note anything that appeared out of SOP (Standard Operating Procedure), as their Westland Wildcat touched down in the furthest reaches of the base.

Back in the air they headed for Fort Bragg, North Carolina and the home base of the US Army Special Forces, Delta Force. Chrissie performed a perfect landing of the extremely modified, all black, helicopter. As the blades slowed, two of the most highly decorated US Special Forces commanders stepped forward. Opening the door Wine, Jacko, Wade, Sammy and Bart climbed out. The Navy Seal commander was the first to speak.

"Wade, Colonel good to see you both," as he shook their hands.

"Thanks Joe," they replied.

"Jackson, welcome back," said Colonel Bacman.

Colonel Bacman, the current Commanding Officer at Fort Bragg and himself an ex Delta Force operative.

Shaking hands with Bacman, Wine introduced everybody as Bacman stepped forward and said, "It is with great pleasure I meet you Mister Ross. Your reputation is extremely well known around here."

"Thanks Colonel but it's not just me. We've all got the same job and I just happen to wind up at the pointy end more often than not," replied Wade smiling.

"Well what can we do for you here, gentleman?" asked Bacman.

Wine explained what they needed and three minutes later the helicopter was on its way to Bethesda hospital. After dropping Morrie and Juan on the hospital helipad they headed for the White House.

Approaching White House airspace, flight control became extremely agitated even though permission had already come from the highest level of command. Two fighter jets had been scrambled and were watching from above.

"Flight six, we cannot see through your windows. I repeat we cannot see through your windows. You do not have permission to land without a visual of you occupants. Turn back. I repeat, turn back. This is your final warning, we will force you down," came the voice through the cabin loudspeaker.

"Now you listen to me you moron. We have permission from POTUS and CJCS to land and we intend to," replied a very annoyed Wine.

"Flight six, please hold your flight path whilst we confirm permission."

"Chrissie just land this bloody thing," ordered the Colonel.

"Flight six, you must not commence your descent. I repeat you must not commence your descent. If you do not hold NASAMS will be activated."

NASAMS (Norwegian Advanced Surface to Air Missile System) the current missile system used by the White House to protect against an air strike. Air space above and around the White House is restricted and a no-fly zone.

Continuing to descend, suddenly the early warning missile detection alarm started to scream as Chrissie yelled, "They've locked on to us Colonel. What'll we do?"

"Arm the missiles. Keep going," shouted the Colonel as the high pitched sound got louder and louder.

Doing as she was instructed the moment she activated the helicopter's Air-to-Surface missile system, the alarm stopped. Keeping the missiles active she bought the wheels to rest on the south lawns of the White House.

Waiting until the blades came to a stop all four doors opened at the same time as the four occupants leapt out.

"Freeze. On the ground. Now or we'll shoot," came the voice over the public address system.

Wade and the Colonel were on the left side of the helicopter and facing the front entry doors as Wade looked around to the sight of at least forty Secret

Service agents with their Sig's aimed at them and another five snipers along the roof line.

"On the ground. Now," bellowed the order.

Chrissie and Jacko were face down with their arms and legs spread while Wade and the Colonel stood half a metre apart.

"You two, last warning," as a sniper fired a round into the grass one metre to Wade's left.

With neither man moving a Secret Service Officer approached flanked by four heavily armoured men. With the guards rifles aimed directly at their heads the officer stopped two metres short.

"I'm in charge here. When I say on the ground, I mean on the ground at that very moment," he bellowed. "Now you two get on the ground."

With still no movement he stepped forward and was about to prod the Colonel, in the chest, as Wade grabbed his shirt, pulled him forward and head butted him on the bridge of his nose. Instantaneously rifles and pistols cocked as Wade dropped the officer and another voice yelled from the balcony, "Drop your weapons. Now. Everybody."

All eyes spun to see the highest ranking officer in the world's most powerful military force order them to drop their weapons. Standing beside General Razen was President Markham. Obeying instantly they lowered their weapons. Wade and the Colonel stepped around the fallen officer and his guards as Chrissie and Jacko raced to catch up.

"Hello Wade," said the President. "You sure know how to make an entrance."

"Mister President, General," he replied. "Let me introduce Colonel Wine and Chrissie. Jacko you've already met."

"Colonel Wine, it's a pleasure," said Razen. "Your exploits are nearly as famous as Wade's."

"Thanks General."

"Come inside and let's talk," said the President as his aides helped shuffle everybody through the doors.

54: Sudley Virginia

"Well, well, well Miss Crystal aren't you a very attractive woman," came the voice from the opposite end of the room.

Swivelling her head and body she saw Thomas Cooper approach as the shackle on her left wrist cut in to her arm. Her captors had left one metre of chain from the shackle to the steel frame of the bed, which was bolted to the floor in the centre of the room.

"I do have to say I have been looking forward to meeting you," he said.

Crystal noticed the riding crop in his left hand and watched as he spun it around.

"Do you ride?" he asked smiling.

Still watching the crop, Crystal shook her head.

Walking around the bed he continued to spin the crop, "I had a visit from lover boy last night but unfortunately he's not going to be able to save you this time. In fact he won't be doing anything ever again."

Crystal tried desperately not to show her feelings but the tears started to trickle down her cheeks.

"Now, now, don't worry. You've got me now."

With her head bent in her chest she hadn't been aware Cooper had walked behind her. With one almighty strike he slashed the riding crop across her back. Screaming out, he hit her again as she tried to get away but the chain pulled against her arm. Cowering over the side of the bed with her head down into the mattress; he hit her again and again.

The pain was unbearable as she heard him throw a key on the bed and say, "Take off the shackle."

Lifting her head the tears cascaded down her face and her body was shaking uncontrollably.

"The shackle. Now," he screamed causing her to shake even more.

Desperately trying to get the key in the hole and struggling to control her reflexes, Cooper walked over. Grabbed the key and opened the lock.

With the shackle off she wrapped her arms around her chest trying to stop the shaking as she backed away from the bed.

Cooper followed two steps behind and with the riding crop raised as Crystal crashed into the wall.

"Clothes off," he ordered.

Still watching the riding crop she stood there shaking. Cooper took one step, lifted the crop higher and brought it down on her shoulder. Falling to the floor, she screamed as he yelled again, "Clothes off or I'll just keep hitting you."

Trying to undo her shirt he raised the crop. "Get up. Get your gear off."

Crawling up against the wall, she tried to undo the first button as he reached forward and ripped the shirt open. The pain on her shoulder was immense as she cried out again. Lifting her head she saw he had removed a knife from his pocket. Flicking the blade open and with the riding crop raised he slipped the knife under her bra and cut it open.

Her breasts fell out of the bra as he screamed, "Off."

Doing as he instructed she slid the bra and shirt of her shoulders. The cuts on her back caused the shirt to stick and trying not to cause herself anymore pain she was slowly pulling it down as Cooper leant forward and reefed it off.

"This is going to be good," he remarked leering at her semi-naked body and gesturing her to remove her pants.

Suddenly the door opened and a man stepped inside.

"We've got a problem."

"What is it? Can't you see I'm busy," said Cooper not taking his eyes off Crystal.

"Well I think you might want to see this. That guy last night, he just walked into the White House."

"What," screamed Cooper as he spun and charged for the door.

55: White House – Situation Room

The President led the group into the executive conference room of the White House Situation Room. The room comprised a large mahogany table, surrounded by thirteen armchairs. Six flat screen plasma televisions lined the walls. A video camera hung on the wall facing the President as it continually scanned. The walls had been lead lined to stop transmissions, both in and out, and this added to the muffled sound that resounded throughout the room.

President Markham took his seat at the head of the table, to his left was Charlotte Bysmith and beside her was General Razen, then Admiral Paul James. To the President's right sat Wine, Chrissie, Jacko and at the furthest end Wade.

"Well Wade what can we do for you?" asked Razen.

Wade explained what had happened and how he felt there must be some link to the White House or at least the CIA.

"And why do you say that, young man?" asked Admiral James.

Eyeing the Admiral and noticing his demeanour had become quite defensive, Wade realised this was the Admiral's area of responsibility and not something he was going to accept without reliable substantiated proof.

"Well Admiral, I'd hate to rain on your party but you tell me how anybody could cause these events to occur, throughout the world, without the help of either the CIA, or the NSC, or at least the Department of the Treasury … and if you're supposed to be in charge of national intelligence, how come you don't know what's going on?"

"That's a wild accusation unless you have proof. The US national intelligence community is one of the most professional, if not the most professional, community in the world and I can guarantee that if there was something to be found we would know about it." Trying to keep his composure, "If you're going to make statements like that why isn't General Forest here to defend himself?"

Grabbing the table. Springing to his feet. Knocking the armchair backwards, Wade leaned across the table and eyeballed the Admiral.

"It must have something to do with all those stars on your shoulders because everyone of you, so called chiefs, is so busy protecting yourselves you can't even see what's happening in your own backyard," calmly replied Wade as he turned and headed for the door.

Approaching the President with Wine, Chrissie and Jacko following; Wade turned his head and said, "Mister President, I'd try the CIA first if I was you."

"Wade. Wait," said Markham. "Tell us your thoughts … please?"

"I respect and appreciate your help so far but our job is to get rid of Cooper and stop the Minuteman missiles. Which we intend to do. We're not interested in politics and all this self-protection crap."

"Okay. I can understand you thinking that but why the CIA?"

Wade looked around the room. Bysmith was trying to look busy studying her notes. James had his head down scribbling on a note pad. Razen was scrolling through the desk mounted laptop. Markham was the only one showing any level of interest.

"Kaitlyn, the Mossad agent who you have met and who is working with us, has at various times sent information that could have only been accessed from within the Warehouse. She has sent and received transmissions, from Director Harel, that are virtually impossible to detect unless you are tapped into her site."

With the mention of Director Harel, head of Mossad, James sprung to his feet and slammed his fist on the table.

"This is outrageous. What the hell are we doing transmitting with Mossad without my knowledge.

Do you people not understand the implications of what could happen to the US when we are directly communicating with a foreign power and that information is not being regulated or controlled," he bellowed.

Directing his attention to Markham he continued, "Mister President, I demand that we immediately cease all communication with anybody that my department is unaware of and these people be removed from our facilities. This is completely unacceptable and borderline treason."

Nodding at James to take his seat, he waited and then calmly replied, "No Paul we will not be taking Colonel Wine and his team off this project … in fact we will be taking their advice on board and using all the facilities at our disposal to help them."

Bysmith and Razen nodded in agreement as he continued, "I want you and Forest here first thing tomorrow and a report on my desk tonight with answers on how this could be happening. Am I clear?"

"Yes, Mister President but I want it on the record that what is happening here is incredibly dangerous to the security of our nation."

"Paul, that has been noted," replied Markham as a knock came on the door and a presidential aide entered.

"Sir, we have an urgent call from a Kaitlyn for a Mister Wade Ross."

"That's me."

"Sir, I will show you to a superman tube," the aide replied stepping aside for Wade to exit.

Superman tube is the name given by the Situation Room staff to the cylindrical telephone booths located outside the conference rooms. The booths are sound proofed and contain both a secure and standard handset.

"We've found Crystal. She had been taken to an old factory facility in Sudley, Virginia. We sent in a Kidon team and they took out seven men, all North American Indians. Crystal has been whipped, quite severely, with a riding crop but she's at a safe house and the doctor said she'd be okay. She told us it was Thomas Cooper who whipped her. She also told us that they had a video feed of you entering the White House," said Kaitlyn.

With anger coursing through his body Wade tried desperately to contain the urge to lash out. Slowly taking large breaths he asked, "Did you find anything in the building?" After waiting ten seconds he asked again, "Kia did you hear me?"

"Wade, I heard you … I have something to tell you and I need you to brace yourself."

"What is it?"

"We found a laptop that had been smashed but we were able to decipher the hard drive. It contained information on all sorts of various people, from all around the world. There were bank tellers to computer programmers to business execs to."

"Kia, cut with the crap. What are you wanting to tell me?"

"On the laptop it mentions a woman's name and apparently she's … your real mother."

"What … how the hell could Cooper know anything about my real mother?"

"The information describes your past including how you got to the orphanage in Alice Springs. It mentions a name, which we ran through the system. Her name is Sylvia and she lives in Portofino, Italy. Her partner was killed under suspicious circumstances about three months ago. She has a twenty four year old daughter Cristina."

"This might all be very true but how does that make her my mother?"

"Thirty four years ago she was working as a cook at a mining camp in the Pilbara in Western Australia when she met an Aboriginal stockman. Apparently they had a relationship and she became pregnant. He wanted Sylvia to go with him to Alice Springs and meet his parents. On the way they were attacked and he was killed. When she arrived in Alice Springs the family did not believe her and sent her away. She gave birth in the shearing quarters of a wealthy grazier. When the grazier saw the baby was not completely dark skinned, as in Aboriginal, he took it to the local orphanage and arranged for the mother to be sent back to Perth. Two thousand kilometres away, no money and grief stricken she used the travel ticket the grazier had given her to return to Italy. I'm sorry Wade but it all seems to fit."

Dropping the handset, Wade slid down the wall. With his head in his hands he slowly swayed his body from side to side as he concentrated on speaking with the spirits.

Seeing his mother he asked, 'Could this be. What do I do?'

'Go with your heart and the spirits will lead the way' she replied.

Opening his eyes he saw and felt Wine trying to force the double action doors. Slowly getting to his feet, the door swung open as the Colonel grabbed him by the arm and with his other hand grabbed the handset.

"What happened?"

With a glazed look in Wade's eyes the Colonel placed the receiver to his ear and Kaitlyn explained.

"We need to get somebody there," stated Wine more to himself than as an order.

"Director Harel has already organised a Mossad team that are en route from Poland. ETA three hours," replied Kaitlyn.

Taking the receiver from Wine, "Do we know where Cooper is?" asked Wade.

"He's currently crossing the Atlantic. We picked up an encrypted message that was directed to Langley and obviously for you. It said 'Hope you like the whip marks. Shame you didn't get to meet mamma. Good effort team but just not good enough. PTAFE.' The transmission emanated over Miami. He has an amazing array of firewalls and diversions he can access but we have been able to get a satellite locked on his plane. He appears to be on a flight path for Spain or southern France."

"Stay on the line," ordered Wade as he and the Colonel headed back into the executive conference room.

"General, can we get Kaitlyn on the loudspeaker?" asked Wade.

Thirty seconds later the Situation Room staff had Kaitlyn on loudspeaker directly to the President's phone.

"Kia, if you're tracking Cooper can you access all his transmissions and his laptop?" asked Wade.

Hesitantly she replied, "Well yes I can but I don't have the skills to hack into the system."

"Okay people. Who would be your best hacker currently in the building?" asked Wade looking around the room.

After some discussion and phone calls Admiral James replied, "I would imagine Koh. She is a North Korean dissident who has shown remarkable skills at infiltrating and then protecting our firewalls.

Three minutes later a young, nervous, embarrassed and worried twenty year old was escorted into the room. Seated at the furthest end of the table, from the President, but the closest to the large screen, she sat with her head down and her hands tucked into her lap.

Wade sat beside her. "Koh, my name's Wade and the woman on the call you're about to hear is Kaitlyn. I want you to talk with Kaitlyn and work out how we can access a laptop that is halfway across the Atlantic, thirty thousand feet in the air and travelling at eight hundred kilometres per hour. Once we gain access we need to be able to download the data." Pausing Wade then continued, "Are you okay with this?"

Nodding her reply, Wade organised for Chrissie to sit with her in one of the adjoining interview rooms.

"General is there any way we could shoot down his flight without detection?" asked Wade.

Thinking for a moment the General, who had spent many years answering difficult military questions without hesitation, replied. "It would depend on how we could keep commercial flights and ground observation out of viewing range."

"Why would we need to shoot it down?" asked Markham.

"As soon as he knows we've accessed his data he could implement 'God knows what'," replied Wade.

"Well, we need to get back to the Oval office," said Markham nodding to Bysmith. "General keep us informed of your intentions."

The President and the Secretary of State exited the room. Ten minutes later a team of planning specialists entered. There was an Airforce weapons expert, Naval commander, Airwing operations commander, oceanographer, meteorologist and computer programmers.

It was standing room only as the six plasma screens lit up. The first had a split screen showing the activity on the flight deck of the USS Harry S. Truman, aircraft carrier stationed in the Mediterranean Sea and the other showing Admiral Boston and his crew in the Flag Bridge.

The second was Cooper's current and projected flight path. The third showed the Canary Islands and in particular the island volcano of La Palma and the active, twelve kilometre underwater volcano El Hierro. The fourth was all aircraft within one thousand kilometres of the west coast of Portugal. The fifth showed various updates of worldwide television reports on the affected markets. The sixth appeared as a rapidly changing undistinguishable gaggle of letters, numbers and signs. Later to be explained as Koh hacking into Cooper's computer.

"Quiet. I want ideas of when, how and where we could down this plane," ordered Razen, as an aide pointed at screen two. "We have thirty minutes and counting." Wade looked above the largest screen to see a digital clock start counting down.

He watched as screens changed, people scribbled notes, phone calls were made, ideas were formed and challenged and a continuous file of personnel came in and out of the room.

At one minute and six seconds remaining, Markham and Bysmith re-entered the room. All unnecessary staff were removed and Naval Commander Wallace Stapleton addressed the group.

"Mister President. It is currently approaching 1500 hours local time and we have been advised that the data will be downloaded from flight G181 by 1730 hours local time. A plan has been devised where we will deploy an E2 Hawkeye from the USS Harry S. Truman, currently stationed twenty kilometres west of the island of Sardinia, in the Mediterranean Sea. Once within range the E2 will disable all comms from or to flight G181. We will activate a relay system that will for all intents and purpose have the pilot believe he is talking to commercial air traffic control."

A screen changed to show a computer-generated image of the volcano on the island of La Palma erupting.

"We will use data from the erupting underwater volcano of El Hierro and images from a previous eruption of La Palma to create a computer generated image that will give the effect of a volcanic dust storm over La Palma. Flight G181 will be instructed to divert further south of the Canary Islands and thus away from commercial flights. We will instruct the pilot to increase altitude to 45,000 feet and this will aid in limiting the chance of visibility from ground level. We have a window of approximately ten minutes to take out the flight before it will enter mainland African air traffic control or be in range of mainland visual detection."

The screen changed again to show the flight deck of the USS Harry S. Truman.

"We have a squadron of FA18 Super Hornets ready with 120 AMRAAM missiles and would be in position by 1740 hours local time," said Stapleton as he took his seat.

Looking around the room the President asked, "Very good but what are the downsides to this idea?"

"We are still trying to divert satellites that will cross the path and we have not had the time to check on shipping or small craft in the expected splash-down area," responded Stapleton.

"General, your thoughts?" asked Markham.

"I feel comfortable with it, Mister President. It would be good to have more time and not have our aircraft at their flight range limits but they can refuel in the air and everybody is trained in this type of operation. So I agree," replied Razen.

Markham looked across to his Secretary of State who nodded in agreement as they both stood. "Good luck," he said as they left the room.

56: Flight G181

Cooper was testing himself on a brainteaser website as the huge Native American Indian approached. Standing six foot eight and weighing in at two hundred and ninety pounds, Akecheta was aptly named. With an English translation of fighter, Akecheta had spent his life using his fists for communication.

"Pilot said. We have problem," stammered Akecheta.

"What sort of problem?" asked Cooper closing his laptop and looking for Tansy, his beautiful Native American Indian personal assistant.

As she approached Akecheta said in a much louder tone, "Big problem."

"Alright. Alright Akecheta … I want you to get the pilot to come down here. Tansy get Portofino on the phone," ordered Cooper.

Thomas Cooper considered himself very controlled and well organised. Problems were for those who did not plan and he believed he was not of that ilk. Whenever anybody mentioned a problem his first point of call was his private and secure webpage. Opening his laptop he went to type PTAFE when he noticed he had no signal.

Brent, his trusted pilot of nine years approached.

"Mister Cooper, apparently there has been a volcano eruption on the island of La Palma, in the Canary Islands. We have been instructed by air traffic control to divert south around the dust plume."

"Why south? Wouldn't north be closer?"

"Yes sir it would but there is a southerly blowing and air traffic control have no idea how far north we would need to go to avoid the dust. We have plenty of fuel and it will only delay us by about one and a half hours."

"Okay … what's happened to our Internet connection?"

"I'm not sure sir. I would imagine due to the volcano. I will advise the moment it comes back on line."

Nodding Cooper waved him off in frustration.

"Tansy, what's happened with Portofino? Why is it taking so long?" he yelled.

Walking down the aisle with the handset against her ear she replied, "I keep getting a recorded message that we are unable to connect."

"It's a flaming satellite phone," he yelled snatching the phone from her ear and listening. Receiving the same response he hurled the phone into the crystal cabinet, shattering glass, bottles, the doors and shelves.

Instantly Akecheta appeared. "Get out. Get out," yelled Cooper.

Without warning the plane nosed up and Cooper was thrown back into his luxurious Club lounge as Brent came over the internal intercom, "Sorry sir but I had been instructed to immediately ascend to 45,000 feet. I apologise for the lack of warning. Hope everything is okay."

The rapid change in altitude had thrown Tansy off balance and wearing high heels she crashed to the floor. Cooper watched as her short mini skirt rose up to her waist and her loose top became skew whiff. Remembering his failed opportunity with Crystal he reached over and grabbed her by the shirt. Reefing her towards him the buttons broke; her top flew open and her arms slid off the sleeves.

Throwing the shirt aside he stood grabbed her by the hair and pushed her face first into the galley wall. Standing nearly eight inches taller he easily restrained her as he ripped her dress and pants off.

"Thomas, please you're hurting me," she pleaded.

By now aroused and with his pants at his ankles.

"Shut up bitch," he yelled as he plunged into her and she screamed.

"No … Mister Cooper … No," stammered Akecheta as he reached to grab Cooper but hesitated. Knowing in his mind he wanted to protect the girl he had feelings for, but his loyalty to his boss was conflicting.

57: USS Harry S. Truman

"Hawkeye. Do you have contact? Lone Warrior over."

"Roger that. Hawkeye locked on. Comms disabled. Charlie approaching Delta Zebra. ETA two mike," came the reply from the E2 Hawkeye 20,000 feet above and three kilometres east of Charlie (Flight G181).

"Lone Warrior to Ragin 1 over."

"Ragin 1. Copy that. Ready and hot," said the Squadron Leader, of the FA18C Super Hornets, sitting above Cooper's private jet.

"Hawkeye. Can you confirm numbers over?" came the order from Lone Warrior, call sign of the USS Harry S. Truman.

"Roger that. Heat detection shows four. I repeat shows four. One pilot and three at the rear over."

"Ragin. You're good to go," replied Lone Warrior.

"Affirmative," said the Squadron Leader as the two FA18C Super Hornets dived into position and unleashed their deadly cargo.

You could hear a pin drop in the Situation Room as Wade, the President and the remainder of the group waited. The clock kept ticking and the screens kept changing for the next sixty seconds, until the static voices of the pilots came back on line.

"Ragin 1 to Lone Warrior. Bandit burnt. I repeat bandit burnt, no remains."

"Good job Ragin. Return to base. Out."

The room sat quiet until Razen's booming voice asked if they had the data they required. A geeky looking computer programmer with spiky hair raised his thumb to acknowledge they had what they needed.

Fingers danced across the keyboards as analysts sent relevant data to the stricken nations to help soften the blow and start the reversal process.

"Thank you General, Wade," said Bysmith as she stood whilst signing operational orders. "Let's hope that's the last of the Cooper's."

58: Mossad Safe House

The Mossad safe house was a typical detached single storey dwelling in the predominately African American, lower socioeconomic community, of Congress Heights, Washington DC.

Darkness had already descended. Wade and Chrissie crossed the road. Hands in pockets. Collars upturned. Beanies pulled down. Nodding to the three homeless dressed Mossad guards standing around the small fire drum, two doors down. Without knocking they entered the front door.

Hardly believing how good it was to see her, Wade grabbed Crystal around the face and passionately kissed her.

"Thank god you're alright," he said.

Smiling and not saying a word she held his upper arm and lead him, hobbling, through the lounge, into the back kitchen. The windows were all blacked over and a large table had been set up with a television going at one end. The floor was covered in a thick, spongy hessian material. The walls and ceiling were lined with layers of hard rubber and numerous laptops, scanners and digital processing equipment sat upon the tattered kitchen benches.

Upon seeing Wine, Jacko, Kaitlyn and Joe, Wade smiled as he put his arm around Crystal's waist and said, "Thanks guys … thanks for everything."

"No problem, mate," replied Jacko in his best attempt at Australian slang.

Food and drink had been bought in. The group all sat down to watch an episode of 'Big Bang Theory'. Laughing, joking and enjoying each other's company Wade noticed Kaitlyn's suppressed emotions.

"Kia. What's up?"

Quietly she replied, "Can we talk?" as the group went silent.

"Is it about my mother?"

"Yes."

"I don't mind. We can talk here."

Joe turned the television off as Kaitlyn started.

"We did some digging on Sylvia and it appears her partner died two hours after an order was sent. We have traced the order and it originated from Washington DC and there's a possibility it might even have been from the Warehouse. The order gave a clear description of him and explained how and where he was to die."

Pausing and looking around the group she continued.

"Twenty minutes ago another order was issued with Cristina as the target. The order is for tomorrow night and gives Sylvia's home address."

"Cooper's partner?" asked Wade.

"Must be … The Mossad team are in position and we can keep a twenty four hour surveillance on them both. Also we believe they have given Sylvia a code name of Sade."

"Thanks Kia," replied Wade as he stood and went to the bedroom with Crystal following.

Sitting on the end of the bed, Wade heard the television come back on and the group laughing.

"Do you believe it's your real mother?" asked Crystal.

"I don't know … as Kia explained it all fits that it could be her."

"Remember you mentioned when we were in Portofino about the weird feelings you were getting."

"Yeah. I've been thinking about that," he replied as he put his hands on her face and kissed her.

"Do you want to know?" Crystal asked holding his hands.

"I'm not sure but I definitely want to protect them. I've been talking with my mother's spirit and she has said to go with my heart. So if you're up to it I would like you to come with me to Portofino and if it is my real mother I want you to meet her," softly said Wade with his head down and choking back the tears.

Wrapping her arms around his neck Crystal replied, "I love you Wade Ross. I love everything

290

about you. I love how you care so much and how you love me. I couldn't think of anything nicer than that beautiful place Portofino. On top of it all, I might even get to meet your real mother."

Standing and clasping his arms around her shoulders, Crystal cried out, "But you're going to have to be careful with my back," as they passionately kissed.

59: White House – Situation Room

Wade, Kia and Wine were escorted into the Situation Room. Already seated were President Markham, General Razen, Secretary Bysmith, Admiral James, Sarah Loll (Presidential advisor on international law) and William Croat (2IC to General Forest).

Forest entered the crowded room with his three aides. Markham instructed all aides, guards and those not directly invited to leave.

"General Forest, please take a seat," ordered the President.

Glaring at Croat and Loll, Forest restrained the urge to explode and demand to know what was going on.

Seated next to James, Forest looked to the President for an explanation.

"General, we have brought you and Admiral James here this morning as we need some explanations and/or clarifications on what appears to be intelligence breaches. Kaitlyn will explain what has happened and we expect you gentlemen to provide answers," said Markham in a stern and authoritarian voice.

"Thanks, Mister President. General, in front of you is a report of everything that has happened so far. As you are aware, Colonel Wine, Wade and their team have been on the path of Samantha and Thomas Cooper. What you don't know is that I have been giving you false and misleading information. Thus you would not know that Thomas Cooper has been killed. He was taken out in an airstrike over the Atlantic yesterday afternoon," said Kaitlyn looking from Wade back to Forest.

Forest sat stony faced as she continued.

"We were able to download data from his personal laptop before the strike and that's now being used to rectify the effected world economies … our major problem is that information is still being released that appears to be part of Coopers plan. Plus funds are still being withdrawn from major financial institutions. The transmitted information is coming from Washington DC and most likely from the Warehouse. We can only assume this is being controlled by his partner," she stated as she took her seat.

The room was deathly quiet as all eyes were on Forest.

Glaring at Kaitlyn he asked, "And who might 'we' be?"

"The combined services of Director Harel and General Razen and their respective teams," replied Kaitlyn.

Springing to his feet and slamming his fists on the table, James screamed, "This is absolutely outrageous. As I said yesterday this is a breach of national security to be dealing with a foreign power and my department not knowing."

"Shut up Paul," said Markham. "Take your seat and keep your mouth shut."

The Admiral returned to his seat with his eyes locked on Markham. General Razen reached across the table and grabbed the Admiral's dictaphone. "I think I'll keep this," said Razen.

"Okay General, what can you say about all that?" asked the President.

Opening the report Forest skimmed over the relevant items as he kept his head down and responded.

"So how long has this been going on?"

"Since we brought Samantha Cooper back from Israel," replied Kaitlyn.

With the mention of the Jewish state James sprung to his feet again. About to speak, Markham yelled over him to get out. Calling security James was escorted from the room. With order restored Razen nodded to Forest to continue.

"Well … why are they here?" asked Forest looking at Loll and Croat.

"I would have thought it obvious why Sarah is here. She is our advisor on international law and this involves many countries which we have an alliance   William is here because he has been working with Kaitlyn and General Razen," said Markham.

"Mister President, I will get to the bottom of this. But I'll need time to read this report."

"Very good General. Tomorrow morning same time, we meet again and we expect some answers."

Wade had been watching the body language of everybody as each bit of information had been released. He noted how Croat had a gentle smile, nearly borderline smirk, at the mention of funds still being withdrawn. He saw Forest not respond at the mention of Thomas Cooper being killed or information being leaked from the Warehouse. Forest was as rigid as a statue throughout the entire briefing and only seemed concerned about Loll and Croat being at the meeting.

His most alarming discovery was the Admiral's reaction to anything associated with Israel and his hostility to Kaitlyn.

The room had been vacated with only Wade, Kaitlyn and Wine remaining.

"What did you make of all that?" asked Wine.

Wade explained his thoughts and asked Kaitlyn why the report had no mention of Sylvia.

"Like you I'm suspicious of Croat but he knows nothing of Sylvia. All the information about her has come from Tel Aviv."

They discussed and decided to put a tail on Croat and get a hacker team, from Mossad, to go through his private life.

Chrissie sat in the drivers seat with Wine beside her. Wade and Kaitlyn were in the rear. Wine answered the secure sat phone on the first ring. Stewie and Bassa advised that everything was in order at Malmstrom.

Scratching his head and slightly perplexed Wade said, "Cooper definitely mentioned Minuteman … Do we know of any other bases?"

Kaitlyn's fingers danced across the small laptop keyboard as she replied, "Warren Air Force Base, Wyoming and Minot Air Force Base, North Dakota."

"What about Indian Reservations near either of them?" asked Wine.

With her fingers still moving like a classical pianist she replied, "Nothing near Warren but there is one near Fort Berthold, southwest of Minot."

Pushing the small star button on the bottom of his phone, Wine lifted it to his ear as Chrissie and Wade's phones vibrated. With all the team listening the Colonel commenced, "Listen up team. Stewie, Bassa same procedure Warren Air Base. Bud, Franco Fort Berthold Indian reservation. Jacko, you and the Delta squad, Minot Air Base. That's the most likely launch point. So you go in black and silent. Chrissie and I will be at 180. Any questions? … Good. Out." As the line went dead.

Turning in his seat, "What now?" he asked Wade.

"Kia and I have discussed and she's going back to the Warehouse. I'm heading to Portofino."

"Do you want anybody with you?" asked Wine.

"Crystal's coming with me. Harel's organised a flight and I think Chrissie should come."

Nodding the group all agreed and the remainder of the trip to the safe house was in silence.

60: Atlantic Ocean

Crystal tried to remain focused on the movie as she lounged in the luxurious sofa. Romantic love stories were her favourite and the one showing was definitely near the top of her list. The injection and dressings the doctor had administered prior to the flight's departure had dulled the pain and she felt quite comfortable.

Looking across she noticed how Chrissie had her head buried in reports, photos and maps. Whilst at the same time she was cleaning her weapons. On the opposite side of the luxurious Gulfstream X unmarked private jet, Wade was struggling to stay awake. Images flashed across the laptop screen that was sitting on his knees. As his eyes were about to close Crystal stood, walked over and lifted the laptop. This startled Wade as he sprung from the seat and knocked Crystal backwards. The laptop crashed to the floor. Realising what had happened he apologised, helped her to her feet and reached for the computer.

"Who's that?" she asked.

"Cristina."

"She is very beautiful," said Crystal bringing the screen closer. "What is that mark on her face?"

He looked back at the severe, badly stitched, irregular line that resembled a crack of ice across a frozen lake. He placed his finger on the screen and ran it the full length; from her left eye to the underside of her mouth.

"It's a scar from a knife attack. When she was fifteen years old and on a school excursion, a teacher in a drunken stupor attacked her. He was trying to molest her when she screamed out. He went into a rage and slashed her across the face with a carving knife and then raped her."

"My god. That's terrible," she gasped. "The scar seems so severe," said Crystal more to herself than as a comment.

"Apparently she deliberately leaves it like that to remind herself of the ordeal."

"So young and so beautiful … What happened to her attacker?" asked Crystal still staring at the screen.

"Never been seen since," replied Wade, as he tightened his hands into fists.

With Chrissie, by now, seated beside her and scrolling through the profile report, Crystal asked, "Do you know anything else about her?"

Chrissie started to read the report out loud.

"Twenty six years ago Sylvia was working in a fashion designer house, in Rome, when an unknown American film producer arrived. He swept her off her feet and three weeks later she moved in to his apartment. Twelve months passed, the movie he was making finished and he returned to the States without knowing she was pregnant. Cristina was born and to this day he is unaware of his daughter. Sylvia has never approached or made contact with Demetrious Cole since."

"Demetrious Cole!" exclaimed Crystal. Looking from Chrissie to Wade. "You both have no idea who he is, do you? He's probably the most famous producer and film studio owner in the world. He produces more blockbusters and attracts all the biggest stars ... I once read where he said he was waiting to meet his true love again ... this is incredible."

Wade raised his eyebrows and smiled as Chrissie continued.

"Sylvia continued to work at the Armani label until two years ago when she moved to Portofino and purchased a small house in the hills behind the town. It is there she met her partner, a yacht salesman. Christina obtained her doctorate in Greek Philosophy and Mythology at Sapienza University of Rome. Due to her dedication and results she has been invited to NYU (New York University), one of the top philosophy universities in the world, to head up the Greek Philosophy faculty. Currently on a three month sabbatical whilst she and Sylvia decide whether to move to the States. She has no boyfriend or known relationships. Since the attack she has been very shy, known to focus mainly on her studies and very rarely seen in public."

"I feel so sorry for her," whispered Crystal. "What about Sylvia?"

"The report seems to have very little on her other than what you've heard. She keeps to herself, she rarely socialises and only with a select group of friends."

Crystal put her head back into the lounge and again tried to focus on the movie but her thoughts were plagued with images of Cristina and her suffering.

Chrissie went back to her reports and Wade fell asleep.

61: Portofino

Wade watched as she walked from the small Patisserie at the entrance to the shops lining the Portofino harbour. A beautiful and elegant woman, she slowly drifted through the crowds. Her long, black wavy hair blew out behind her as the breezes floated off the water. Her skin and body as smooth and firm as somebody half her fifty two years of age.

Men casually glanced over their shoulder as she floated past. Women admired her grace and poise, as she seemed not to notice their stares. She spent the next hour wandering in and out of stores buying vegetables, bread and all the necessary items, but nothing extravagant. Walking from the flower shop she turned, kissed the proprietor on both cheeks, looked at her watch, stepped onto a Moped and slowly scooted along the harbour edge. After travelling four hundred metres she stopped, looked at her watch again and waited.

Sylvia had her back to the shops and people as she stared out into the waters of the Mediterranean. From his hiding spot, on the launch, Wade peered through the high powered binoculars and felt he could sense the pain in her eyes. Her eyelids slowly started to close. She dropped her head, ever so slightly, and a tear formed on the outside of her left eye. With her hands clasped she didn't appear to hear the other Moped approach until the rider shouted her name. Turning she smiled. They hugged and headed back along the foreshore.

Wade put down the binoculars and motioned to the captain to take them around the headland to the preplanned position so they could watch Sylvia's house. With resounding confidence in the Mossad agents who were now following them, he sat down on the highly polished foredeck.

"She's very beautiful," said Crystal sitting beside him.

Smiling he nodded in agreement.

"Wade you there?" came the static voice from the small handset in Wade's pocket.

"Yeah, what's up?"

"I think they've got a tail. White van. Two males. Northern European. Passenger taking photos with a long range scope. About three hundred metres behind and not closing," came the male reply in heavily accented Hebrew.

"Okay. Keep me informed. Stay with the women," ordered Wade.

Springing to his feet he looked up to the captain and shouted, "Double time. We need to be there, now."

The huge V12 engine kicked in and the cruiser threw Wade and Crystal back into the cabin wall as they frantically tried to get their footing and hurry back to the cockpit.

The night sky was closing in fast as the boat raced across the smooth as glass waters. Rounding the second headland the captain killed the engine and lights and the boat commenced its levelling process. Ten minutes passed. Two hundred metres from the rocky cliff face, slowly bobbing like a cork on the calm seas. Wade heard the two Mopeds before he saw the small dull lights trying to cut through the trees high up the hill.

"Itamar, what've we got?" asked Wade.

"The two women are in the house. We can see movement. They don't appear to have noticed anything. The two in the van have made no contact and are waiting," replied the Mossad agent.

"I'm coming in. If they move, follow," he ordered.

The captain had spotted an old derelict jetty further along the coast. With the boat just beyond idle speed he expertly manoeuvred the large vessel alongside as Wade leapt onto the rickety timbers and the boat continued back to its anchor point.

Like a cat on a hot tin roof, Wade sprung from support to support as the timbers crumbled behind him. In his all black outfit, camouflage cream and black carry-all slung across his body; he looked like the perfect cat burglar.

Itamar and his partner nearly had a heart attack as Wade opened the rear door and dropped inside their car.

"How the hell do you do that?" asked Itamar, getting his senses back under control.

Ignoring the question Wade watched as the trio sat in silence. All three men were highly trained Kidon assassins and all had worked for Director Harel. Sitting for hours, waiting, was part of the surveillance process, so nobody commented as they watched the two men continually enter and exit the van. The large, scruffily dressed, shaved-head Europeans were oblivious to their watchers. They took turns having a cigarette, wandering around the van, urinating, drinking Vodka and making stupid gestures towards each other.

0100 hours the man in the passenger seat answered his phone and they both hastily climbed from the van. Looking up and down the road Wade watched as they both shoved a 9mm Grach pistol into their rear waistband. Wade was aware the Grach was a favoured weapon of choice by the Russian Mafia.

Considering their size, Wade was surprised how quickly they crossed the road and darted into the trees leading down the common driveway to Sylvia's house.

The three men leapt from their vehicle and headed in their predetermined routes. Wade was following the Russians and as he turned into the drive, he saw they were already in the house.

Speaking into his throat mike, "Double time. They're in the house," he told the two Mossad agents.

Sprinting down the asphalt driveway he took four steps at a time as he raced up the front stairs and burst through the partly open door. The first Russian spun to the sound as Wade's fingers smashed into his windpipe. Grabbing the falling body he lowered it to the floor. Using only the light of the moon Wade crept on the balls of his feet along the corridor. The door to the first room was open and the room was empty. The second door was only slightly ajar. He peaked in and saw the semi-naked body of Cristina with the sheet draped over her legs and the curtains blowing in the light breeze.

As he approached the third door the barrel of Itamar's silenced Beretta Model 71 appeared at the opposite end of the hallway. With the door open and the sound of rustling, Wade was about to look in when he felt the spirits tell him to act, not observe. Focusing on these thoughts, he rounded the door jamb, took two steps and leapt to his left, half way up the wall. Using his Parkour skills he bent his knees and like a frightened monkey sprung off the wall. By now half a metre above the Russian, who was standing over the stunned Sylvia, Wade brought his elbow down and smashed the pistol wielding arm. The Russian crashed to the floor as Wade's heel embedded in the side of his temple, killing him instantly.

Sylvia screamed as Itamar turned on the light. Her scream alerted Cristina who raced from her room. Stunned and about to scream herself at the sight of two armed men standing in their hallway, she watched as they stepped aside and gestured for her to enter the room. Watching the two men closely and keeping against the wall, she covered her breasts as she stepped into the room.

Upon seeing Wade, standing over another man on the floor, and her mother shaking violently, cowering on the bed, she screamed, in Italian, "Who are you? What do you want? Leave my mother alone."

Replying in Italian Wade said, "We are not here to hurt you but to help you."

Cristina scampered to her mother, not taking her eyes off Wade whilst trying to cover herself.

Wade backed towards the door, as he said, "My name's Wade Ross and we're her to stop these two men from killing you both. Please believe me. I will explain the whole thing." Pausing and looking into their eyes he continued as he pointed at the Russian. "We'll remove him. Please get dressed and we'll wait in the other room."

The two women sat huddled together as the Israeli agents picked up the Russian and all three men departed.

The agents had removed the two bodies and Itamar's partner had taken them in their van. Itamar stood guard outside the front door. Twenty minutes had elapsed as Sylvia and Cristina entered the small kitchen. Waiting until they were both seated, Wade commenced.

"I work for an organisation that believes you have both been targeted. I'm sorry the way this has all happened but we hadn't expected them to act so quickly."

"Who are they?' asked Cristina.

"We believe Russian hit-men but we think their orders are coming from somebody within the United States," quietly replied Wade.

"Why us? Why Russian Mafia? And what do you and those other men have to do with all this?" she asked again, becoming more comfortable with Wade.

"You have to believe me when I tell you we are here to help and I will tell you everything I know. But we have to get you both out of here."

"Please Mister Ross, this is scaring me," stammered Sylvia.

"Sylvia. I understand but I insist we must leave now."

"How do you know my name?"

"Please … let's go," ordered Wade as he stood and motioned towards the front door.

The thirty minute drive to the Mossad safe house, on the opposite side of Portofino, was in silence except for the occasions when Cristina would whisper to her mother, 'It will be alright … sssh'.

61: Northern Portofino

The five level classical Mediterranean style villa sat perched on the cliff face with uninterrupted views across the water. Built two hundred years earlier its narrow verandahs and large neo classical arches blended beautifully into the wooded surroundings.

With six storey mansions to either side it was the home of the rich and famous that came to Portofino. Billionaire's yachts littered along the cove tied to their moorings. The hills were exceptionally steep and the trees dense; perfect for seclusion.

Itamar parked the car in the garage. Wade, Sylvia and Cristina crossed the perfectly laid tessellated tile entrance. The light came on. The door opened and a beautiful brunette welcomed them.

"Hello, you must be Sylvia and Cristina?" said Crystal.

Shaking hands the two ladies, still clasping each other, entered.

Crystal led them past the magnificent staircase, under the huge chandelier and out into the luxuriously decorated living room. Cristina and Sylvia looked around in utter amazement at the ballroom size area. The white marble floor and the larger than life paintings, all independently lit, gave the impression of an art gallery. A white leather lounge, capable of seating twenty four people, sat towards the full height glazed doors, opened to the sea.

"Please have a seat," motioned Crystal.

The two ladies sat with their backs to the water. Wade and Crystal sat opposite. Itamar, Chrissie and an extremely lean, fit looking female entered from a side door carrying trays. Placing the food and beverages on the table between everyone, they sat.

"Sylvia, Cristina thank you for trusting us. I'm going to tell you some things that unfortunately you can never divulge. No matter what happens," said Wade, waiting for them to acknowledge.

"Believe me, it's for your own good," said Crystal quietly.

Looking from Crystal, to each other, to Wade they nodded.

"Good. These two people," pointing at Itamar and his female companion, "and the man outside work for an Israeli intelligence agency. Crystal is an American Navy helicopter pilot and we," looking toward Chrissie, "are ex soldiers who work with a private agency that in turn works for governments. Everything we do is classified and usually not even acknowledged as having occurred," he paused. "Over the last six months we've been working on a mission that involved some extremely wealthy and powerful individuals. To the point they nearly

311

caused a collapse of some countries economies. We thought we had caught the last of them when your name came up," said Wade looking at Sylvia.

"Mine," she replied. "Why me?"

"Do you know or have you heard of a Thomas Cooper?"

"No … should I?" she asked.

Wade dropped his head, took a deep breath and then looked her straight in the eyes. "Sylvia, I'm going to ask, and tell you things that will be uncomfortable but for yours and Cristina's safety we need to know."

Crystal lightly placed her hand on Wade's thigh as he continued. "Thirty four years ago you were working as a cook in Australia when you met a man and became pregnant. You were heading for Alice Springs when he was killed. After arriving you gave birth to a boy and were then sent back here, to Italy."

Sliding her hands down her face, Sylvia gasped as she listened. Looking at Cristina, her eyes glazed over as the tears trickled down her cheeks. "I'm sorry … I'm truly sorry."

"Mum, it's okay … Really it's okay."

Getting her composure Sylvia replied, "How did you know this?"

"We found it on Thomas Cooper's laptop. It mentioned how he was coming here to kill you. But the problem now is we've traced a kill order that has been issued for Cristina."

Cristina's eyes lit up with the mention of her name.

"What can we do?" pleaded Sylvia.

"We have people in Israel and the US working on finding who issued the order. Until then we stay here and make sure you are both safe."

Wade explained how he needed Sylvia, Cristina and Crystal to remain in the main bedroom on level two. Nava, the female Mossad agent and Chrissie would stand watch. Itamar and Wade spent the remaining night hours adding further early warning detection devices and ensuring the existing ones were fully operational.

The light of the first rays of morning started to splash across the ocean as everybody gathered in the lower basement kitchen. Sylvia and Cristina had not slept a wink. Spending the hours talking about Wade's news. With their blood shot eyes peering over their coffee mugs, Crystal was trying hard to distract them from the situation.

"I believe you worked at the Armani house for many years?"

"Yes, it was very nice," softly replied Sylvia.

Wade's secure sat phone beeped shattering the tranquillity of the light conversation.

"Wade, we have a development. One of the Russians you took out last night had an encrypted

313

message on a phone we found in their van. With the help of Koh we were able to decode it. It said 'ensure Sade dies'. We then traced the message and it was definitely sent from the Warehouse," said Kaitlyn.

"What about Croat?"

"It turns out he was with General Razen, in the White House bunker, the whole time. No message could have been sent from there ... I don't think he's the one," she replied.

"Blast," muttered Wade to himself. "Can you get to the Warehouse and take Joe. We need to find out how and who the messages are being sent," he ordered as he disconnected the call.

62: Warehouse

"Wade, are you there? Can you hear me?" whispered Kaitlyn into the sat phone.

"Sure. What's up?"

"Joe and I have just arrived at the Warehouse. General Forest has shot a guy who in turn had shot Samantha Cooper."

"Are you sure?" responded a surprised Wade.

"I'm sure. It happened inside the Interrogation Room. The CCTV had been disabled and a high frequency noise emitter was found on the shooter. Apparently the General walked in as the shooter put a round in her head and one in her chest. Forest then fired a single shot into the back of the shooter's head. They're still trying to identify him but could take a while. Forest used a 44 hollow point."

"What … that's ridiculous … a Magnum 44 with hollow points," he said shaking his head. "Do they know how the shooter got into the Warehouse?"

"Not really. The theory at the moment is that he was one of the satellite analysts. The building is being cleared and everybody's security passes are being checked."

"What about Forest?"

"Gone back to Langley."

"Thanks," replied a frustrated Wade as he disconnected the call.

Approaching midday the group was restless. Crystal was talking like an auctioneer nearing the end of a sale, trying to distract Sylvia and Cristina. Asking questions about fashion, love, life in Italy and any other female topics she could think of.

"It must have been wonderful working at Armani with such talented and artistic people?" asked Crystal.

"Yes it was. Everybody was so friendly and caring. It was like a big family," replied a smiling Sylvia.

"You must have met some very famous models and movie stars?"

"Models, yes. Movie stars, no. The film industry doesn't use fashion clothing. Their designers produce the clothes as they're required."

"Really," responded a bemused Crystal. "I would never have guessed. They always seem to be wearing the latest fashions. How do you know this?"

"Over the years I've had many dealings with the industry," replied Sylvia in such a matter of fact way that Crystal was surprised.

The three women continued their conversation with Chrissie watching completely disinterested. Itamar's partner was hidden on the roof, scanning

360 degrees while Itamar and Nava checked and rechecked entry and exit points.

Wade was digesting Kaitlyn's news. Head shot and body shot were classic Special Forces double tap. Satellite analysts were highly educated and extremely unlikely to be Special Forces trained. If he were Special Forces, he would have heard and reacted to General Forest's entry. He would also have known better than to have his back to the only exit or entry point to the room. Why was Forest using a 44 with hollow points? What could be gained from murdering Cooper?

Dropping his head into his hands, he thought how ironic that though they should be nearing the end of the mission, instead the questions were multiplying. Even concentrating on the spirits was not helping.

Wade contacted Wine. They spent thirty minutes discussing the latest events and decided to bring Forest up to speed. Wade waited for the call to be answered.

"Wade. How interesting that you have called," said Forest tersely.

"General … I appreciate you're probably pretty pissed with us but unfortunately in our line of work we try to keep as much information as possible to ourselves. It tends to keep us alive."

"I understand. What can I do for you?"

Wade went on to explain everything he knew including information on Sylvia and Cristina. The

Mossad safe house location. The Russian mafia hit-men. Data from Thomas Cooper's laptop. Where and what Colonel Wine and the team were currently involved in. He explained how he needed to get Kaitlyn and Koh into the Warehouse server without anyone knowing so they could set a trap.

"Very good. As you're probably aware we've had a security breech. Soon as the Warehouse is back up running, I'll arrange for Kaitlyn and her access … Are you and Crystal currently at the safe house?" asked Forest.

Wade thought this a very unusual question considering what he had just divulged.

"We're in Italy but not near Portofino. We hope to be there some time tomorrow."

The General advised he would get a team to Sylvia's house, go through Cooper's data with Kaitlyn and check in with Colonel Wine. Disconnecting the call Wade could hardly believe that one of the world's most economically destabilizing situations with billions of dollars missing and Forest had not asked or mentioned about it once. Shrugging the thought aside he assumed maybe as the situation had now been averted or resolved, the CIA than forgets and moves on to the next problem.

63: Mossad Safe House

Approaching 2300 hours the sea breeze had picked up as the trees rustled and the small waves lapped against the rocks. Cristina had fallen asleep with her head on her mother's lap. Sylvia was propped up against the bed head and Crystal was lying on the adjoining single bed.

Sylvia was becoming very comfortable with the American and was enjoying their conversations. They had spent hours discussing their lives, adventures, misgivings, loves and yearnings. During one such conversation Sylvia mentioned her passion for writing.

"Now that you have more free time you'll be able to pursue it more actively … maybe take classes," suggested Crystal.

"Thank you Crystal. That is very nice of you to say but I've actually been writing for nearly twenty years."

"Really … have you had anything published?"

"No. It's screenwriting for films," softly replied Sylvia lowering her head and checking Cristina was still asleep.

"I'm sorry. I wasn't trying to pry."

"Please don't apologise. My stories have been quite successful and many have been made into movies. It's just that nobody knows I'm the writer. I write under the pseudonym of Dan Kar which is short for Dandaloo Karawi."

"Why a pseudonym and what is the significance of Dandaloo Karawi?" asked Crystal as she sat up on the bed, becoming fascinated with Sylvia's story.

"It's aboriginal for 'pretty boy'. Every time I write I think of him and how much I miss him," she replied as a tear formed.

Crystal fought to hold back her own tears and the thought of her mother, as she stood, walked over and hugged Sylvia. Not another word was said as Crystal left the room. The two women lay on their beds and remembered those they loved and missed.

By 0300 the cloud cover had increased and the moon was hidden. Wade opened his eyes as he heard the steel framed windows creaking in the now stronger breeze. After years of Special Forces training he had developed the ability to go for days with only ten minute micro naps. The dull thud of a hard object hitting a ceramic tile instantaneously alerted his senses. Springing from his position squatted and leaning against the wall, he inched his way to the balcony doors. Peering through the rustling curtains he saw the two black ropes that continued up the side of the building to level two. It was a rubber coated grappling hook and they had company.

Slowly bringing the night vision monocle over the balcony edge he saw the two black clad figures scampering up the wall. Another two had moored an IRB to a neighbouring pontoon and were scaling the adjacent building. He spotted a fifth vanish into the lower basement.

"We've got company," said Wade through his throat mike as he explained where the intruders were.

"Another east of the drive," said Nava.

"Chrissie top floor. Nava the women," ordered Wade.

"We've got the basement," whispered Itamar.

Wade saw the first of the small, lean agile figures leap on to the balcony and roll across to the wall. Two seconds later the second figure appeared. Repeating the same procedure. He watched as they looked at each other and drew swords from behind their backs. As they stood he fired his silenced 45mm round into the head of the closer assailant and swung his H&K USP Tactical at the body of the second.

Falling face first, the closer figure crashed on to the tiles with the sound of the metal sword echoing through the night. Wade was not taken back by the noise but more the speed the second attacker had moved when he fired the first shot. His second shot missed. A skilled marksman and very controlled under pressure Wade followed the attackers movement as he leapt for the open balcony door. Letting his hand, eye and pistol work as one he pulled the trigger and the round lodged above the attackers ear.

Wade raced across and pulled off the dripping wet, blood soaked fibre light wetsuit hood. Stunned he grabbed the sword and studied the handle. Out on to the balcony and he repeated. Dropping the sword he unzipped the wetsuit. Pushed the woman's jet black hair aside and saw the spiral tattoo on her shoulder. He opened the backpack and emptied the contents.

"Their Kunoichi. Be ready," said the surprised Wade.

Kunoichi, the name given to a female trained ninja. Rarely seen in modern day western civilization they are reputed to be used cryptically throughout north Asian countries. Kunoichi are renowned for carrying a short ninja sword, a Wakizashi. Are very adept at the use of the Shuriken, throwing stars. Sometimes known to have also mastered the double bladed Tanto knifes.

"Remember they're very silent and brilliant with the Shuriken. Don't hesitate," whispered Wade.

Lying against the balcony ledge Wade slid the blowpipe through the concrete baluster. With the deadly dart he took aim and fired across the twenty metres separating him from the closer of the two on the neighbouring wall.

Having heard the sound, of the flight of the dart, the second climber dropped from the rope and dived at two trees. The poison acted instantaneously and the first plummeted to the rocks below. By now out of range Wade ordered Itamar to activate the early warning sensors.

Charging across the marble floor, constantly scanning for movement, he was halfway up the giant staircase when he heard the sound of the electrification from the upper level balcony. The wetsuits and their rubberised boots stopped the Kunoichi from being electrocuted as they crossed the charged balcony floors but were not helpful as they grabbed the door handles.

Reaching the level one landing he heard a body hit the floor followed by a pistol bouncing on the tiles. On the balls of his feet Wade came up behind the fireplace. The night vision monocle showed the outline of Nava with the Shuriken lodged in the side of her neck. Aware the Kunoichi was still in the room and could remain silent for extended periods, he looked for a distraction. With his pistol in his right hand, he lent to the right and using his left rolled a lime across the tiles. The lime had covered only half a metre as the Tanto pierced its skin. Wade was not watching the lime but listening for the sound of wet suit movement as the Kunoichi threw her weapon. The slight creasing was all he needed and the double taps found their mark.

Lifting his monocle he saw the amount of blood that covered the white marble floor and knew Nava was dead.

Years of war zones, death and mayhem had made Wade very accustomed to dead bodies. He could cope with the blood, gore, smell and dismembered body parts but whenever he saw an Aboriginal or Israeli death it felt like family. With only able to allow himself four to five seconds, he looked at her body, shook the image from his head and ran from the room.

Racing to the second level, taking three steps at a time he tried to raise Itamar.

"Itamar … Itamar. Come in," he gasped between breaths.

"They are dead," came the whispered Danish accent of Chrissie. "I heard sounds as the mic died."

"Where're you?"

"Roof."

"Can you see any others?"

"Negative," she replied as they both heard the muffled sound of C4 and a scream from the driveway garage entrance.

"Alright. Level two, cover the stairs. You should have one coming from the basement," ordered Wade whispering and panting to get his breath.

Stepping into the doorway of Sylvia's room, within a nanosecond he had analysed the situation. To his right and four metres ahead a Kunoichi had her left arm around Cristina's chest. A Wakizashi across her throat. In the middle against the far wall Sylvia sat huddled to the bed head. Another Kunoichi stood two metres adrift of her, side on to Wade and wielding a Tanto.

With his weapon aimed at the first Kunoichi Wade heard Crystal, who had been aroused by the scream, step into the doorway behind him. Pivoting on his left leg he dropped to the floor as he spun around and with his left arm knocked Crystal back behind the wall. The whistling razor sharp Shuriken skimmed above Crystal's head and clanged into the opposite wall.

Wade continued his pivot, leapt to his feet as he saw the Tanto wielding, Shuriken throwing Kunoichi backflip across the room towards the door. Landing on her feet, in the hallway, she whipped her head round as Wade, who had Parkoured off the adjacent wall, slammed his elbow into the back of her neck.

Rolling with the blow the agile assassin hit the wall and catapulted into the air. Wade had expected her reaction and used the opposite wall to Parkour back. With his night vision monocle gone he was depending on sound, instinct and the ability for his eyes to naturally adapt to the darkness.

As he hit his attacker he used the opportunity to grab his Ka-Bar knife from his leg scabbard. Like atoms on a collision course, they both flew through the air and their respective knifes found their targets.

Landing back on his feet Wade saw the Kunoichi's wetsuit peel, like a blistered tomato, as the cut opened up from shoulder to shoulder across her chest. The slow trickle rapidly developed into a cascade. Her heart tried desperately to pump blood through her oxygen depleted body. He watched as her knees shook like a learner on stilts. Desperately trying to lift the Tanto she crashed sideways.

"Wade, your arm," said Crystal.

Her words snapped him back to reality as he felt the blood reach his right hand. Holding up his left hand signalling not to move he wiped the right on his shirt. Picked up his H&K and turned into the room.

His natural night vision had returned. With both hands clasping the pistol, held at full length he walked towards the bed.

With a Shuriken now in her left hand, Wade knew the Kunoichi could kill both women before he could get to her. Calling her bluff, with the pistol held rock steady aimed between her eyes; he continued forward. He felt the blood flowing down his bicep and into his sleeve. Concentrating hard, he called on the spirits for their help as the blood increased.

"One more step, Mister Ross, they die," said the highly accented Japanese.

326

The quarter sized moon appeared from behind the clouds and the room was bathed in dim obscured light. Focusing like a cobra starring down its prey he saw the sword pushed harder into Cristina's throat. The Kunoichi's vice like grip held her steady, as the cut grew wider and wider. The blood was trickling down between her breasts. Sylvia clamped her hands to her mouth as she watched in horror.

"Not my problem. But you'll be dead as well," softly replied the stone faced Wade.

"You don't care if your mother dies?" questioned the expressionless Kunoichi.

Wade didn't flinch. Sylvia spun her head and gasped as her mouth dropped open.

"You didn't know," said the surprised killer.

Still staring at the highly trained ninja, Wade minutely dropped his left arm. The slight shift in focus, from the Kunoichi, was his signal and the bullet found its mark. The impact of the 45mm round forced her head back, killing her instantly. The backward falling motion dragged the blade across Cristina, slicing from her neck to her shoulder.

Wade was rapidly losing consciousness as the blood poured from his arm. Dropping to his knees he heard the distinctive silenced double tap of Chrissie's semi-automatic pistol. Crystal charged into the room, turning on the light as she entered.

Sylvia was frozen to her spot, eyes transfixed on Wade.

"Sylvia … Sylvia," screamed Crystal. "Help Cristina."

Tearing the buttons from Wade's shirt she tried desperately to remove it. Blood covered the floor, his legs, his chest and arms, her hands and everything was getting more slippery by the moment.

"Sylvia," screamed Crystal. "Help her or she'll die."

Finally able to free his arms from the shirt Wade's head crashed into her lap. With all her strength she wrapped the sleeve above the cut and pulled the tourniquet tight. She then wrapped the remainder of the shirt round and round over the cut until it looked like a ball of wool. Looking up, Chrissie had entered and was surveying the scene.

"Cristina. It's her throat," yelled a panic stricken Crystal.

Rapidly and calmly Chrissie applied a makeshift dressing, lay Cristina down and called Wine.

Ten minutes had passed. Chrissie had given Wade and Cristina adrenaline shots and had set up temporary intravenous drips. Applied butterfly sutures and more suitable field dressings, as Wade opened his eyes.

Having not moved, Sylvia watched as Wade's head lolled about and his eyes tried to accustom to the lights.

"Are you really my son?" she asked in disjointed Italian.

Still opening and shutting his eyes Wade heard the question but was unable to answer. Sylvia had risen from the bed and was hanging on to the chair. Trying to get her composure.

"How can it be? How do you know?" she asked again in Italian, looking at Crystal for answers.

"Sylvia, I don't know what you've said. I don't understand Italian."

"She asked is Wade really her son and how we know," softly answered Chrissie.

Looking up at Sylvia's swollen tear filled eyes and shaking hands, Crystal replied.

"I'm sorry Sylvia but apparently it all fits."

"No … No don't be sorry. If it's true, it's a godsend," she said as she fell to her knees.

64: Mossad Private Jet

By sunrise the Mossad extraction team had removed the bodies, cleaned the walls and floors and the neighbours awoke to what appeared a normal day.

The Mossad medical team had done an exceptional job of stitching Wade's arm and Cristina's neck. They slid the heavily sedated Cristina and her gurney with all the attached tubes and machines into the back of the unmarked van. Sylvia, who had spent the previous three hours unable to take her eyes off Wade, Crystal and Chrissie climbed in. Wade had insisted on another adrenaline shot and the removal of the drip as he climbed into the passenger seat. The huge, wild-looking driver smiled.

"Wade you look worried," said Jamshid in his heavily accented Hebrew. "How do you feel that she could be your real mother?"

Lifting his injured arm and placing his hand on Jamshid's huge bicep. "Thank you my friend. I appreciate your honesty. I'm not sure how I feel. If she really is, then I hope we can learn about each other's lives."

The big man smiled again as they accelerated up the steep drive.

Wade had relayed events to Kaitlyn who in turn had passed on to Director Harel. After many phone calls and rejected plans it was decided that Site 180 was the safest location for Sylvia, Cristina and Crystal. Kaitlyn was ordered from the Warehouse and Wine agreed to meet them at Dulles International Airport, Washington DC.

The unmarked van arrived at Genoa Christoforo Colombo International Airport thirty minutes later. The royal blue Embraer Legacy 600 private unmarked jet glistened in the morning sun. The medical staff secured and made ready Cristina. Sylvia was given a sleeping injection and tucked into one of the luxurious beds. Crystal and Chrissie collapsed into the lounge chairs. Wade and Jamshid sat at the small conference table in the partitioned area.

Twenty minutes after arriving. The obligatory customs checks completed. The plane approached cruising altitude. Crystal and Chrissie had fallen asleep. The waitress was busying herself in the separated galley and Kaitlyn's face appeared on the small screen at the end of the conference table.

"What've you got for us, Kia?' asked Wade.

"Thomas Cooper's data has been a dead end. The Warehouse is still off limits and Samantha Cooper's interrogation tapes have gone missing."

The three Israeli trained assassins sat looking at each other. The quiet was disturbing but necessary.

They each digested the information and looked for a clue.

"Where do we think the Kunoichi fit in?" asked a puzzled Jamshid. "You can't just call them up and say 'hey do you want to come and kill some people for us' … I'm sure there would have to be contact lines or something."

"Do we know how they operate? Do they work for money or for principle or what?" asked the bewildered Wade.

Kaitlyn agreed to do some digging. With a flight time of nine hours to Dulles they decided to reconnect before landing.

Leaning back in his chair Wade looked to his huge friend for help.

"I'm finding the psychology of this entire mission hard to fathom. With your fresh eyes, any ideas?"

Thinking whilst flicking through the piles of notes and photos that were spread across the table, he stopped and held one to Wade's view. President Markham, General Razen and General Forest sitting in the Oval office couches in deep discussion.

"Is it possible that those who you think are helping you, are really blocking and hiding things from you," he said fiddling with the photo.

"Well sure it's possible … who are you thinking of?"

"What about the President or Forest?"

Analysing his thoughts Wade responded, "The President would need outside help, and quite a lot, to pull this off. I don't think so. Forest on the other hand, could … If he did, he is one hell of a good actor."

"Well, think about it. What's the one thing that is beating you every time?"

"They always know where and what we're doing!"

"Correct and who has the best opportunity to do that?"

"Okay. I take your point. But this is about money. Billions at that. How could he possibly hide it?"

The big man lent forward in his chair as he softly replied, "You said there was some Indian chief who had numerous accounts with millions of dollars. Why couldn't there be thousands of those accounts totalling billions of dollars."

"Sure, there could. How's that help?"

"Wasn't the Indian's name something to do with trees? Hence couldn't see the forest for the trees."

Wade sprung out of his chair.

"You're a genius. Of course. It was right in front of our eyes."

With renewed enthusiasm he dialled Kaitlyn and arranged an immediate teleconference. They spent the waiting time discussing options with the Colonel.

Three hours later the screen beeped to register an incoming call. Hitting the button President Markham's face appeared.

"Hi Wade. Kaitlyn said this was urgent."

"Mister President," replied Wade as the screen split into multiple faces. "General Razen, Secretary Bysmith thanks for being so prompt. The man next to me is Jamshid, Israeli Secret Service and as you can see Kaitlyn and Colonel Wine are on line."

Watching the concerned faces of the three most powerful people in Washington he continued.

"The news I'm about to give you might be very hard to digest," paused Wade. "It appears our man responsible is General Forest."

"Forest!" exclaimed Markham, looking at his chief advisors seated opposite him in the Oval office.

"Are you sure?" asked the astounded Razen.

"Jamshid was the one who figured it out. Since then we have been able to trace the hidden accounts. We've found over forty thousand bank accounts with approximately a million dollars in each account. Our analysts have estimated there could be another forty to fifty thousand accounts. We also found a common suffix to all the accounts. Koh was able to hack into Forest's private computer and the suffix is his password."

"My god. Do we realise the ramifications of this," said Razen staring at his colleagues.

Allowing the information to sink in, Wade watched as Markham ran his fingers through his short greying hair. Bysmith stood and paced the room.

Sixty seconds had passed when Wine cleared his throat, "Mister President. If I may."

"Please. Please by all means Colonel."

Wine explained they had a plan but they needed the President's help to distract Forest from following their movements. The details for the White House administration's part of the plan was sketchy and they hoped Bysmith could fill in the gaps.

"Colonel. You are asking us to arrange a visit for the Israeli Prime Minister and the Palestinian President, here in Washington, to discuss peace talks. Correct?" asked Bysmith.

"That's correct, Ms Secretary."

"And how do you expect us to get them to agree to come to Washington?" asked a stunned Bysmith.

"Actually Wade has already spoken with Director Harel who has spoken with Prime Minister Asimov, who has agreed."

"Unbelievable," replied Bysmith. "What about Malouf? How do you intend to get the Palestinians here?"

"That's slightly more complicated," replied Wade. "I assume you have heard of the movie 'The Hurting Sand'?"

"Yes, I have … what does that have to do with any of this?" asked the slightly annoyed Secretary.

"'The Hurting Sand' is a controversial story that became a world-wide cinematic success. The story focused on the plight of an Arabic woman living in New York City. Married to a successful Arab businessman, who was highly regarded within the US Arab religious community, the woman lived a life of fear. Physically and mentally abused every night by her husband, she developed an unlikely relationship with a female, Christian, psychologist neighbour. Their friendship became sexual and the psychologist helped the woman escape to a secret Idaho commune. The psychologist leaves her husband and also goes to the commune.

The story is well told and compelling watching but it raises many issues. The Arab community is mortified that such a show could be made and shown and their extremists are hunting worldwide for the writer.

If you were to advise Malouf that if they attend these talks, we will give them the writers name; I'm sure they'd be there," said Wade.

"Possibly but we don't know the writer."

"Well we do and we'll tell you when you're all together."

"Mister Ross, this administration does not play games. If you want our help you release the name.

Then we will see what we can do," sternly replied Bysmith.

Sitting back in his chair Wade smiled, slowly shaking his head.

"Firstly, if you think, while you sit there in your little white castle, that this is a game than we are not the people for you. Secondly, we have already finished our job. So you won't be getting any names. Thirdly, you haven't got too much right recently so I would've thought you'd be taking all the help you can get. Obviously not," softly said Wade hitting the disconnect button.

Numerous attempts were made at reconnecting, with Wade ignoring each time. He arranged with the pilot to redirect to Denver Colorado International Airport. Wine organised a transport helicopter and easy customs access on their arrival.

65: Oval Office

"Burt any ideas? What do we do now?" asked the US President to his chief military advisor.

"Mister President. I think we handled things with Wade completely wrong. He's very unconventional but he gets results. I believe him when says he has the writers name and I do feel their idea is a good one. From our previous dealings, with them, I would imagine they will go this alone," replied Razen sitting back in the Oval Office lounge chair, all the while glaring at Bysmith.

"Are you blaming me for this General?" she asked defensively.

"Calm down. Both of you," ordered Markham. "If Forest is the culprit why don't we just let them take him out?"

Sitting in silence all three took a swig of their scotch as they watched the flames leap above the logs in the fireplace.

Razen lowered his glass, stood from his chair and straightened his jacket.

"The major problems I see are when they take somebody out they cause so much damage and we don't want or need that in the middle of DC right at this time," looking toward Markham. "As you're aware your popularity isn't so great at the moment

338

and more deaths and mayhem in our capital, won't help … plus they're so silent we'd never be able to pin the blame on them if everything went pear shape. Then we're lumbered with trying to explain how and why the leader of our major international intelligence organisation has been killed."

"Well not just that. What about the cost that's been put into this Warehouse … probably billions," added Bysmith.

Stony faced the President poured himself another drink. Loosened his tie, scratched his head.

"This might all be very true but doesn't answer my question. What do we do now?"

Two hours later after many more scotch's and discussions with, Rick Majors, head of the Presidential Secret Service, a clandestine operation had been organised. Rick used some old contacts from his time at the CIA and his current association with the President to arrange a SOG team to eliminate Forest.

SOG (Special Operations Group) a classified department from within SAD (Special Activities Division) the covert operations component of the CIA. Extremely secretive and made up of the best intelligence and paramilitary personnel available from all US Special Forces and operations groups.

The six man SOG team had been issued a kill order on Forest and any known affiliates.

Lying back in his chair, Markham felt very comfortable with himself.

"Well at least that's over," he said with Bysmith nodding in agreement.

66: Site 180

Site 180 had the electronic firepower of the US Fifth Fleet. From high level surveillance, instant satellite access, to a high speed secure server. Completely undetectable from land or air whilst able to track a man walking across a desert on the opposite side of the planet. With its own miniature nuclear reactor as a power source and an abundance of water from the mountain it was the perfect hideaway.

Wine had ensured whenever his team were at the facility they were afforded only the best. Saul, the ex British SAS Sergeant and Sarah, his Polish doctor wife, were responsible for the fresh food, medical equipment, daily requirements, cooking, cleaning and armoury. The retired couple lived and worked within Site 180 with their IT wizard daughter, Sharna and her farmer husband Ted.

They provided the team with comfort and joy whilst also given, in return, the utmost respect. Sharna would ensure everything IT ran smoothly. Any problems were solved instantly to the gratitude of the team. She kept firmly abreast of the latest advancements. She hoped one day to be able to go out with the team and hence trained during all of her free time to the delight of her father and dismay of her mother. Ted's uncanny knack of fixing things had him as the team go-to man. He self-taught an understanding of the helicopters, the drones, all the different weapons, the site air conditioning system, the power generators right down to the kitchen appliances.

After manoeuvring through the labyrinth of an entry they came to the last bomb proof door that led into the main control centre. The door slid open as Wade, Crystal, Sylvia, Wine and Cristina, being pushed on her gurney by Chrissie, entered. The room was beautifully heated and flooded in light. Wine made a beeline for Saul who was bent over one of the dozens of computer screens. Wade wrapped his arms around the short, grey haired, rotund Sarah.

"Hello, my gorgeous little man," she said only able to get her arms to his chest.

"Sarah. It's good to see you."

With Cristina still sedated Chrissie headed to the medical room, giving Sarah a kiss as she passed.

"And who are these beautiful ladies?" she asked as she watched Crystal and Sylvia's eyes darting around the enormous room.

After the introductions Sarah stepped forward and gently grasped Crystal's hands.

"I love this man like a son and I can see how happy you make him … so thank you for that."

"Sarah, leave the poor girl alone. She's just got here," yelled Saul from across the room.

Smiling Crystal knew she was going to like this grandmotherly figure. Sarah took Crystal and Sylvia to show them their new short term home.

Five hours later the team had all arrived and were seated around the large Perspex table in the centre of the main control room. Having showered, fed and stowed his or her gear, everybody was in a jovial and carefree mood. The noise was thunderous as they all tried to be heard over each other. The Colonel allowed the banter as he watched his team relax knowing it was short lived.

Sarah approached the table with the largest tray of home-made chocolate cookies Crystal had ever seen. She placed the tray and hands arrived like octopus tentacles.

"One at a time, you lot," she said.

Without another word spoken those who had grabbed two, three or even six replaced them and took one. Crystal looked on in bewilderment at how these highly trained killers who appeared as tough as nails and as hard as concrete were always so respectful.

Enjoying the biscuits, that were the size of their hands, the Colonel started the meeting. Bud and Franco explained how they found nothing at Fort Berthold. Stewie and Bassa had the same at Warren Air Base. Sammy and Bart advised that he and the

Delta Team found an implant in one of the terminal launch pads and it was ready but had not been activated. They explained that it could have been activated remotely. He also advised that the Delta Team had returned to base. Jacko and Seal Team 6 had conducted a reconnaissance and surveillance of the Warehouse with nothing further to advise. Jacko produced a hand-sketched map showing the location of all CIA spotters, their respective equipment and weapons. Wade explained events in Italy and everybody was surprised at the mention of the Kunoichi.

"Okay," started Wade looking around the table at all his friends. "I know our team is probably the furthest from a democracy you could imagine but I'm asking you this time to decide if we should go any further on this mission. We've finished and been paid for what was expected of us. We should all be getting on a flight to New Zealand for Kiwi's funeral … so what'll it be?"

Without hesitation they all raised their fists as Chrissie said, "You know we have to finish this for him."

Feeling the shackles run up his back and the tears start to swell in the back of his eyes, Wade nodded.

The noise rose again but this time the discussion was serious as they started to plan their attack. Sitting at the back of the room Sylvia looked to Crystal.

"Who is Kiwi? He obviously meant a lot to Wade."

"He was Wade's best friend. He got killed in Switzerland not long ago," softly replied Crystal lowering her head.

Three hours later with paper strewn across the table and floor, drop down screens scribbled all over and dozens of computer images displayed throughout the room, Wine called everybody to order.

"Listen up. We go in tomorrow night. Team 1 Wade and Jacko will take the kites. Team 2 Stewie, Bassa and Bart you need to blend in as the homeless. You're to make sure you've taken out their spotters by 2300, at which time Team 3 Morrie and the SEAL Team will come from the water. Team 4 Bud, Franco. I want you on the west flank as support fire for the SEALS. Team 5 Sammy will be sniper on the roof of the old silo."

Looking across Sammy nodded in agreement.

"Surveillance is showing two, or possibly three, in the silo tower. Are you going to be okay with taking them out plus carrying all your gear?" asked Wine.

"No problem Colonel," smiled the big black man.

"Right," muttered Wine. "Remember this is silent. I don't want you doing a Wade and taking out half the building."

"Can't help himself Colonel. Hands are too big. Just keeps firing. Thinks he's back in Africa

345

hunting poachers," joked Stewie, Sammy's best friend, and the team burst into laughter.

"Alright, alright," said Wine bringing the meeting back on track.

"We'll run a silent drone, which will be controlled from the van, from 2230. The drone will kill all surveillance, early warning detection, cameras and radar emission from the Warehouse. That'll give Teams 2, 4 and 5 thirty minutes to get into position. Team 6 will be Kaitlyn, Joe and myself and we'll be in the van. We know the Warehouse detection is only effective around the building to three hundred metres. So we'll be on the southern side, two blocks across halfway down Sixteenth Street."

Walking around the large table Wine came up behind Chrissie and put his hand on her shoulder.

"We need some distractions and Chrissie has agreed to act as a street prostitute. She will be our eyes and ears from ground level … we know you're not comfortable with this, so thanks."

"Yeah, Chrissie thanks from the rest of us," added Wade as the team all agreed.

Walking back to face his team, Wine ran his fingers through his short black hair. With his hands clasped behind his head he looked up at the satellite image of the Warehouse roof and its surroundings.

"Well that's probably the easy part. This is where this whole plan could go pear shape. All yours Wade."

346

Not bothering to stand he grabbed a laser light pointer and aimed at the Warehouse image.

"At the northern end we've detected something different about the roof structure. We can't pinpoint exactly what it is but we've had a guess that it might be the old roof sheets over the toilet area and they haven't been braced and relined like the rest of the building. We know the roof is wired to detect the slightest movement and we also know it can be electrified from below. So you all need to be in position by 2300, as Jacko and I will float in on the kites at 2310. The drone will give us protection from the sensors and cameras but only for three minutes. Team 6 then needs to recharge the drone and that will take another two minutes by which time it will all be over."

Moving the pointer to the drop down wall he continued, "Team 3 needs to be ready to punch through the wall, on my command at 2313. At the same time, we'll blow the roof and rope down. Remember we can't kill the power to this building from outside and we have no idea of what other weapons they might have inside. We don't know who are friendlies or not, so identify your targets first."

"Good luck everybody," said Wine as the group stood and went to ready their gear.

"One last thing," shouted Wade over the noise. "If you see a group of hoodies drive in, light a fire and just appear to be hanging around. They're a distraction I've organised and will be gone by 2220."

Crystal sat and watched the group disperse and head off in to their military rituals. Wade approached and sat down beside the two women.

"It seems like a lot could go wrong," said Crystal.

"True," nodded Wade. "But we're running out of time so it has to happen now."

Looking across at Sylvia he continued, "I know we haven't had much time to talk and I guess we're both a little confused but when I return I would like the three of us to spend some time together."

"*Grazie*," she smiled.

67: Warehouse – External

Stewie had gone in early the next morning and was lying against the doorway of a derelict shop with old newspapers scattered across his body. The sun was trying desperately to break through the clouds as the wind whipped up and lashed against the rusty corrugated walls. With his tattered beanie pulled tightly over his head he glanced toward the CIA spotter who had positioned himself behind the large dumpster.

The spotter was perfectly situated to watch any movement in or out of the drop-down wall. As the wind increased and the temperature dropped, the spotter became less and less interested and eventually buried his head in his coat.

Stewie was the perfect actor as he spent the day wandering throughout the vicinity of the Warehouse and watching the spotter's movements. Approaching 1700 hours, with darkness blanketing the area, the five spotters in their various locations were so cold, tired and bored they didn't see Bassa and Bart slip in under their noses. The three men of Team 2 found secure locations with a perfect line of sight to their targets and setup for the wait.

Sammy quietly lowered the black box beside the upturned table as he activated the invisible beam.

He crept across the broken glass scattered floor as the rats scurried. With the black sack, carrying his sniper rifle, tripod, scope and rounds, slung across his back he drew his silenced H&K USP SD 9mm pistol.

Halfway up the rusty fire stairs he came upon two of Forest's men playing cards. With efficient double taps he continued. The top of the stairs opened on to a large, rusty, chequer-plated landing. On the opposite side a ladder led vertically into the cylindrical silo that sat atop the rectangular warehouse. Looking up the ladder Sammy realised the twenty metre climb would be suicide if he was detected.

"Yo bro, stop with the shit man," he said, dragging a battered timber stool across the landing. Standing at the base of the ladder he aimed his pistol straight up.

"What the hell are you two doing?" asked the spotter from above as he bent his head into the ladder opening.

Sammy fired two perfectly directed shots into his head and he fell forward. Unaware he was holding his rifle, the spotter crashed on to the steel floor and the noise was deafening as it echoed through the building.

Scampering up the ladder he quickly set up and waited for the repercussions.

"Team 5. You there?" whispered Stewie.

"All good," said Sammy.

"My god what was that noise?" asked Stewie. "They're all spooked now."

"Three tangos down. Site secure."

"Quiet," came Wade's voice through everybody's earpiece.

Team 2 and 5 watched for the next four hours as the CIA spotters eventually relaxed and once again became more interested in keeping warm. Sammy was able to disguise his presence by responding to Sitrep requests with double clicking his radio.

At 2130 the beaten up Lincoln drove into the adjacent carpark. Its four occupants got out, music blaring and proceeded to light a fire in an upturned drum. All eyes watched as they smoked joints, drank beer and kept turning their music louder and louder.

Team 4 used the distraction and got into position. At 2220 with the fire roaring and music still playing the car squealed its wheels and raced out on to the street. The four occupants knew not to take any notice of the blond as she rounded the corner.

The short, tight mini skirt kept riding up the fish net stockings as Chrissie made out she was adjusting her top that only slightly covered her breasts. Her jacket was half down her back and the blood red lipstick was smudged across her cheeks. The six inch heels had her well over six feet high. The huge diamante sparkling bag slung over her left shoulder gave her an Amazonian presence. Stumbling down the rubbish strewn footpath she stopped and leant against the filthy graffiti covered brick wall beside the first spotter.

"Hey sweetie," she said in her strong Danish accent.

"Fuck off bitch," growled the spotter nervously looking down the road hoping nobody was watching.

Turning side-on Chrissie slid her hand into the bag, gripped her pistol and fired a single silent shot between his eyes as she stepped to cover his fall. Using the cover of the dumpster she heard the silenced rounds find their targets of the remaining spotters.

2230 and now back in her operational gear she looked up to see the silhouette of the silent drone float past. Thirty three minutes later the drone passed again.

"Team 3. I have a visual," said Sammy as six wet black clad figures appeared at the corner from where Chrissie had come.

Everybody strained to hear any sounds above the wind and moving rubbish. Listening for the drone or kites, the minutes ticked by.

"Team 3. Sixty seconds from … now," said Wade as they all looked on in bewilderment that he had got into position without any of them hearing.

The five SEALS and Morrie stood and were about to charge across the concrete hardstand when Bud's voice exploded in their ears.

"We've got company. Black SUV. Stopped on Seventeenth. Six in black, heavily armed, SCAR Lights, NVG's, moving your way. They look pretty serious."

"Okay. Everybody hold back. 6, turn away the drone. 4, I want commentary," ordered Wade.

"Roger that. They're in typical Sierra Foxtrot (Special Forces) leapfrog formation heading straight for the wall. Should be coming into 5's visual … now," said Bud.

"Copy that. Heads down. Straight at the wall … there now. Looks like they're placing Semtex … stepping back. Here goes," said Sammy as the explosion threw the wall into the Warehouse.

Smoke and dust covered the opening as the six men opened fire and threw grenades into the building.

Believing it was a hit squad Wade had already instructed Jacko to prepare the roof for detonation. When he heard the six rifles open fire indiscriminately seconds after the blast, he yelled into the throat mike.

"Take'em out. It's a hit squad."

Two seconds later the six SOG operatives were falling to the ground as the carefully placed explosives caused the roof section to drop one metre on to the toilet block.

"Listen up. Our element of surprise is gone. Team 3, I want you to go in and clear the north end. There's multiple rooms and no idea what to expect. Stewie, Bassa watch their backs. Sammy, Bud, Franco hold your positions. We can expect emergency crews any minute and I want you to hold them. I don't care what it takes they are not to get to the building. Chrissie, Bart same on the east flank. Jacko and I will cover the south end. Colonel we need an eye in the sky and a chopper for evac," ordered Wade.

"Roger that. On its way," he replied.

"Remember the building could be wired. Smoke ready? On my command," ordered Wade again as Jacko dropped the rappelling ropes and they clipped on their carbineers.

"Smoke," screamed Wade as the smoke canisters were dropped from the roof and fired through the door. Waiting for the smoke to do its job the building was plunged into darkness.

"NVG's (Night Vision Goggles)," yelled Wade. "Ready ... Go. Go!"

68: White House

President Markham was known for not wanting to be disturbed whilst sleeping. The phone chirping on the bedside table startled him as he reached across and picked up the handset.

"What," he mumbled trying to get his bearings. "This better be important," sitting up trying not to wake his wife.

"Mister President, we have a serious problem. You might want to turn on the television," said Razen.

"What are you talking about?" he asked hitting the remote.

The television sprang to life and the President watched as a news crew helicopter image showed a police helicopter, fire engines and police cars being shot at. A siege situation had developed around the secret CIA Warehouse. The news story showed a long range image of six black clad bodies lying outside a blown wall.

"Christ, Burt. What are you doing about this," he yelled startling his wife.

"Unfortunately it's now out of my control. CIA personnel. FBI jurisdiction and the SOG team all dead."

The President climbed out of bed, ran his hands over his head as he paced the room. Cursing and swearing his wife tried to calm him down.

"Get Charlotte and Paul James on the phone," he yelled back into the phone.

"Here, Mister President," they both replied in unison.

After a torrent of accusations flew between all four parties eventually Razen calmed everyone down.

"This is obviously Wine and Ross's work. I think we need to let the FBI guys on the ground handle it as they see fit. When it's over we devise a strategy that limits our association and distances us as far as possible," said the General.

Everything was quiet except for the television noise in the background. The three people on the phone listened as they heard the President's wife begging him to sit down and relax. Reminding him of his blood pressure and weak heart condition.

"I hope you all realize the severity of this. The media will want blood," said Markham pausing. "What if Forest comes out on top?" he asked suddenly realizing this could be a worse situation.

"I'll get our spin doctors on to this immediately," replied Bysmith.

69: Warehouse – Internal

Kaitlyn tapped into the Warehouse public address system and initiated the command 'everybody down' that kept screaming through the building. Smoke was being swirled around by the downdraft of helicopters and the wind roaring through the two openings.

Looking like black aliens, with NVG's, gas masks, throat mikes and body hugging wetsuits, they stormed through the building. Kicking down doors, prodding and forcing people to the floor and shooting anybody showing resistance. The SEAL team and Morrie had reached the far end of the building and were back at the blown opening when Wade ordered the lights back on. Stewie and Bassa had exited and were adding support to the outside teams. Jacko and Wade had split as they circled the huge fortress like main operation centre.

Jacko was halfway along the rear windowless wall. Wade rounded the opposite corner as the building lit up like a Christmas tree. Jacko slung off his NVG and Wade grabbed his monocle NVG. With their vision still adjusting neither man saw the sniper. The round tore through Jacko's thigh and the sound reverberated along the walls. Having used a monocle Wade's right eye adjusted quickly enough for him to see the sniper move in the roof rafters. Bringing his H&K G36 in to his line of sight, he executed a perfect double tap with the shooter crashing on the roof of the operation centre.

"Jacko's down," yelled Wade. Stewie advised he was on his way.

While scanning the rafters he saw, from his peripheral vision, Jacko cutting his pants, grabbing for a field dressing and signalling for Wade to keep going. Doubling back he stepped up to the plate glass and saw Forest, with his back to him, snatch up his laptop. His Desert Eagle in his right hand Forest was barking orders at the two heavily armed men standing either side.

Firing five rapid-fire, circle formation shots into the glass; Wade dived back behind the wall. Forest and his men spun and pumped rounds into the glass. The combination of shots from both sides shattered the highly resistant glass. Wade heard the two rifles click as the magazines emptied. Rolling from his cover across the glass strewn floor he hit the closer man, between the eyes, with his first shot. The second shot missed and the third skimmed Forest's elbow.

Leaping to his feet and charging in to the room, Wade saw Forest drop the laptop and pistol as he grabbed for his arm. With his weapon aimed at the second man's head, Wade looked at Forest.

"Why?" he asked. "How the hell did you ever expect to get away with this?"

Smiling and slightly shaking his head he stared into Wade's eyes as he replied, "The rich have the power and the poor get walked on. I will never be walked on again."

Wade watched as the General looked down at the blood running down his arm and through his fingers. He raised his head and nodded. Believing this to be a signal Wade spun to see the second man reach for his pocket. Wade's pistol exploded in his hand as the man's head was thrown backwards.

The high-powered rifle round tore through his shoulder and spun him one hundred and eighty degrees as the second round smashed through his hip bone. Spread-eagled on the floor, the blood flow quickly intensified as Wade tried to remain focused. Forest looked down. "You idiot Ross. I was always going to beat you because I've got the money. But I will say I enjoyed the battle and the opportunity to manipulate you and your team. I spent forty years grappling with the political and hierarchal bureaucracy of the military and the intelligence communities and their respective incompetency. So when you came along the challenge of battling wits was too much for me to resist." Laughing he said, "But hey, the best man won."

His size twelve boot crashed into Wade's face shattering his nose, jaw and cheekbone. Turning to leave he spun like a mad bull and slammed his boot into Wade's ribs, shattering the ribcage and sternum.

With a smile of success he stepped out of the main operation centre knowing that he now had the current White House Administration in his pocket. With the SOG attack sanctioned by Markham and Razen and Wine's mission failed he would use the media to show incompetence and his ability to lead the CIA through adversity. Once the dust had settled he would take his money and live the perfect life in his luxurious South American hideaway. He thought how ironic it was that his major problem, Thomas Cooper, had been eliminated by those who were going to be blamed for the whole thing.

"General," said the female voice behind him as the cold hard steel barrel pressed against the back of his head.

"Kaitlyn. Don't be stupid. You'll never get out of here."

The noise of the five rifle shots was tremendous, bouncing of the walls and roof as the five snipers fell from the rafters.

"If you kill me you'll be locked up forever," stammered Forest.

In typical Kidon fashion Kaitlyn pulled the trigger of the silenced pistol and without batting an eyelid turned and ran for Wade.

70: Hospital

Wade opened his eyes and the white light was blinding. Squinting, his focus returned as Crystal leant into and blocked the light.

"Hello beautiful man," she said.

Wade tried to lift his arm, move his head, open his mouth but nothing would happen. Flicking his eyes from side to side he tried to figure where he was. Placing her hand on his arm Crystal explained he was in hospital and had undergone three operations. How the doctors had to reset his broken nose, fractured cheekbone and dislocated jaw. Not only that, they had had to tend to two gunshot wounds and place pins in his ribcage.

With Wade unable to speak or move, Crystal talked repeatedly for half an hour. Stopping mid sentence she looked toward the door as Sylvia entered. Once again touching his arm she looked at Wade as she said, "I want you to spend some time with Sylvia. I know you can't talk but we spoke about things last night and you should hear what she has to say. I'll be outside."

Sylvia stepped into Wade's vision as she looked at his beaten body.

"I'm sorry Wundurra I do not know where to start," she said as tears slowly started to trickle down her cheeks. "When you first arrived and told me the story about my time in Australia, I was shocked you would have known this. But I was more taken back by Cristina being present to hear. I have had the time to absorb the information and after a lot of discussion with Crystal, whom I must say is a truly beautiful person, I decided to have a DNA test. The doctors in here were very helpful and obliging … and apparently I," she stammered and lowered her head. "I … I am your mother."

Wade's eyes sprung open at the realization of these words. He stared at his mother wanting so hard to say something.

"I'm sorry … I'm truly sorry," she said as she loudly wept.

Crystal ran into the room, closely followed by Wine, Kaitlyn and Chrissie.

"No don't say that Sylvia. This is a beautiful thing and I know Wade is thrilled to know this," said Crystal as she looked across at Wade who had tears flowing like a waterfall.

The women all hugged as Colonel Wine looked at his friend and whispered. "Remember what I told you about what happened to me. Don't let that happen to you. We'll always be here but you need to look after them."